Andrea started to scream...

A dark and obviously male figure was rising from a chair in the corner. Andrea fumbled in her purse, trying to find her pepper spray. Her fingers closed around the can, but the intruder moved quickly, grabbing and flinging it away.

"I'm not here to hurt you, Andrea," he said softly.

He knew her name! She spun around and ran for the door, but before her trembling fingers could loosen the chain, he'd gripped both her arms in a steel-like vise.

Just as suddenly, he released her and ran his hands through his disheveled hair. Then his mouth twitched with amusement and he began to laugh.

"By the way," he said. "I'm Michael Borelli. We haven't officially met."

ABOUT THE AUTHOR

Saranne Dawson is a voracious reader and has an avid interest in current events, which, she says, stems from "living in the middle of nowhere" in central Pennsylvania. With a master's degree in public administration, she works as a human-services administrator. In her spare time, Saranne sews, bikes, plays tennis, gardens and tends three "hopelessly obnoxious and pampered cats." She also visits her children on a regular basis.

Books by Saranne Dawson

HARLEQUIN INTRIGUE
286—IN SELF DEFENSE

HARLEQUIN AMERICAN ROMANCE
180—INTIMATE STRANGERS
222—SUMMER'S WITNESS
364—A TALENT FOR LOVE
448—BETWITCHED
480—DECEPTION AND DESIRE

Her Other Half
Saranne Dawson

Harlequin Books

TORONTO • NEW YORK • LONDON
AMSTERDAM • PARIS • SYDNEY • HAMBURG
STOCKHOLM • ATHENS • TOKYO • MILAN
MADRID • WARSAW • BUDAPEST • AUCKLAND

ISBN 0-373-22307-2

HER OTHER HALF

Copyright © 1995 by Saranne Hoover

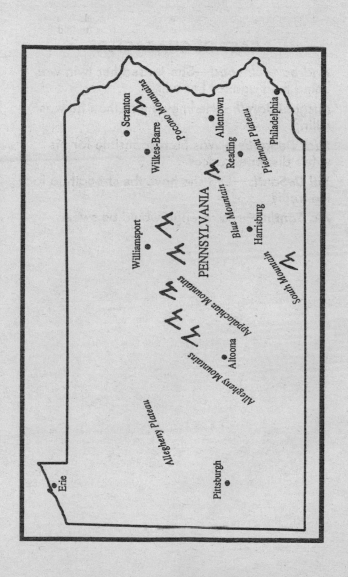

CAST OF CHARACTERS

Andrea Lockwood—She sensed her twin was being held against her will.

Michael Borelli—He knew more than he was telling.

Nick DeSantis—Was he responsible for his wife's disappearance?

Val DeSantis—Did she have the strength to face the truth?

Mr. Santini—His revenge would be sweet.

Prologue

The feeling settled upon her like a cloud over the hot Caribbean sun. Andrea Lockwood stirred uneasily, then opened her eyes to stare out at the wide expanse of clear blue sky and shimmering turquoise water. Her two friends dozed beside her, beneath their own gaily striped umbrellas.

She began to shiver. She stared in disbelief as goose bumps rose up on her newly tanned skin. A cold feeling settled in deep, to her very soul.

A tall, dark-skinned young man, wearing the resort's distinctive uniform of white pants and pastel madras plaid shirt, wheeled a heavily laden bar cart toward them. On either side of Andrea, her friends stirred.

"Is it too early to have a drink?" Robin asked, squinting up at the sky.

"The rules don't apply when you're on vacation," Susan intoned.

"You sound like a student," Robin retorted, forgetting for the moment that any talk of college and classes was off-limits by mutual agreement.

Andrea felt reassured by the banter, by the normalcy of it all. The uneasiness she felt had to be from a bad dream when she dozed off. It couldn't be anything else.

They all ordered drinks, then settled back again. Conversation floated out from beneath the row of umbrellas, hovering in the warm, salt-scented air. She noticed that her goose bumps were gone as quickly as they'd come. But she still felt a jumpy, jittery feeling deep inside her. She tried to contribute to the conversation, but part of her had begun to slip into the distant past—remembering, and trying to block out, that other time she'd felt this way.

"What's wrong, Andy? Too much sun?" Robin leaned forward and stared at her friend and colleague.

Andrea shook her head automatically, but with each passing second the certainty was growing within her that something *was* wrong. She tried to ignore it, but that only added to her discomfort. She got up suddenly, her body having made the decision that her mind was still avoiding.

"I'm going back to the bungalow for a minute," she told her two friends as she slipped into her flowered caftan and sandals, then began to make her way across the gleaming white beach.

She was at war with herself all the way back to the bungalow. It was absurd! She was overreacting to an unremembered bad dream. It *couldn't* be happening again!

Still, she went immediately to the phone, her hand already outstretched to pick it up as though her body was determined to ignore her brain. Only when she realized that she didn't remember the number did she drop her hand.

And then the waves of guilt and anguish inundated her. How could she not recall her twin's phone number? Such a simple thing—and yet so difficult. She found her purse and got out her address book.

You don't remember it because you don't call her more than three or four times a year—carefully spaced intervals so that she wouldn't seem to be intruding into Val's life.

Andrea had called her sister only a few weeks ago, just before Christmas. As she stared at the name and phone number in her book, a wave of shame washed over her. The truth was that she'd harbored a secret hope that she might be invited to spend part of the holidays with Val; she'd let herself believe that things were improving between them.

She stood there uncertainly, replaying that conversation. Val had sounded happy, if a bit guarded as well. But of course, she'd been fine that other time, too—probably right up to the moment it had happened.

That thought propelled her to the phone with renewed determination. But in the few moments it took for the call to go through, she began to waver again. What could she say? "Hi! Wish you were here." She *did* wish that—and a whole lot more—but saying it was out of the question.

The phone began to ring. Andrea's heart leaped into her throat. What if she was right? What if . . . ? Her brother-in-law's voice answered.

"Hello, Nick. It's Andy. Is Val there?"

Into the brief pause rushed all her worst fears. She gripped the phone tightly. The goose bumps erupted again.

"Uh, no, she isn't. But I'll tell her you called."

Andrea wanted desperately to ask if her sister was okay. But the question would sound foolish. If she wasn't, wouldn't Nick tell her? A simple inquiry could shatter the fragile bonds that might be in the process of re-forming.

She said goodbye to Nick and hung up, but the image of her brother-in-law stayed in her mind—and with it came a memory of that feeling she'd had when she'd first met him. She pushed it from her mind. That was more than two years ago, and Val was happy.

Was it simply the *memory* of a feeling—or the same sensation *again?*

She clenched her fists in helpless frustration. She hated it, loathed the uncertainty, the inability to control that dark part of her mind. But she could not deny it. She'd tried to once—and had lost her twin.

Her mind now made up, Andrea picked up the phone again to call the airline. Outside were mango trees and bright red hibiscus, hot sun and beaches, but Andrea's thoughts had turned to winter-bare oaks, dark pines and the snow-covered landscape of Pennsylvania.

Chapter One

The heavy gray skies were beginning to leak a few snow-flakes as Andrea pulled up in front of the big old farm-house. Off to the left were row after row of long green-houses, their windows misted over in the cold. To the right and lining the driveway itself were the striking ornamental grasses—a new line of business for Val and Nick.

Between the house and the greenhouses was a triple garage. Two of the doors were open. In one, Andrea saw the truck they used for their business. In the other was Nick's classic, cherry red Corvette. She hoped that meant that Val's Volvo was in the closed bay.

Leaving her own car in the graveled parking area in front of the garage, Andrea got out and started toward the house, then stopped and went instead to the closed garage door. She had to stand on tiptoe to see through the small windows, and when she sank back down again so, too, did her hopes of finding Val at home. The space was empty.

She went on to the house, even though it was more likely that Nick would be out in the greenhouses or in the office attached to the closest one. Then, when her knocks produced no response, she started back across the gravel to the greenhouse office. The snow had begun to fall more thickly and the wind picked up, whipping her long, loose auburn hair across her face—a far cry from the soft Caribbean breezes.

Moist warmth surrounded her as she opened the office door. A young woman looked up from a computer and grinned, then hesitated uncertainly. Her behavior touched painful memories in Andrea, thoughts of times when quizzical looks had been a normal part of both her and Val's lives.

"You're Andrea," she said, now smiling again. "For a minute, I thought you were Val."

Andrea nodded, her throat suddenly constricted. "I guess my sister isn't here," she said. "I saw that her car is gone."

A frown appeared on the woman's face. "Oh! Then you don't know?"

Andrea felt herself falling into a black, endless abyss. Something *had* happened! She was too late! But then, even as the woman began to speak again, she realized that Val had to be okay or the girl wouldn't have mistaken her for her twin.

"Val left for Florida the day before yesterday. Her...your mother is in the hospital."

Their mother? Was *that* what she'd felt? But she'd spent Christmas with her in Naples and she'd been fine then.

"I've been away," she explained to the still-frowning woman. "Is Nick here?"

Andrea's mind was spinning. The woman said that Val had left two days ago, but she'd spoken to Nick only yesterday and he'd said nothing about it. Something was wrong here.

"Nick's with a customer. He might be tied up for a while."

"I'll go over to the house," Andrea told her. "Please let him know I'm here."

She hurried through the swirls of wind-driven snow to the back door of the house, assuming it would be unlocked. It was, and she stepped into the big country kitchen, then went directly to the phone.

Her mother's answering machine came on. Andrea decided not to leave a message and instead dug out her address book and called her aunt, who lived in the same condo complex. She answered on the second ring.

"Charlotte, it's Andy. I'm trying to reach Mother. Is she there?"

"No, dear, but I was just on my way to meet her. We're having lunch at the club. She played golf this morning, but my arthritis has kicked up again, so I didn't go. Is anything wrong? I thought you were in the Caribbean."

Yes, something's wrong, Andrea shouted silently, all the while assuring her aunt that everything was fine. "Tell Mother I'll call her later."

She hung up and stood there, looking around the neat, charming kitchen that was decorated exactly as she would have done it herself. Then her gaze fell on the dishes in the sink and she frowned. Two coffee mugs, two plates, two sets of silver. If Val wasn't here, who was? And why did the woman in the office think their mother was sick when clearly she wasn't?

All her fears about Nick DeSantis came rushing back at her again, but she still didn't know if they were new suspicions or simply memories of that time when they'd been first introduced.

Andrea hadn't met Nick until just before the wedding. When their mother had told Andrea of her twin's impending marriage, she'd at first feared that she wouldn't even be invited. She'd known that she wouldn't be asked to participate, and she'd always suspected that their mother had insisted she attend.

She should never have told Val what she'd felt when she met Nick, but the sensation had been so powerful she couldn't keep it inside.

Nick DeSantis was a handsome, charming man, and to all appearances was in love with Val. But Andrea had felt something dark and frightening when she met him. Val had told her scathingly that what she felt was jealousy.

Andrea closed her eyes, unwillingly recalling the conversation that had quickly deteriorated into a shouting match as both of them had dredged up the past.

For the first few months of Val's marriage, Andrea continued to worry about that feeling, but as time passed and it became apparent that Val was happy, she reluctantly concluded that perhaps her sister had been right. Maybe it *was* simple jealousy—made all the worse by the fact that Andrea had never had cause to envy her twin before.

She was still staring uneasily at those dishes when the back door opened and Nick walked into the kitchen, bringing with him a wave of cold air that seemed entirely appropriate, given the direction of her thoughts at the moment.

"Hello, Andy. I thought you were still on vacation."

She ignored the smile and the attempt at pleasantries. "Where's Val? The woman in the office said that Mother is in the hospital and she went down there, but I just called Aunt Charlotte and she said that Mother was out playing golf."

Andrea didn't even try to hide her accusing tone as she glared at her brother-in-law. He didn't say anything for a moment as he walked over to lean against the counter, his hands thrust deep into the pockets of his jeans. She noticed that he was standing directly in front of the sink and thought again about those extra dishes.

"She isn't in Florida. I don't know where she is," he said finally in a low voice as he ran his hands through his thick black hair.

"What do you mean, you don't know where she is?" Andrea's voice rose as her fear escalated.

He looked at her, then glanced away quickly. "We, uh, had an argument and she just took off—two days ago."

"And you haven't heard from her?"

He shook his head. "Look, I'm sure she'll be back. It's happened before."

"Have you called the police?"

He nodded. "You have to wait three days to file a missing-person report on an adult, and even then they won't really do anything."

"You said she's done this before?" Andrea asked incredulously. "What's going on here, Nick?"

Her sharp tone drew his gaze back to her and she saw his expression harden. "Listen, Andy, this has nothing to do with you. Val's...insecure. She'll be back after she's had some time to think."

Andrea hesitated. She wanted to insist that it *did* have plenty to do with her, but Nick knew that was a lie. The fabled closeness of twins just didn't apply in their case.

"Maybe I should check my machine to see if she called me," she said into the tense silence.

Nick said nothing as she picked up the phone and punched in her own number, then the code that activated her machine. They both knew that Val would never have called her.

There were several messages, but none from her twin. Andrea hung up the phone and turned back to her brother-in-law, keeping her expression and her voice carefully neutral.

"I'll be at the Holiday Inn. Please call me right away if you hear from her."

"Look, Andy, there's no need for you to hang around. She's okay and she'll be back. I'll have her call you."

Andrea didn't respond as she walked out the door. If she'd had any doubts about her feeling, Nick's tone of voice had ended them. He was nervous and scared; she was sure of that. Was it merely his concern about Val—or was he worried about her sudden appearance on the scene?

AFTER CHECKING INTO the motel, Andrea sat down at the desk and picked up a pad of motel stationery. As a college professor, she was accustomed to writing important points on a chalkboard, but in the absence of that, paper would do.

Unfortunately her thoughts refused to let themselves be organized. She kept hearing echoes of Nick's assertion that this "had nothing to do with her." With each repetition in her mind, his tone became more and more sarcastic, though to be fair to him, she didn't think he'd actually sounded that way.

It was her own guilt; she knew that. *Nothing* her twin did had anything to do with her anymore. She had become, at best, peripheral to Val's life.

It was all so damnably unfair! Even their mother seemed to have abandoned any hope for a reconciliation between them.

Thoughts of their mother made Andrea glance toward the phone. It was possible that Val might have called her, but she doubted it. Their mother's past attempts to bring them together had caused a rift there, too, though nothing as serious as the chasm between Val and her.

No, she thought, *I can't call Mother—at least, not until I have a better sense of what's really going on.*

Andrea abandoned the paper and instead got up to pace around the room; she tended to do that in her classrooms where she taught psychology.

She paused to stare at her reflection in the big mirror over the dresser, recalling Nick's secretary's first assumption that she was Val. That mistake had evoked an odd combination of pleasure and pain that lingered with her even now.

The face that stared back at her was both hers and her sister's—a classic oval face with a slightly upturned nose, high cheekbones, a wide mouth and heavily fringed gray-green eyes. Both of them were tall and long-legged, and retained the grace and athleticism resulting from years of ballet and figure skating.

But the painstaking, multiple surgeries had altered those features for Valerie, shifting them subtly. Her nose had less of a tilt and her cheekbones weren't quite so prominent. They were small differences, but noticeable when Val and Andrea were together...

Andrea wondered what her twin saw when she looked into the mirror. Did she see herself as being disfigured—even though she wasn't? Yes, she thought sadly, knowing that when Val saw *her,* she was actually seeing herself as she *should* be.

Andrea turned away from the mirror and the tormenting questions. Where was Val? Was it possible that she was making too much of this, that Nick was right and she should just stay out of it?

Her rational mind told her that this was entirely possible—but her instincts continued to tell her that something was wrong. She knew she had to trust those feelings this time, as she hadn't done all those years ago.

She began to review the situation. Okay, so she could understand that Nick had apparently lied to their staff about Val's sudden departure. He wouldn't want their personal problems to be revealed to their employees. But his explanation to Andrea simply hadn't rung true. She was very adept at picking up the subtle signs of lying—the too-rapid speech, the change in intonation, the shifting eyes.

And what about those extra dishes in the sink? Was she making too much of that? Maybe Nick just wasn't inclined toward neatness, and what she'd seen were the leavings of two solitary meals.

It was curious, too, now that she thought about it, that Nick hadn't questioned her sudden appearance here a day after she'd called him from the Caribbean.

Although she'd never known for certain, Andrea guessed that Nick knew that she'd told Valerie about him. He probably thought she fancied herself a psychic. But only twice— no, *three* times now—had Andrea ever experienced what could be called "flashes," and all had been connected to Valerie.

Her research into twins suggested that this sort of thing wasn't at all unusual. Twinship was a strange and little understood phenomenon.

She stopped her pacing and peered out the window. The snow that had earlier been threatening to pile up had almost stopped. She felt a powerful need to *do* something, to take some action instead of just thinking. But what could she do?

She couldn't go to Val's friends because she didn't even know who they were—a thought that produced yet another sharp twinge of pain. And since Val worked with Nick, she couldn't go to her place of employment as a start.

She ruled out the police, too. She could just envision herself marching into the police station and saying that she had this feeling that something had happened to her sister. She'd probably be lucky if they only laughed at her, instead of calling the local mental-health authorities.

She began to search through her memories of their infrequent phone conversations, seeking a clue that would give her a starting point. Andrea always made the calls—and she was the one who did most of the talking, as well.

Then suddenly she had it—the health club! Val had told her that she'd joined a new club in town and was working out every morning. She'd even referred to a group of women there. It wasn't much, but it *was* a beginning.

She left her room and went down to the front desk. Val hadn't mentioned the name of the club, but she had said it just opened. Perhaps the desk clerk could provide some information.

She got the name immediately, and it turned out to be on the far side of town. Driving through Centre Valley became an excursion into nostalgia for her, because she'd spent precious little time here since her high school days. There were so many changes, not the least of which was the growth of the place. From a small town with a large university, it had expanded tremendously.

She drove past the main gate to the campus and thought about the offer she'd had to teach here. She'd been so tempted, nearly convincing herself that proximity to her twin would bring them close again. But then she'd thought about the torment of living here if there was no reconciliation, and she'd refused the position.

Memories surrounded her as she spotted familiar places— all of them inextricably linked to Val and divided into "before" and "after" with a chilling finality.

She found the club on a road that hadn't existed when she'd lived here. It was named for a family that had once owned a huge dairy farm and a stable where she and Val had often ridden.

Since it was the middle of the day, there were few cars in the parking lot when she pulled in. She knew that in order to speak to the women Val worked out with, she would have to return in the morning, but what she planned to do now was to see about obtaining a membership so she could join them.

She approached the entrance to the club, her face turned toward a neighboring field where she and Val had often raced their horses. Then suddenly she collided with a very solid wall of flesh!

Dazed from her bittersweet memories and the sudden, unexpected contact, Andrea found her arms being gripped firmly and her gaze meeting a pair of very shocked dark eyes.

"Sorry," she murmured as she regained her balance and the man let her go. But she found herself talking to empty air. The stranger moved quickly through the door and headed toward a blue Jeep Cherokee.

She stared after him for a moment, her arms still tingling from that brief contact. He turned her way briefly before getting into his vehicle, then drove off quickly. She felt slightly embarrassed at her reaction to him, although it was understandable. A little over six feet tall with a trim, muscular build, he had thick, dark hair and a ruggedly handsome face, complete with a cleft chin. Even in that briefest of contacts, he exuded an easy sort of masculinity, the kind that was bound to set any woman's nerve endings aquiver.

Proof of that awaited her when she entered the club and saw the trim blonde at the desk staring out the window in the direction of the departing stranger, wearing a slightly wistful expression that Andrea hoped hadn't been on her own face, as well.

The woman shifted her gaze to Andrea and smiled. "Hi! Have you decided to make up for lost time?"

Andrea saw the clerk's look become less certain as she approached, although it was clear that she still believed her to be Val.

"Val is my twin sister," she announced. "I'm visiting for a few days and I was wondering if it's possible to take out a temporary membership."

"Gosh!" the blonde exclaimed, staring unabashedly at her. "I didn't know she had a twin. You really *do* look alike." She continued to study Andrea. "But I guess there *are* some differences."

Yes, thought Andrea as she had a sudden, unwelcome flashback to those days she'd spent with Val and the doctors. The surgeons had been pleased to have her, instead of the photographs they usually worked from.

"Sure. We can fix you up with a pass. We do that all the time. How long will you be staying?"

"I'm not really sure. My sister is away, but I'm expecting her back very soon, so it will probably be no more than a week."

The blonde nodded as she consulted her computer screen. "I thought she must be away, since she hasn't been in. She'd been coming every day."

"I understand she works out with a group of women, so I thought I'd just join them, if that's possible."

"That's right. They call themselves the Sunrise Sisters because they all come in when we open at six-thirty."

Andrea stifled a groan. She was *not* a morning person. She struggled mightily to avoid early-morning classes for that reason. But she paid the fee and then let the woman show her around.

The club *was* nice, and it even boasted a pool, which appealed to her far more than the exercise equipment. She'd never really been into the health-club scene, preferring instead to ride her mountain bike and ski.

As she left the club, she found her thoughts straying back to the handsome stranger. But only briefly, because she had far more important things on her mind.

MICHAEL BORELLI FOUND that the image of Andrea Lockwood floated in his mind's eye the entire way back to the house. He could even still smell the scent she'd been wearing—something soft and elegant.

He'd damned near had a heart attack when he saw her, though she couldn't have known that. It hadn't taken him more than a second or two to realize that she wasn't Valerie. The differences weren't all that great, but they were definitely there.

And he thought that the difference wasn't just physical, either. Despite the briefness of their encounter, Michael sensed a self-confidence in Andrea that was missing from her twin. He wondered idly if that had always been the case. If so, it was no wonder that the two of them didn't get along.

But what the hell was she doing here? He didn't like it. Nick couldn't have known she was coming, though he'd mentioned that she'd called.

Michael pulled up in front of the garage, then went into the greenhouse office. Nick was on the phone, but the look he gave Michael suggested he already knew that Andrea was here. Michael signaled that he was going over to the house, knowing Nick would follow him when he got off the phone.

The image of Andrea Lockwood was still with him—that curvy, long-legged body, the auburn hair whipped by the breeze. Pleasant though the picture was, she still spelled trouble.

By the time he'd opened a beer and was starting to make himself a sandwich, Nick was there, looking damned worried.

"I already saw her—at the club," Michael told him before Nick could say anything. "Why is she here?"

Nick ran a hand distractedly through his hair. "She was at the club? Why would she be there?"

"Well, I hope to hell it isn't because she's decided to play detective. What's she doing here?"

"She didn't say—but I know," Nick said unhappily. "She senses something has happened."

Michael stared at him. "What are you talking about? Don't tell me that you think she's had another psychic episode? You know I don't believe in that garbage."

"I never told you what she said about me, did I?"

When Michael shook his head, Nick went on. "I met her right before the wedding, and she told Val that something about me 'bothered' her. She said there was something 'dark' in me, something I was hiding."

Michael swore and took a drink of some beer. He'd heard the story about the accident, but he hadn't believed the part about Andrea. Still, they *are* twins, he thought uneasily.

"What did you tell her?"

"Betsy in the office told her what I'd told all the employees—that Val's in Florida because her mother's sick. But Andy knew that wasn't true, so I told her we'd had a fight and Val took off."

Michael nodded. "Good thinking. Since they're not that close, she might buy that."

"I don't think she did. She's planning to hang around—and she went to the club. She could be trying to find some friends of Val's to talk to."

"She's not staying here, is she?" Michael asked, alarmed.

"No, she said she'd stay at the Holiday Inn. But she's going to be trouble, Michael. She's no pushover, believe me."

"Yeah, somehow I guessed that," Michael said as her image flashed through his mind yet again. Andrea Lockwood was definitely going to be trouble—especially if she was bent on playing Nancy Drew.

THE FIRST PERSON Andrea saw when she walked into the club was the handsome, dark-haired stranger. He was working out on an exercise machine, and from what she could see—which was plenty, since he wore only gym shorts and a T-shirt—he looked as though the gym was his second home.

"Val! We've missed you! Where've you been?"

At the sound of her sister's name, the stranger's head turned in Andrea's direction. Their eyes locked for one brief moment, and then she turned to the tall woman who'd spoken. Once again, she saw a welcoming smile drain away into uncertainty.

"Oh, gosh! You're not Val! You're her sister!"

Andrea acknowledged that she was, turning her back on the man across the room even as she registered his reaction to Val's name.

"Where's Val? Isn't she coming?" The woman asked after introducing herself as Beth.

"Actually, she's away for a few days. I came for a surprise visit, and since she's not here, I've decided to wait until she gets back."

"Oh." Beth looked vaguely troubled, but before Andrea could think of a way to pursue that, she was introducing her to the other women who'd gathered around and were staring at her with open curiosity.

At this early hour, there weren't many people at the club, and the women arranged themselves on the various torture devices. Andrea chose a stationary bicycle, since that would require the least effort and perhaps afford her the opportunity to pursue some conversation.

But it also meant that she was facing the stranger, who had by now moved to a bench closer to her, where he was lifting weights. A petite blonde was working out next to him and, even with the effort required to press weights, he was still managing to talk with her. Unfortunately the chatter around Andrea prevented her from overhearing it.

The man was beginning to interest her for more than the obvious reason. Yesterday she'd written off the startled look in his eyes to their accidental collision. But now she wondered if she could have been wrong. The way he'd turned so suddenly when Beth had called out Val's name suggested a connection.

She pedaled away, trying to avoid looking at him, even though their glances seemed to snag on each other's regularly. The more she tried to ignore him, the more she became aware of him.

She tried to figure out how she could elicit information without sounding as though she were worried about Val. She was very much aware of the delicacy of her situation. If she was wrong about Val's being in trouble, she certainly wouldn't be helping their strained relationship by making a rash move here.

She decided to wait until they went to the locker room, hoping that some inspiration would strike by then, and also that the conversation among the women would give her an opening to ask about Val.

The stranger moved on to the punching bag in the far corner, his back now to her as he donned gloves and began to pound at it rhythmically—obviously not for the first time. The blonde he'd been talking to was paying far more attention to him than to her own exercise routine.

"More power to her." Beth chuckled from her bicycle nearby, apparently in response to a comment from someone else. "I wonder who he is."

Since there were only two other men there at the moment, and they were working out together some distance away, Andrea knew she must be referring to the stranger. She was surprised at Beth's comment, since she'd assumed she must know him.

"Why don't you give her some competition, Beth?" one of the others teased.

"Not me," Beth stated firmly. "I've given up on men. Cats are much better company—in and out of bed."

"I don't know," another woman said. "There are men—and then there are *hunks*. And that one definitely fits into the latter category."

"Yeah," Beth acknowledged. "A body that doesn't quit and probably a brain that never got started."

They all laughed as the object of their attentions continued to thump the bag. Andrea wondered—not for the first
time—why women got so upset when men treated them like
sex objects. Her own experiences had taught her that women
were just as bad. In fact, she suspected that most men would
be shocked to hear how women talked about them.

Who is he, she wondered, and why didn't the others seem
to know him? She'd figured that he knew Val because he was
a regular here, but clearly that wasn't the case.

Don't get carried away, she warned herself. *And don't
start looking for another mystery when you've already got
one on your plate—even if this one does come wrapped in a
sexy package. Besides, Beth was probably right about him
having nothing upstairs.*

They finished their workouts and got some fruit juice
from the bar. The others started off to the locker room, but
Beth lingered behind.

"Are you in a hurry?" she asked. "If not, why don't you
join me for a swim?"

"Exactly what I had in mind," Andrea told her, and they
went off to change into swimsuits. But she couldn't quite
resist casting one last glance at the stranger—and once
again, their gazes locked.

Between the noise of the showers and the sound of blow
dryers, conversation in the locker room was all but impossible, and in any event, it was obvious that the others were
in a hurry. Andrea decided that her first attempt at playing
detective was a disaster—unless she could get something out
of Beth.

At first, they had the pool all to themselves. Then the two
men who'd been working out together came in, and not long
after that the stranger followed, now wearing a pair of brief
black trunks that left even less to the imagination.

Andrea had just reached the end of the pool when he
walked in, and once again everything around them blurred

into insignificance. It seemed that her hormones were getting a better workout than her muscles. She pushed off the end of the pool and began to stroke her way to the far end.

After swimming their laps, Beth and Andrea sat down at the edge of the pool. She was still trying to think of a way to broach the subject of Val without risking too many questions when Beth surprised her by asking one herself.

"It's probably none of my business, but is Val okay?"

Andrea's head swung toward her so sharply that Beth started to protest that she hadn't meant to pry.

"No," Andrea said as her heart began to pound in her throat. "You're not prying. I just wondered why you might think she's *not* okay. I've been away for a while, so I haven't talked to her."

Beth sipped at her fruit juice and shrugged. "It's just that she seemed kind of worried the last time I saw her—or maybe *distracted* would be a better description."

"When was that?"

"Tuesday. That's the last morning she came here, and she didn't say anything about not coming the next day. I called and left a message on her machine, but she never called back."

Tuesday. According to what she'd been told by the girl in Nick's office, that's when Val had supposedly left for Florida.

"Did she say anything about what might be bothering her?" Andrea asked, trying to keep her tone just right—slightly concerned but not panicked.

"She just said something about a meeting that she wasn't looking forward to. She must have been going to it straight from here, because she dressed up, and she usually just leaves in her sweats."

"But she didn't say what the meeting was about?"

Beth didn't answer for a moment as she stared at Andrea. "Something *is* wrong, isn't it?"

Andrea sighed. "I'm...not sure. Nick says that they had a fight and Val took off. He doesn't know where she is."

Beth gave her a shocked look. "A fight—those two? I can't believe it. She adores him, and from what I've seen he feels the same toward her. Everybody has arguments, but I can't see her taking off like that."

Andrea didn't know what to say. She was reluctant to admit that she didn't believe Nick, even though she was increasingly certain that he'd lied. If Val *had* taken off after a fight, it just didn't make sense that she would have come here before leaving. And what was this business about a meeting she "wasn't looking forward to"? Was that just a smoke screen to avoid telling Beth the truth?

She saw Beth's gaze flick briefly toward something behind her and turned to see the dark-haired stranger treading water not far away. As she turned, he moved toward the side of the pool and levered himself out. He didn't look her way this time.

"Val never hinted to me that there were any problems between them," Andrea said, not adding that she'd be the last person her twin would tell.

"Me, neither," Beth replied. "We haven't known each other all that long, but we've gotten to be pretty close."

"Do you know where she might have gone for this meeting?"

Beth frowned. "There are any number of places she might have gone, but I know that Trellises is her favorite for breakfast. We go there sometimes if I'm working the afternoon shift." She explained that she was a nurse at the local hospital.

"You really *are* worried about her, aren't you?"

Andrea nodded. "I can't explain it, but I just have this feeling that she might be in trouble. But I could be wrong," she added hastily.

"Let's go get some breakfast ourselves," Beth suggested. "We can go to Trellises. They might remember if she was in there on Tuesday morning. It's not a very big place."

As they got up to go to the locker room, Andrea saw that the stranger had taken a seat at one of the tables behind them. He was sprawled casually, drinking some fruit juice, a towel slung around his neck as he watched someone dive into the pool at the far end.

When they walked past him, his head turned slightly and his gaze swept casually over her. She found herself wishing that she'd worn her new suit, instead of the nondescript tank suit that was great for swimming, but didn't flatter her much.

Come off it, she told herself disgustedly, now getting really irritated at her overreaction to him. But that didn't prevent her from asking Beth who he was.

"I don't know. I've never seen him here before. But he certainly livened up everyone's morning," she added with a grin.

"What about the blonde he was with?"

"Suzie? He wasn't with her. She usually joins us, but she latched on to him the minute he came in."

THE RESTAURANT, which Andrea had never seen before, was certainly appropriately named. White-painted trellises were everywhere, covered with shiny green vines that Andrea had to touch before she could be sure they were fake. They served an excellent breakfast buffet, and after the two women had loaded up their plates and laughed about undoing their earlier efforts, they found a small table.

"Ahh, there's Terry, the cashier," Beth said. "She'll know if Val was in here on Tuesday."

Beth got up and went over to the older woman. Andrea saw the cashier take a surprised look in her direction, and then a moment later shake her head. By the time Beth got back to the table, she was prepared for the bad news.

"She's sure Val wasn't in on Tuesday. She said the last time she saw her was last week, when she came here with me."

Beth sat there, staring off into space for a moment. "I've been trying to remember if I actually saw her leave the club that morning, and I'm pretty sure that I came out just as she was pulling out of the lot. And if that was Tuesday, she didn't turn toward town."

"But you're not really sure?"

Beth shook her head. "Unfortunately no. It could have been some other day. Do you think Nick is lying to you?"

Andrea hesitated. She liked Beth and she trusted her instinctively, but she was still very reluctant to divulge anything more. She knew that if she wanted to ask questions, she had to be prepared to answer some herself. And at this point, Beth seemed to be her only source of information.

"Nick and I don't really get along all that well," she admitted. "And frankly, Val and I haven't been that close, either."

"Yeah, I already knew that. Someone who went to school with you told me that it all went back to a bus accident Val was in, but she didn't give me any details."

Andrea nodded sadly. "That's right. When we were fifteen, we were supposed to go on this church youth-group trip to Washington, D.C. The night before we were to leave, I had this terrible nightmare that we were in a bus that crashed and there was fire everywhere.

"When I woke up in the morning, I was still scared from the nightmare and afraid to go on the trip. But I didn't want to admit that it was because of a bad dream, so I pretended I was sick and stayed home."

Andrea paused, shuddering with the memory. "Anyway, I didn't go, and Val did. The bus was hit head-on by a runaway truck on a mountain road. It was one of those big gasoline tankers and it caught fire. Three kids, the bus driver and a chaperon were killed, and many others were burned and injured—including Val. She was the worst of the ones who survived.''

"And she blamed you for not warning her?" Beth asked incredulously.

"Yes, but no more than I blamed myself. It's just that nothing like that had ever happened to me before. Still, I thought that I should have known it was a premonition, and not just an ordinary nightmare. When I woke up that morning, I had this absolute certainty that I shouldn't go on the trip—and I should have stopped Val from going, too."

Beth shivered. "How awful for you—for both of you. But it seems to me that she should have understood—at least when she got older."

"Oh, I think she *does* understand—deep down, at any rate. But it was really hard on her. When they started to do the reconstructive surgery, the doctors used me as a sort of model, and I think that made things worse."

Beth nodded slowly. "And when she sees you, it's a reminder of what she did look like. She's very attractive, and I never would have guessed that she'd looked differently— until I saw you."

Andrea nodded sadly.

"You said earlier that you had a feeling she was in trouble. Did you mean that you had another nightmare?"

"It wasn't a bad dream this time—just a feeling. But it came literally out of the blue, so I had to come. But I'm worried that I'm too late."

Chapter Two

"Andrea, I just remembered something else Val said that morning."

They were in the parking lot outside the restaurant. Andrea was about to get into her car, her thoughts already on what she should do next.

"I was telling her about an old college roommate I'd heard had just been arrested for stealing drugs from the hospital where she worked, and how shocked I was, and she said something like, 'It's so scary to think you know someone really well and then find out that maybe you didn't, after all.'

"It wasn't *what* she said as much as the way she said it—like she was relating it to something that had just happened to *her*. I think that's why I remembered it."

Andrea got into her car and watched Beth drive away, her final words echoing through her brain. Was it only a comment meant to sympathize with Beth—or *had* Val been talking about herself? And if she was, who could she have meant?

The person who came to mind immediately was Nick, and she was back to thinking about that feeling she'd had when she first met him. Maybe Val had learned something about Nick that had driven her away. But what about the supposed meeting? Was it real—or just an excuse to cover up the fact that she was dressed up to leave?

As a psychologist, Andrea had seen many people in crisis, and she knew that their behavior often seemed irrational to others. Val might very well have gone to her workout that morning simply out of habit, and then taken off.

She drove out of the restaurant lot and started back toward the health club. The road was new to her and she wasn't exactly sure where it went. Since Beth thought that Val had gone in that direction, she decided to check it out. Maybe there was a restaurant out there.

As she passed the entrance to the club, she saw a dark blue Cherokee waiting to pull out. The handsome stranger. She hadn't noticed the vehicle in the lot this morning, but she knew that was what he'd been driving yesterday. She watched in her rearview mirror as he pulled out after she had passed. He turned in her direction and she frowned, certain that she'd seen his signal blinking in the other direction, toward town.

He stayed well behind her, even though she drove slowly, staying under the speed limit as she passed through an area where a lot of construction was going on and a sign indicated a new industrial research park. She recalled Val's having mentioned it. They'd won the contract for landscaping there—their biggest job yet.

The road made a wide curve around a hill—and then Andrea saw where she was. Directly ahead was the crowded interchange to the interstate.

Soon she was driving through a congested area filled with gas stations, motels and restaurants. If Val had come here, it could have been either to get something to eat or to go to the highway.

The Cherokee was still tailing her, although it had now fallen far enough behind so that another car was between

them. Andrea decided to test her theory that he was following her and pulled into a gas station. The Cherokee went
past, but as she sat at the pumps, she saw it pull into a motel parking lot farther down, circle around and then stop in
a space near the exit. But he didn't get out.

After filling the tank, she pulled out again, this time
heading back toward town. She had already decided that she
was going to check the restaurants in the hope that someone might remember Val, but at the moment, the stranger
took priority. She was still thinking about that startled look
on his face yesterday and his reaction this morning at hearing Val's name.

Before long, she saw him again, still maintaining a dis-
creet distance as he followed her back into town. Now she
knew that he *had* to be following her.

She wasn't really frightened, since there was nothing he
could do except follow her at this point. She thought about
driving back to her motel, but then quickly ruled that out
because she didn't want him to know where she was staying. So instead, when she reached the downtown business
area, she pulled into a parking lot. He drove a short distance down the street, then pulled into a space along the
sidewalk.

She knew he could see her from where he'd parked, and
she didn't want him to know that she'd spotted him, so she
got out of her car, fed the meter and walked out of the lot.
Resisting the temptation to look in his direction, she walked
along the street, casually browsing in store windows. When
she crossed the street to the side where he was parked and
started toward him, he suddenly pulled out and disappeared down the street. She noticed that he'd been parked
in a bus-stop zone.

She was rather disappointed, since she'd been tempted to
walk up to him and demand to know why he was following
her. But now that the opportunity was lost, she admitted it

would have been a foolish thing to do. Just because he set her hormones soaring didn't mean he couldn't be dangerous. In fact, that only made him *more* deadly.

After strolling for a block or so, Andrea returned to her car, carefully scanning the lot and the street for any sign of the Cherokee. Then she headed back to the cluster of restaurants near the interstate.

She didn't really hold out much hope of gaining any information about Val here, since all the restaurants probably had a high volume of business. But she was at a loss for anything else to do, while at the same time being afflicted with a powerful urge to do *something*.

Still, if Val *had* been here, she had a distinct advantage. Instead of having to bother with descriptions or photographs, she could take advantage of their twinship. Even the fact that they were both redheads helped.

Her hopes hadn't been high to begin with, but after receiving negative responses at the first four restaurants, she was depressed. There were only two places left, one a rather seedy-looking motel whose oversize parking lot was half-filled with big trucks.

She decided to go to that one first and get it over with. Numerous male heads turned in her direction when she entered the restaurant, breathing in the unpleasant odor of cigarette smoke and grease, combined with the fragrant aroma of coffee.

There was no hostess here—instead, a cashier perched on a stool behind a small counter near the entrance. Andrea walked over to the heavily made-up and very buxom blonde, thinking that she must have been a very attractive woman before time had done its unpleasant work.

Surely, she thought, Val would never have come here. This was a waste of time. But then her certainty began to fade as the woman looked up and began to smile in a way that suggested she'd seen her before.

"Hello," Andrea said. "I wonder if you could help me. Were you here Tuesday morning during breakfast?"

"Sure. I remember you. Did you forget something?"

After her lack of success at the other restaurants and her doubts that Val could have come here, Andrea was so surprised that she just stared at the woman.

"I mean, I noticed that you left in a hurry and all," the woman said, giving her a sympathetic smile.

"It wasn't me," Andrea told her when she had recovered from her shock. "It was my twin sister. So she *was* here Tuesday morning?"

"Sure. She was here. She kind of stood out, you know?" The woman laughed.

"You said she left in a hurry?"

The woman nodded. "She seemed pretty upset. I didn't go after her, though, because the guy she was with got up right after her and he paid the bill."

"Did you know him?"

"No, never saw him before, either. And I'd have remembered him. He was a good-looking guy."

Two men came up to the counter to pay, then stood there joking with the woman for a few minutes while Andrea was left to try to assimilate what she'd just learned. The only reason she could think of that Val would have come here was to avoid being seen by someone she knew. The patrons were mostly truckers, and it didn't seem to be the kind of place locals would come to.

But who was the man? The woman's comment about his being "good-looking" conjured up an image of the dark-haired stranger. As soon as the men had gone, she asked the woman to describe him.

"Like I said, he was a good-looking man—and the kind who acts like he knows it, too. Dark hair, dark eyes—those bedroom eyes, you know? About six feet tall, well-built. I'd say he was in his mid-thirties."

The stranger definitely fit that description, Andrea thought. But to be fair, so would a lot of other men. Except that none of them were following her around. Who was he and what was his connection to Val?

"Is your sister in some kind of trouble?" the woman asked solicitously.

"She might be," Andrea acknowledged. "I'm not sure. Do you remember anything else about him. You didn't happen to see what kind of car he was driving, did you?" She could see that the woman had a partial view of the parking lot from where she sat.

"No, it was pretty busy at the time. The only other thing I remember is that they didn't come in together. He came first—maybe ten minutes before she did. And he told me he was meeting someone and gave me your sister's description. Oh, and I'm sure he had a New York accent. I'm pretty good with accents, because we get them from all over."

Andrea turned to look at the tables, wondering if she could find out more from their waitress. "Do you remember who their waitress was?"

"Let me think. Yeah, it would have been Judy, but she's off today. Truth is, she isn't exactly here when she *is* here, if you know what I mean. Too many late nights."

"When will she be working again?"

The woman consulted a schedule on a clipboard. "Not till Monday, unless she's switched with someone. Sometimes they don't let me know, even though they're supposed to."

"Could you give me her home phone number?"

"Gosh, you really *are* worried, aren't you? We're not supposed to give out the girls' numbers, but I can try to get in touch with her for you."

"Thanks," Andrea said, reaching into her purse for her card. She wrote the name and room number of the motel on the back. "Please tell her that it's very important, even if she doesn't remember much."

After thanking her again for her help, Andrea left quickly to avoid any further questions. It was clear that the woman was growing more and more curious.

One thing seemed certain at this point—Nick had lied to her. If Val had simply run away after an argument, it just didn't make sense that she would have come here to meet someone. It was even more troubling that the man Val met fit the description of the stranger who'd been following her.

THE WOMAN at the restaurant was obviously as good as her word, because by the time Andrea got back to her motel there was a message from a Judy Davidson. She returned the call right away.

"Sure, I remember her," the girl said. "Dolly told me she might be in trouble."

"Yes, that's right," Andrea acknowledged. "I was wondering if you might have overheard anything."

"No, not really—but that sort of tells you something right there, doesn't it?"

"What do you mean?" Andrea asked, confused.

"Well, most people just go on talking while you're serving them—like you're invisible, you know? You wouldn't believe some of the stuff I've heard. But they just shut up every time I came to the table. I mean, it was like they'd even stop in the middle of a sentence."

"Did my sister seem upset?"

"Yeah, she sure did. She didn't even eat anything, just drank some coffee. I got the impression that whatever he was telling her, she didn't want to hear. He seemed to be doing most of the talking."

Andrea thought back to Beth's recounting of that remark by Val. Was *that* what had upset her? Had she heard something negative about Nick? She'd said that before meeting the man at the restaurant, but he must have contacted her to set up the appointment.

She asked Judy to describe the man and got the same description, almost verbatim. "Do you remember anything else about him—any scars or anything?"

"No. I'm sure he was from New York, though. And he was good-looking, all right—but that kind are usually scum."

In spite of herself, Andrea smiled. Handsome men certainly seemed to be taking a trashing these days. She made appropriate sounds of agreement, then asked if she'd happened to see what kind of car he was driving.

"No, we were really busy. We always are at that time of morning."

Andrea thanked her and hung up after asking her to call back if she should remember anything else, no matter how unimportant it might seem.

It was time to confront Nick with what she'd learned. If he'd been uneasy lying to her before, she was going to make him *very* uncomfortable now.

NICK WAS ALONE in the small greenhouse office when she marched in, and his expression was scarcely welcoming.

"I haven't heard from her, Andy."

"You've been lying to me, Nick—and I want the truth! If I don't get it, I'm going to the police."

"What makes you think I'm lying?" he asked, his expression giving nothing away.

"Because I've found out a few things on my own."

"Such as?"

"I'm not telling you until you tell me the *truth*."

"Look, Andy, I know you've never liked me, but I swear to you that I'd never do anything to hurt Val. I love her. She's the best thing that ever happened to me. Whatever you found out, you probably misinterpreted it."

Andrea hesitated. Try as she certainly did, she couldn't deny the sincerity in his voice. But she knew that he could still be withholding some information.

"She met someone—a man."

"What'd he look like?" Nick demanded. "Where'd she meet him?"

"That's not important," Andrea replied, already regretting her outburst. "She went to the health club the morning she left—and then she went to meet someone. That seems like pretty strange behavior for a person who was running away after an argument."

Nick was silent for a long moment, then got up and stood with his back to her as he stared out the window. "I think maybe she was having an affair," he said without turning. "That's what we were arguing about. Val is…insecure. You know that. She accused me of having an affair last fall, and I think she thought she was getting back at me. Maybe that's who she met.

"And as to her going to the club, she's gotten to be really obsessive about it. She hasn't missed a day since she joined."

"*Were* you having an affair?" Andrea asked, too curious not to pose the question, but still beginning to feel rather embarrassed at having intruded into this situation.

He turned to her in an abrupt movement. "No, I wasn't—and I never have. I told you I love her. Go home, Andy. This has nothing to do with you, and if Val finds out that you're involved it'll only make things worse. She'd even started to talk as though she was ready to patch things up with you. On New Year's Day, she said that maybe it was time for a new start."

His words struck Andrea hard. She hesitated, and Nick pressed the point.

"There's nothing you can do here. I've already checked our bank accounts, so I know how much money she has with her. It wasn't a lot, so she'll soon have to use her charge or automatic-banking-machine cards. And when she does, I can find out where she is. I'll keep you posted. I don't think she'll stay away long.''

Andrea felt deflated. Her self-righteous anger had drained away. Nick was right. If Val was ready for a reconciliation, she shouldn't be risking that, by involving herself in this.

''You're right,'' she admitted reluctantly. ''There's nothing I want more than to have my sister again. And I *don't* dislike you, Nick. I know that Val's been very happy with you.''

''Then let me deal with it. I promise I'll keep in touch, and when I find Val, I'll tell her that you dropped in and then left when she wasn't here.''

Andrea drove away from the farmhouse awash in shame and embarrassment. By the time she reached the motel, she had decided to take Nick's advice and go home. In fact, she was appalled at how she'd let her thoughts get so out of control.

She decided to leave first thing in the morning. That way, she wouldn't have to make the long trip after dark.

ANDREA WAS ON THE ROAD in the strange half-light of pre-dawn, eager to get home and try to forget her foolishness. For that reason, she ignored the nagging sensation that she'd overlooked something. She continued to ignore it until it virtually screamed at her in the gravelly voice of Dolly, the cashier at the truck-stop restaurant.

''He came first—maybe ten minutes before she did. And he told me he was meeting someone and gave me your sister's description.''

Andrea frowned. Nick had said that the man Val met must have been her lover—or at least he'd certainly implied that. And in her shock at discovering her twin's affair, Andrea hadn't really questioned that.

But why would he have had to give Dolly her description? Andrea remembered the layout of the restaurant quite well. It wasn't very large to begin with, and every table was clearly visible from the entrance. Val should have been able to spot him the moment she walked in—unless she didn't know him.

That revelation forced her to face the supposed fact of Val's affair, something she'd tried not to think about. It was certainly true that Val wasn't the most secure person in the world, but the one security she *did* have was her marriage.

Some people might engage in a game of tit for tat, having an affair just because they suspected their spouse of infidelity—but not Val. They might not be close any longer, but Andrea certainly knew that Val wouldn't do such a thing.

As she continued to drive east, Andrea's thoughts went back to Nick and the way in which he'd told her of Val's supposed infidelity. He'd had his back turned, and his voice had been slow and halting. At the time, she'd interpreted it as being embarrassment on his part—wounded male pride—and that had lent credence to his words. But what if she'd misinterpreted his behavior? What if he'd been lying to her?

A green-and-white sign announced an upcoming rest area. Andrea moved over to the right lane and signaled for the exit. A part of her was saying that she should just keep on driving, but she pulled into the rest area nonetheless, then went into the building to find a phone, hoping that Dolly would be working again this morning.

She breathed a sigh of relief when the phone was answered by her familiar voice. After identifying herself and telling Dolly that she still hadn't heard from her sister, she asked her about that statement.

"You told me that he gave you Val's description. Did you mean that he didn't expect her to recognize him?"

"Right. At least, that's what I figured. He said he was meeting someone, then gave me her description."

"And my sister didn't recognize him when she came in?"

"I don't think so. She looked around, but I caught her right away and pointed him out."

"Thanks, Dolly. I'm sorry to have bothered you again."

"No trouble—and listen, I was thinking. You wondered about the car he was driving or if anyone saw her leave. A lot of the guys who stop here are regulars, you know. They stop going one way and then stop again coming back. I'll start asking around to see if any of them might have seen what he was driving, or if they saw her leave."

"Yes, that's a good idea. Thank you. But I'm not staying at the Holiday Inn anymore, so I'll have to call you back."

"I'll be off for the next two days, so call me Tuesday. Maybe I'll have some news for you then. But I sure hope you hear from her before that."

Andrea thanked her again and hung up, then walked out into the predawn chill. The sky was just beginning to lighten off to the east. There was no one else in the rest area. Despite the penetrating cold, she began to walk along the sidewalk that ran the full length of the big parking area.

Facts, she told herself. No speculation. What are the clues here? Val vanished. She went to the club the morning of her disappearance, where she seemed distracted and said she had a "meeting she wasn't looking forward to."

Then she met a man at a restaurant where she was unlikely to be seen by anyone she knew. And she'd left very upset, followed by the stranger she'd met there.

And one final fact, though not positively related to the others, was that a man answering the description of the one Val had met had been following her.

She reached the end of the sidewalk and turned back to her car, now facing both the cold wind and the chill of her own fears. Something *had* happened to Val. She was once again sure of it. She had to stay now, regardless of the risk she was taking if she was wrong. It was better to destroy any hope of a reconciliation with Val than to make the same mistake she'd made all those years ago.

Headlights swept the parking area as a big truck pulled in, rumbling to a stop between Andrea and her car. The man who climbed down from the cab looked almost as big as his truck. When he saw her, he stopped, blocking her path to her car.

Andrea hesitated as fear squirmed along her spine—a fear out of all proportion to the moment.

"Pretty deserted to be walking around, isn't it?" the man asked. "You might think these places are safe, but they're not. All kinds of creeps hanging around. You oughtta be more careful, miss."

Andrea had to restrain a smile. "You're right. I just wasn't thinking."

"Take my advice. Don't get out of your car at any of them unless there's plenty of people around." Then he gestured to her blue Miata.

"Cute little bug you got there. My kid's been asking for one as a graduation present. You like it?"

"I love it," she said sincerely.

He scratched his graying head. "I dunno about buyin' a car that's hardly no bigger than I am."

She laughed. "Thanks for your concern—and your advice. I'll keep it in mind."

Back in her car, Andrea breathed a sigh of relief, then thought about her overreaction to the trucker's appearance. He was probably right about the danger, but still she'd definitely overreacted. Could it mean that her subconscious was trying to warn her of other danger—the handsome stranger, for example?

As she drove to the next exit to turn around, she thought about him. She had to assume it was the same man who'd met Val—and she needed to find out who he was. When she had that answer, she might know what had happened to Val.

By the time she reached Centre Valley, she'd made two decisions. She would not stay at the same motel and she would register under a different name. And she would temporarily give up her cherished Miata in favor of something less noticeable.

ANDREA'S HANDS GRIPPED the wheel of the rental car tightly as a chill of recognition shot through her. There, coming toward her, was a dark blue Cherokee. Before she could do more than turn her head slightly, it had passed her. She peered into the rearview mirror apprehensively. Could he have seen her?

She couldn't be sure that it was the dark-haired stranger, and even if it was, he wouldn't be expecting to find her driving a gray Chevy. Besides, her telltale auburn hair was tucked beneath a knit cap.

Still, as she continued on toward Val's home, the image of the Cherokee lingered in her mind. And then, just as she reached the driveway with its handsome sign announcing Centre Valley Gardens, it struck her.

The Cherokee bore New York license plates! She hadn't paid any attention to it before because, living as she did in southern Connecticut, she was accustomed to seeing New York plates. Surely, though, here in central Pennsylvania they were far more rare. Another connection made!

She passed by the driveway and began to look for a place to leave her car. Not far beyond the driveway, she discovered an old dirt road that ran into the open fields. But near the highway was a grove of pines that would hide the car from the house. She pulled in and got out, her thoughts still on the stranger.

But the mysterious man was not her objective at the moment. She'd decided that she needed to establish if Val had, in fact, taken off on her own—and the way to do that was to get into the house. Instead of returning to the highway and then going up the driveway, she set off across the snow-dusted field. She was assuming that at this time of day Nick would be busy in the greenhouses, which lay on the far side of the house.

It seemed to take forever to get across the windswept field, which had been plowed under and was now a series of deep ruts and small mounds, some of which were frozen, while others were slick with mud. And all the while, she feared she might be wrong—that Nick would be in the house, watching her. Of course, he wouldn't be likely to know who it was, but he'd surely be curious about someone out walking through the fields on a day like this.

Finally she reached the house and angled toward the rear, expecting to come face-to-face with Nick at any moment. But no one appeared, and she found the back door unlocked as before.

She slipped quickly inside, then paused for a moment, holding her breath as she listened carefully. But the only sound she could hear was the low whir of the refrigerator.

Her glance settled on the sink. There it was again—two of everything. She walked over to look more closely and discovered traces of egg yolk on two plates. Either Nick was eating a lot of eggs, or once again he'd had company for breakfast.

The big old house boasted two sets of stairs—one in front and a much narrower set that led up from the kitchen. That could come in very handy if she had to leave in a hurry.

She crept quietly up the back stairs, then paused at the top, listening. She was sure she was alone in the house, but that extra set of dishes remained on her mind. Moving very cautiously, she made her way down the carpeted hallway to the big master bedroom at the front of the house.

Val and Nick had done extensive renovations to the house, which included creating a huge walk-in closet for the master suite—and it was to that closet that Andrea hurried.

The luggage was all there! Andrea stood there for a moment, actually willing it to disappear. Their parents had given them each an identical set of very good luggage as graduation presents, and Val's matched set was stacked on a shelf.

She didn't know her sister's wardrobe, but a glance suggested that nothing much could be missing. Not yet ready to face the consequences of her discovery, Andrea reached out to touch some of her twin's clothes, smiling as she saw things that she herself might have bought.

Then from outside came the sound of a car. The engine abruptly grew silent and a door slammed. After that, there was silence again. It was probably a customer, she decided. She was afraid to go to the windows, because she might be seen from the office.

Still, she knew she shouldn't be lingering, and she'd found what she came for, so she started back down the hallway—then stopped as something caught her eye. The door to the guest room she'd used on her rare visits here stood partially ajar—and, inside on the floor, she saw a man's suitcase and an attaché case.

She pushed the door open, thinking about those extra dishes. The bed was neatly made, but it was obvious that someone was using the room. There was even a very faint trace of a pleasant masculine cologne in the air, emanating from the attached bath.

Her gaze fell again on the attaché case and she knelt down to try to open it. Locked. She turned her attention instead to the closet. Several sweaters were hanging there, together with a handsome navy blazer and an assortment of casual pants. Whoever he was, it looked as though he'd come prepared to stay for a while.

Then two other things caught her eye. Wrapped around the hanger that held the blazer was a leather strap that upon closer inspection turned out to be an empty shoulder holster. And propped against the wall, nearly hidden by the pants, was a rifle in a leather case.

She stared at them in shock. Who was this visitor—and why had he come "loaded for bear," as her grandfather would have said?

Then she started nervously and stifled a cry as a door slammed below her. Someone had come into the house! Was it Nick—or his well-armed guest?

Whoever it was, she didn't want him to find her here, so she left the room and then paused in the hallway, listening for footsteps. When she heard nothing, she decided to risk going down the back stairs. But just as she reached them, she heard sounds in the kitchen below.

Fighting panic, Andrea crept back down the hallway. And then she heard footsteps on the back stairs! Certain that she couldn't get down the front stairs in time to avoid being seen or heard, she slipped into another bedroom, then left the door cracked open just a bit.

The footsteps came closer as she peered through the crack. Then they stopped just outside the guest room, which was beyond her line of vision. Could he have heard her up here? Then suddenly she remembered that she'd left the door to the guest room wide open, instead of just slightly ajar as it had been. She held her breath, wondering if he'd notice. Then she shifted her position carefully, hoping to get a better view. And what she saw was part of an arm—and a hand with a gun!

For a dangerous moment, Andrea was simply too stunned to move. It felt as though she'd walked into a movie. Even as she began to back away from the door, she could still see the sleek, deadly weapon in her mind's eye.

Her heart now thudding in her throat, Andrea stripped off her down jacket, then shoved it under the bed and crawled under herself. He would probably come in here and he might even check the closet—but surely he wouldn't look under the bed!

The footsteps came closer and the door opened. With her cheek pressed to the floor, Andrea could see his shoes as he stopped in the middle of the room. Then he moved toward the closet and she congratulated herself on her decision not to hide there.

There was dust under the bed and her nose began to itch. She pinched off her nostrils and began to breathe through her mouth—very quietly. The closet door opened and closed again and the shoes became visible once more as he paused near the bed. She expected a face—and a gun—to appear at any moment. Holding her breath now, she stared at the rugged brown suede-and-leather shoes and willed them to disappear. And finally they did.

She heard him move on to the other bedrooms and then finally retreat down the front stairs. A few moments later, the back door opened and closed. She permitted herself a heartfelt sigh of relief and slid out from under the bed. He'd probably gone out to the greenhouse, but he could be back at any moment. She put on her jacket, once more tucked her hair beneath the cap and hurried down the back stairs herself, then ran out the door and around the side of the house into the field.

MICHAEL SHOVED HIS GUN into his back waistband as he left the house. Someone had definitely been in his room. He was sure that he'd left the door only slightly ajar. Noticing details like that was part of his business.

The girl in the office told him that Nick was out in the greenhouses, and Michael pushed through the connecting door into the moist, tropical warmth, scanning the long rows until he spotted Nick.

"Someone was in my room."

Nick looked surprised. "It wasn't me. Are you sure?"

Michael nodded. "I think I'd better make sure Andy left town like she told you."

Nick looked doubtful. "The motel clerk said she checked out early this morning. And even if she *is* still in town, I don't see why she'd be creeping around the house. Knowing Andy, if she decided that I was hiding something from her, she'd just come back and tell me so—like she did before."

"She could have been checking to see if Val took clothes with her," Michael suggested.

"She wouldn't be able to tell," Nick protested. "They hardly ever see each other."

"What about luggage? Where does Val keep hers?"

Nick gave him a stricken look. "Damn! I didn't think about that. Her luggage is on the shelf in the closet—and Andy has the same set. I remember noticing that when I carried Andy's bags in once."

Michael swore and hurried out of the greenhouse. He hadn't been gone very long, so it was possible that she was still somewhere around. She couldn't have parked her car that close to the house or he would have seen it, and he hadn't passed it on the road.

He got into his Cherokee. Just as he was about to start down the driveway, he caught sight of someone in the field on the far side of the house. He stopped and reached into the back for his binoculars. By the time he got them trained on the distant figure, it was moving into a grove of pines—and was definitely female.

He scanned the grove and caught sight of a car, but not the bright blue Miata he'd expected. Could it have been someone else? No, he decided. The figure he'd seen looked too much like Andy. And if she'd switched cars, that could mean that she was aware of his following her. He was surprised. Obviously he'd underestimated her.

He backed up quickly to the office door and ran in to ask the secretary if he could borrow her car for a while. She handed him the keys, making apologies for the condition of the interior. He thanked her and jumped into the gray hatchback. It looked as though she were using it for a dump, but at least it was inconspicuous.

He'd gone only about a half mile on the highway when he saw the gray Chevy up ahead. He slowed down to stay a safe distance behind. There would be time enough later to confirm if it was Andrea.

He followed her into town, then let a couple of cars get between them. Then, when she turned onto the road that led out to the interstate, he got directly behind her again. She'd removed the cap…and her long, auburn hair tumbled over her shoulders.

Michael smiled in spite of himself. Andrea Lockwood was a damned big problem, but she was also very interesting. He liked resourceful women and he admired her determination—but he still had to figure out a way to get rid of her.

Chapter Three

A glass of wine, an excellent dinner and a leisurely stroll through several antiques shops proved to be fleeting pleasures as Andrea returned to the motel.

She had hit the proverbial brick wall. The only options she could see for herself now were to confront Nick again and hope she could get the truth out of him, or go to the police and try to convince them that Val was in trouble.

What do you do when all your options are bad ones? she asked herself as she pulled into the motel lot. It was an eerie echo of a question posed by one of her clients in the college psych clinic not long ago. In that case, she'd been able to help him generate other options—something therapists were often able to do. But she could come up with nothing for herself, except for going home and waiting to hear from Nick, which she wasn't going to do.

As she was about to get out of her car, her bleak thoughts were interrupted by a woman's laughter. She turned and saw a couple staggering toward the motel. It was impossible to tell if the woman was drunk or merely unable to navigate properly in her stiletto heels and skintight leather mini.

She watched as they went into one of the rooms. This wasn't the first evidence she'd seen that the world's oldest profession was alive and well in Centre Valley. She'd chosen the motel because it seemed the least likely place that

Nick would look for her, but now, as she headed for her room, she wondered if she might not be putting her personal safety at risk. Perhaps she'd better change motels again tomorrow.

Her mind returning to her dilemma, Andrea unlocked the door to her room and walked in, pulling it shut behind her and fastening the safety chain. The blinds were partway open and the room was dimly lit by the huge motel sign outside. She started across the room to switch on the lamp— and froze!

A dark and obviously male figure detached itself from the chair in the corner. She tried to scream, but managed only a surprised squeak. At the same time, she fumbled in her purse for the can of pepper spray she'd been carrying ever since they'd had a series of rapes on her campus.

Her fingers closed around the cylinder and she brought it up. But the intruder moved quickly, grabbing it from her and flinging it away.

"Calm down, Andy. I'm not here to hurt you."

The fact that he knew her name should have been reassuring, but instead, it only increased her terror. This wasn't some drunk looking for a prostitute—this was someone after *her!*

She jerked her arm from his grasp and spun around, trying to reach the door. But before her trembling fingers could get the chain loose, he had come up behind her and gripped both her arms in a steel vise.

She kicked backward, landing a solid blow to his shin as she struggled to free herself. But that put them both off-balance and they tumbled to the floor in a tangle of arms and legs, rolling about as each of them tried to gain the upper hand.

His superior size won out all too quickly, and he grasped both her hands and held them imprisoned over her head while he reached for the lamp switch. She started to scream again, but it died in a gurgle as she stared into the face of the dark-haired stranger!

He released her, then got to his feet and sat down on the edge of the bed, running his hands through his disheveled hair. His wide mouth twitched with amusement—and then he began to laugh.

"What are you doing here?" she demanded, clumsily getting to her feet. Her fear was temporarily replaced by anger. He'd broken into her room, manhandled her—and now he was *laughing?*

"Waiting for you—obviously. I fell asleep. You surprised me as much as I scared you."

"Do you expect me to apologize? This is *my* room. How did you get in here?"

"I picked the lock. That's what happens when you stay in cheap motels. You should consider yourself lucky that it was *me* waiting for you, and not one of this place's usual customers."

His dark eyes gleamed with amusement. "Bedroom eyes," the waitress had called them. And they were in *her* bedroom. Andrea's gaze went to the can of spray on the floor nearby and she began to edge toward it. But he obviously saw it, too, and moved with lightning speed, grabbing it before she could get to it.

"I told you I'm not going to hurt you," he said, examining the cylinder before slipping it into the pocket of his leather jacket.

"By the way, I'm Michael Borelli. We haven't officially met."

Michael Borelli. The name was vaguely familiar. She'd been edging toward the door, but now she stopped in confusion. Where had she heard that name before?

"The same Michael Borelli who failed to make your acquaintance at Nick and Val's wedding, thanks to a foolish miscalculation."

"You'd been shot," she said, remembering it all now. He was Nick's friend and should have been his best man. As she belatedly recalled, he was a former New York City police officer and a private investigator.

"Like I said, a foolish miscalculation." He grinned at her. "So now that you know who I am, will you stop acting like I'm going to attack you at any moment?"

She said nothing. Knowing who he was didn't exactly reassure her. That meant he was the one staying with Nick—the very well-armed man. She wondered uneasily if he had a gun with him now.

"I'd like you to leave, Mr. Borelli."

He made no move to do so. "Actually, I came over here to invite you out to dinner. But I assume you've probably eaten by now, so why don't you join me while I grab something?"

"Are you in the habit of breaking into the rooms of women you don't know to invite them to dinner?" she inquired acerbically.

"No, I knocked first. It was too cold to wait outside." He took her arm. "Come on. I'm hungry. The choices are pretty limited at this time of night, but there's an all-night diner with decent food."

She shook off his hand. "Give me one reason why I should trust you."

He made a show of scratching his head. "Damned if I can come up with one. But don't let that stop you. You're the adventurous sort."

Andrea turned away to pick up her bag—and hide her smile. She still didn't trust him any farther than she could throw him—which he'd already proved wasn't far—but she had to admit that, among other things, he was very amusing.

They left the motel room and walked along the covered walkway, then went down the stairs to the parking lot. She looked around, but didn't see his Cherokee—and that prompted the question she should have asked before this.

"How did you find me?"

"I followed you back here from Nick's earlier."

"You couldn't have," she stated flatly. "I would have seen you."

"I did just what you did—switched cars."

She came to a stop. There was a lie in there somewhere. She'd passed him on her way to Nick's, and he was headed toward town. And if he was the one staying at Nick's—the man who'd returned while she was there—where did he get a different car? She would have recognized Nick's truck or his Corvette.

"Were you still in the house when I came back?" he asked.

"I was under the bed in the room across from yours. Aren't you a private investigator?"

He chuckled. "I'm supposed to be, but apparently I'm not a very good one."

She did her best to ignore the twinkle in his eyes and that sexy chuckle. In spite of his self-deprecatory statement, she would have bet her tenure that he was, in fact, *very* good. The only question was what he was doing here.

"I saw you in the field and borrowed a car from one of Nick's staff," he told her, taking her arm again and leading her around the side of the motel to the small rear lot.

It was very dark, but she immediately saw his Cherokee, parked beside her Miata, which she'd hidden there. She pulled her arm from his grasp and announced that she would meet him at the diner. He stared at her for a moment, then shrugged.

"Okay, but I want you to know that my feelings have been hurt. Do I look like the kind of guy who goes around attacking women?"

She ignored him and dug out the keys to her car. No, he didn't look like the kind who attacked women. Instead, he seemed like the type who could sweet-talk them into anything.

As she followed him to the diner, Andrea tried to recall what little she knew about Michael Borelli. It wasn't much. Val had seemed to like him, and she'd said that he and Nick had been best friends since childhood. Nick had been very upset that Michael hadn't made it to their wedding.

Don't trust him, she warned herself sternly. He may be handsome, sexy and funny—but he's still Nick's friend.

The diner was nearly empty, since most of its late-night clientele tended to be college students and they were gone for semester break. Michael led her to a table in the rear, far from the other customers. After ordering moussaka, a house speciality for as long as she could remember, he leaned against the high back of the booth and stared at her.

"So tell me what you've found out."

She shook her head, avoiding his dark eyes. "First, you tell me why you're here."

"That's simple enough. Nick called me because he's worried about Val. He wants me to find her."

"Why did she leave?"

He looked surprised. "Nick said he told you. They had a fight and she took off. He wants me to find her and talk to her—make sure she's okay. Whether or not she comes back is up to her."

You did talk to her, she said silently, *and it didn't work.* Now she understood the situation that Dolly had described to her. But that *couldn't* have been Michael Borelli! Val hadn't known the man she went to meet. Confusion swarmed over her. Could Dolly have been wrong?

"What did they fight about?" she asked, wondering if it was even remotely possible that Nick could have lied to Michael.

"I thought he told you that, too. She accused him of having an affair. He hadn't, but he thinks she is—or was—having one in retaliation." He shrugged. "The usual joys of marriage."

"Val wouldn't do that."

"How do you know? The two of you haven't been that close, from what Nick told me. And besides, you're a psychologist. You know that people frequently do things you don't expect them to do."

"She's not just my sister—she's my *twin*. And I know she wouldn't do something like that."

"But you told Nick that she met a man somewhere."

"She did. A man whose description fits yours."

"It wasn't me," he said quickly—but she saw something flicker briefly in his eyes. "Did she meet him at that truckers' restaurant out at the I-80 interchange. That would explain a few things."

"What things?"

"I went there this afternoon because I figured someone at the club must have pointed you in that direction. That's where you were headed when you spotted me following you. The woman I talked to at the club said Val told them she had a 'meeting,' but that was all she knew.

"Anyway, I thought that Dolly Parton wannabe was lying when she said Val hadn't been there. But I couldn't get her to talk, despite my best efforts to charm her."

Andrea smiled inwardly at his description of Dolly. She herself hadn't made the connection. And she guessed that Michael was just a bit put out that his "charm" hadn't worked.

"Doesn't it strike you as being rather strange that Val would have gone to the club that morning? And how do you explain the fact that her luggage isn't missing?"

She threw in that last in the hope of catching him out, but he merely smiled.

"So that *is* why you were snooping around the house. Pretty good thinking. Nick told me you two have matching luggage. He says Val also has one of those big canvas bags, and it's missing, along with some of her clothes."

Andrea wasn't about to take Nick's word for anything, but she didn't tell him that. "But what about her going to the club that morning? That seems pretty strange to *me*."

"*Nothing* seems strange to me anymore, lady. To coin a phrase, I've seen it all. She'd been going there every morning, so she just went there out of habit. Most of us are very predictable. It's the one thing that sometimes makes my work a bit easier. But why do I keep getting the impression that you don't believe Nick?"

Andrea wasn't sure *what* she believed at this point. "She never even hinted to me that she and Nick were having problems."

"But she wouldn't, would she? From what Nick said, you two haven't been close ever since the accident."

Andrea nodded, unable to meet his gaze. He hadn't spoken harshly, and he certainly hadn't said anything she didn't already know—but it still hurt. Then she started nervously as his hand suddenly covered hers warmly. He pulled it away quickly.

"I'm sorry, Andy—and from what Nick told me, Val was beginning to regret it, too. But now that I've met you, I think I can understand why things have stayed the same all these years."

"What do you mean?"

"Well, first of all, there are the physical changes. From the pictures I saw of the wedding, I wouldn't have been able to tell you two apart if it wasn't for the dresses. But there *are* differences, and if I can see them, they must be even more obvious to Val.

"Then there's the personality difference. I'd be willing to bet that you were always the leader and the more popular one—and that only makes it worse."

Andrea was stunned at his assessment of the situation. His words weren't new to her, but the fact that he'd so easily figured out the situation came as a shock. Whatever else Michael Borelli might be, he was certainly a shrewd judge of character.

"I think that Val had begun to gain some self-confidence the past year or so—after she married Nick. And that's why she may be ready to become friends with you again."

Andrea nodded. She couldn't dispute what he was saying, since she, too, had detected a slight thaw in Val's attitude toward her. But the nagging thought remained that Nick—and now Michael—could be using that to get her to leave.

"If she was gaining self-confidence, then why would she have an affair?" Despite what Michael had said, Andrea knew that Nick had lied about that.

"Like I said, she was probably trying to get back at Nick. That's not uncommon."

"You sound like a man who speaks from experience," she remarked, recalling that he'd made a similarly cynical remark about marriage earlier.

He laughed. "No, just from observation. I've never been married. And the more I see of it, the less I like the idea, even though I *do* like kids."

"Is that what you do in your work—spy on cheating husbands and wives?"

He shook his head. "No, I leave that part of the business to the slimeballs. There're plenty of them around. Most of my work is corporate. Remember how shocked the public was when Ross Perot admitted that he'd used private investigators in his businesses? Well, they *all* do it—and it pays well, too."

"Is that why you left the police force?"

For one brief moment, a shadow passed across his face. It was gone very quickly, but Andrea knew that she'd struck a nerve, and she wondered why.

"Yeah, that was most of it. But I also got tired of locking up scum, only to find them out on the street again in a couple of months."

His dinner arrived, along with her slice of shoofly pie and coffee. After the waitress had gone, he looked at her.

"Okay, enough history about me. Tell me what Dolly told you."

"Val *was* there that morning. She met someone and Dolly's description had convinced me it was you." She watched for that flicker she'd seen before when she mentioned the other man, but he just made a sound of disgust as he dug into his moussaka.

"Did she leave with him?"

"No, but Dolly said she seemed really upset when she left. And he left right after she did."

"Maybe that means they broke it off—or that he gave her an ultimatum—leave your husband or I disappear."

Andrea knew that the man Val met couldn't have been her lover, and she very much wanted to tell him that—to prove that he was wrong about Val and that Nick must be lying. But that meant that either Michael was not telling the truth, or that Nick was keeping something from him. In either case, it seemed prudent to keep that bit of information to herself for now.

What was going on? And who was deceiving whom? Nick must certainly know what happened to Val—but did Michael? She was shocked to realize how much she wanted to trust Michael Borelli, and how easy it would be to do that. There was something so reassuringly solid about him—a quality she suddenly realized she saw in so few people and one she prized greatly.

"Well, we should hear from her soon," Michael said after a pause. "She didn't have much money with her, and the credit-card companies will let Nick know if she uses them. Same with the banking card."

"Surely Nick must have some idea where she could have gone?"

"He doesn't. I've checked with most of her friends, too. I know that they could have been sworn to secrecy, but I asked them to get in touch with her and tell her I wanted to talk to her. I think she'd talk to me, even if she doesn't want to talk to Nick. I gave them all my twenty-four-hour service number."

"She couldn't have gone far, though. If she had, she would have run out of money by now," Michael said.

Andrea thought about Beth from the health club. Michael must have talked to her. She began to wonder if Val might have contacted her friend, or if Beth knew she'd called someone else. Beth would have had no way of getting in touch with her, so she should call her tomorrow.

"So what are you going to do now?" she asked.

"Nothing—unless you have an idea."

"*You're* the detective," she reminded him.

"I know, but waiting for something to happen is a big part of investigative work, despite what all the movies show. So can I assume that we'll work together?"

"I don't know."

He shrugged. "Well, if you keep on playing detective on your own, at least you'll keep me busy."

"What do you mean?"

"Simple. I'll follow you. So why don't you save yourself some money and make my life easier? Give up the rental and go back to your cute little blue bug."

"Doesn't it hurt your ego to be following me around to see if I find out something you haven't?"

"Not at all. I discovered long ago that women are often better at certain types of investigative work than men are. That's why I hired a female investigator for my agency.

"And in your sister's case, the fact that you're twins helps, too. Just seeing you can jog someone's memory and make them more cooperative."

"Does Nick know I'm still here?"

"Sure. What have you got against him, anyway?"

"Nothing," she said, perhaps too quickly.

"He says you told Val before the wedding that there was something about him that bothered you."

"I don't want to talk about it, Michael. I know that Nick has made Val very happy—up to now, that is."

"Are you psychic?" he asked. "Is there some sort of psychic connection between you two? I know the story about the accident. But did you come here because you had another premonition or whatever?"

Andrea wasn't prepared for that particular question. She started to shake her head, then stopped, unable to think of another explanation for her unannounced arrival here.

"I'm not psychic," she stated firmly. "But I *did* sense that something was wrong—so I came."

"It must have been a pretty powerful feeling, since Nick said you were in the Caribbean on vacation. Or did you just overreact because of that other time?"

"Maybe I did," she said, not meaning it, but once again surprised at his perceptiveness. "But I *had* to come—even if I was wrong."

She hadn't intended that her words should be a plea for understanding, but what she saw in Michael Borelli's eyes was just that. A pleasant warmth flowed through her, and in that moment, she became convinced that he would never lie to her.

When they left the diner, he insisted upon following her back to the motel to see her safely to her room. He also urged her to find another place to stay.

"And no more 'disappearing' acts, please." He grinned as he opened her car door for her.

On the way back to the motel, Andrea kept glancing into the rearview mirror, even though she couldn't really see him. But she didn't have to—his image was burned into her brain. Michael Borelli was quite possibly the most attractive man she'd ever met—and not just in the physical sense, either.

He walked her to her door, and there was a brief hesitation on both their parts, into which flowed sensual possibilities that it appeared neither of them was yet willing to confront. Then he said good-night and reminded her to put on the safety chain.

When he had gone, Andrea could feel his absence almost as strongly as she'd felt his presence. She wished that she didn't like Michael so much. Her undeniable attraction to him was certainly clouding her judgment.

But she dared not forget that he was Nick's best friend—and despite his attraction to her, she knew exactly where his loyalties would lie.

NICK WAS WAITING impatiently when Michael returned to the house, and even before he spoke, Michael knew that something had happened.

"I got a call," Nick said, brandishing a piece of paper. "Just about an hour ago. When can you check on it?"

"First thing in the morning," Michael assured him. "Now tell me about the conversation."

Nick repeated it verbatim. It had gone pretty much as Michael had expected.

"We were right," Nick said. "She isn't that far away."

"That still doesn't mean that I can find her," Michael reminded him. "They could be on the move."

Then he told Nick about his conversation with Andy. "I think she'll cooperate, but I still haven't figured out how I'm going to get rid of her."

"You'll think of something," Nick said confidently.

"Yeah, I will," Michael agreed, his mind turning from the tangled relationship of the twins to his own, equally complex relationship with Nick.

Nick's confidence in him was an echo of their long-ago childhood. They were distantly related and Michael was only a little over a year older, but as children, that had seemed like a big difference to them both. They'd lived next door to each other and learned a lot on the streets of Brooklyn in a working-class Italian neighborhood where being tough was the only thing that counted. Grown up and then apart, until the day that...

He left off those thoughts because they were still too painful, even after six years. He wished hopelessly that he were in New York, and not back in his past. The only good thing that had come of this was Andrea Lockwood—and that was a decidedly mixed blessing.

Later, as he lay in bed, Michael thought about Andy. She was bright and funny and gutsy—a dynamite combination, as far as he was concerned. She was also vulnerable, haunted by a mistake she hadn't made—and that, too, was part of her appeal. Add to that her obvious physical charms and...

But he didn't trust her. He was pretty sure she hadn't told him everything, which meant that she didn't trust him, either. She must have found out something that convinced her Val hadn't left on her own—and he needed to know what it was.

"BETH, IT'S ANDY Lockwood."

"Hi, Andy. Have you heard from Val?"

Andrea's hopes plummeted. "No, and apparently you haven't, either. Is there anyone else you think she might have called?"

"I suppose she could have called another friend, but if she had, I think I'd know about it."

Andrea thought that if Val had called anyone, it would most likely have been Beth. There was something about Beth that made people naturally want to confide in her.

"Did Michael Borelli call you?" she asked.

"Who?"

"He's the man who was at the health club," Andrea told her uneasily. "An old friend of Nick's who's also trying to find Val. He's a private investigator and he's been contacting her friends. He seems to think that even if Val won't talk to Nick right now, she'd talk to him."

"Well, he didn't call *me*, and he couldn't have called Sally, either. I talked to her last night and she would have told me. And the two of us are certainly among her closest friends."

"Oh." Andrea didn't know what else to say. She thanked Beth and promised to keep in touch.

Kind, sympathetic Michael with the warm, understanding eyes. *Lying* eyes, she thought disgustedly. But why would he have lied about such a thing? It certainly made sense for him to contact Val's friends to see if they'd heard from her—unless he knew they *couldn't* have heard from her.

Andrea felt sick. Despite the evidence to the contrary, she'd still been hoping that Val *had* taken off on her own. But how much more evidence could she ignore?

She was about to go take a shower when she remembered that Dolly was going to try to get some information from their regular customers at the truck stop. Andrea didn't know how likely it was that she would turn up anything, but she was desperate. So she called her, and the tone of the woman's voice suggested that she had indeed found out something.

"I was hoping you'd call, because I just got some information, and I for one don't like the sound of it. A trucker I know pretty well came in a little while ago and I remembered that he'd been here that morning because he'd made some remark about your sister. He left just a few minutes before she did.

"Anyway, he said he saw her come out, and he could tell that she was really upset. She got into a green Volvo, but she didn't start the engine. He thought it looked like she was crying. Then the guy she was with came out and got in on the other side. He said they seemed to be arguing. She was trying to get out of the car.

"At that point, a truck pulled in and blocked his view. He said he thought about going over to make sure she was okay, but he guessed it was between them, you know. He figured that since she'd been with the guy inside, she could have gotten help then if she'd needed it.

"Still, he waited to see what would happen, and a couple of minutes later, she pulled out. The guy was still in the car, and a black Chevy Blazer pulled out right behind them. He remembered that the driver was sitting in it when he came in for breakfast, and he was still there when he came out."

"Did he get a look at the other man—the one in the Blazer?"

"Not a good look. All he remembers is that he had gray hair. And he can't be sure that he was following your sister and the other guy, but he thought he might be."

Dolly paused, then said, "Oh, yeah—and one other thing. This real hunk was in here asking if your sister'd been here that morning. I didn't tell him anything, but he left me his card. He's a private investigator from New York."

"Yes, I know who he is."

"Honey, I don't know what's going on, but it sounds to me like you oughtta go to the police."

"Thanks, Dolly. I really appreciate your help."

Andrea sank onto the bed. She'd only been up half an hour and already the day was getting worse and worse. She checked her home answering machine by remote, but wasn't surprised to find that there was no message from Val. Then she went into the shower, her mind whirling with possibilities—none of which were good.

She couldn't yet quite bring herself to believe that her sister had been kidnapped, but neither could she dismiss the possibility. Who were these men and what did they want with her? And what had they used to lure Val to that meeting?

As she stood under the hot spray, Andrea recalled Val's statement to Beth about thinking you know someone well and then finding out that you don't. Beth had thought it was more than mere sympathy—and now Andrea did, too. Her sister could have been lured to the meeting with information about Nick's past—the darkness in him that Andrea had sensed!

It has to have something to do with Nick, she told herself. Nick is lying, and Michael almost certainly is, too. But why hadn't Nick gone to the police? Was it only that he trusted Michael to handle the situation—or was there another reason?

Suddenly she recalled Val's having said once that Nick believed the "sun rose and set" on Michael Borelli, that he'd told her he owed Michael more than he could ever repay. Val either hadn't asked Nick what he meant, or she hadn't wanted to tell Andrea.

Andrea was just toweling herself dry when she heard a knock at the door. Fearing that it might be a prospective "customer," she ignored it. But the rapping continued and even grew more insistent.

"Andy, it's Michael! Open up!"

Wrapping herself in the skimpy towel, which barely covered the essentials, she opened the door a crack, keeping the chain in place.

"You really do know how to knock first," she commented dryly.

"I was just about to get out my burglary kit." He sniffed ostentatiously. "You smell good."

She'd used the frangipani soap she'd brought back from her abbreviated vacation and knew that she must be enveloped in the distinctive scent. "I just got out of the shower. You'll have to wait until I get dressed."

"Let me in and I promise I'll keep my eyes shut. If I stay out here, I might get propositioned—and you know how we men are."

Andrea laughed, unable to resist his humor even in the midst of her mental turmoil. She undid the chain and he walked in with his eyes closed. She grabbed her clothes and hurried back into the bathroom, where she quickly applied some makeup and dressed, then dried her hair.

Basically it all came down to two choices. Either she could confront both Michael and Nick with her knowledge, or she could keep what Dolly had told her to herself and pretend she accepted Nick's story. Confronting them was no guarantee that she would get the truth, but concealing her information just might allow her to get closer to it.

"Val called Nick last night," Michael announced as soon as she came out of the bathroom.

"She did? What did she say?"

"Not much, apparently. He said she sounded pretty upset and wouldn't say when she was coming back."

"Did she tell him where she is?" Andrea asked eagerly as relief flooded through her. She'd been wrong, then—apparently about everything.

"No, but I had attached a caller-identification device to Nick's phone and I checked out the number this morning."

"So?" she asked impatiently.

"It was a pay phone located at a gas station near some Podunk place about an hour's drive north of here."

He produced a road map. "I thought we'd take both cars and start checking out that area. She's probably at a motel nearby."

"But if she's at a motel, why would she call from a pay phone?"

For a moment, Michael appeared to be surprised at her question. Then he shrugged. "I don't know, but that's where she called from. Maybe she'd gone out somewhere to dinner and it was just a spur-of-the-moment thing."

"Were you there when she called?"

"No, I was with you. Why?"

Andrea hesitated, then decided to risk it. "Michael, can you be sure that Nick is telling you the truth?"

"Of course," he responded curtly. "Why would he lie? He's going nuts, worrying about her."

"Exactly what did she say?" Andrea asked, already doubting that Val had made the call.

"Not much, apparently. She just said that she'd called to let him know that she was okay, and that she hadn't decided what to do yet."

You're lying, Michael Borelli, she said to herself. Either Val didn't call at all, or she'd said something else. She saw that same inability to make eye contact and heard the slight change in tone that she'd noticed with Nick.

"I thought we'd go find the pay phone first," Michael said. "If the gas station was open at the time, someone might have noticed her and could tell us which way she went."

She nodded, wondering if this was all a wild-goose chase. But what would be the point? It seemed likely that *some-*

one had made a call from that phone. And in any event, what else was there for her to do? Even with the information Dolly had given her, she really had no useful leads.

"What's wrong, Andy? I thought you'd be pleased that we've finally heard from her."

"I am," she replied, forcing a smile. "But I'm still worried about her."

Chapter Four

"Help me to understand something," Michael said, regarding her across the small table at a fast-food restaurant. "Why don't you think Nick's telling the truth? And since you don't believe it, what do you think has happened to Val?"

Andrea carefully maintained eye contact with him—not an easy task when the eyes she stared into were so dark and utterly sexy. She was surprised and amused to hear him use a phrase that every therapist used regularly. "Help me to understand" was so much less threatening than "I don't believe a word you're saying," or a simple, "You're crazy."

"Did you study psychology in college, Michael?" she asked.

"I took a few courses. Now answer my question—and not with another question."

"I've never actually said that I don't believe Nick. I just have some doubts, that's all—and I think for good reasons."

"Such as?"

"Such as a marriage that seemed to be nearly perfect—and Val's timing. Why would she run away just when they've gotten their biggest business contract yet? Val cares about the greenhouse as much as Nick does.

"And there there's this supposed affair of hers. I've already told you I don't believe that. It isn't like her, Michael—and please don't tell me that I don't know her anymore. Values are something that don't change."

"But we both know that she met a man the morning she left," he pointed out neutrally.

"So? How do you know she couldn't have met him for some other reason?"

"What other reason?" he asked, his voice now taking on a slightly sharper tone.

"Suppose he lured her there... to kidnap her?" Andrea asked, deciding to go for the shock value.

But Michael's reaction wasn't what she'd expected. Instead of surprise, she got a smile, then a chuckle. "Andy, you watch too many TV movies. But let's just suppose you're right, for the sake of argument. *Why* would anyone want to kidnap Val?"

"I don't have the answer to that yet," she replied, bristling at his patronizing tone.

"Well, it sure can't be money," Michael said. "They're stretched about as tight as they can be right now, with that expansion into ornamental grasses and this new contract. It's temporary, of course—in the long run, they'll do very well."

"But what if the kidnappers don't know that?"

"Andy, if you're going to kidnap someone, you do your homework first."

"Then what if it has something to do with Nick's past?"

Michael heaved a sigh. "Your psychic antenniae aren't infallible, Andy. There's nothing in Nick's past."

He gave her a level look. "Besides, we're still back to the money thing. You're suggesting blackmail."

"I think we should go to the police."

"Fine. We'll go the police. What do you intend to tell them—that you have this 'feeling' your twin is in trouble? I was a cop—remember? I know exactly what they'll do, which is nothing. You can't waste valuable police resources on 'feelings.' Val is an adult, and unless you have strong evidence that she didn't disappear on her own, there's nothing they can do."

She said nothing. Even if she told him what the trucker had told Dolly, it wouldn't add up to "strong evidence." Val had come to the restaurant and left of her own free will. And as the trucker had said, if she'd felt threatened she could have gotten help.

Still, she thought about telling Michael about it. There was no reason not to, except that little inner voice that kept telling her to keep it to herself for now.

He opened the road map and spread it out as they finished their breakfast. "The place where she called from is very rural. There can't be many places she could stay, and anyone who saw her is likely to remember her. I got you a map, too."

She followed Michael north out of town into the sparsely populated region. It was a very different world from Centre Valley.

There was so much poverty in this area. Centre Valley and its immediate environs were prosperous, but out here was the desolate rural poverty of a place that time had left behind. Scattered farms that mostly appeared to be clinging to little more than hope, isolated homes in need of repairs, power lines marching across barren fields and over forested hills, trailer parks and forlorn dogs chained to doghouses. Abandoned cars and appliances littered the landscape.

Why would Val even come to such a place? Andrea asked herself. But a kidnapper would find it the perfect place to hide someone. There was little police presence in rural areas like this. Mostly they were patrolled by the state police, if at all.

They found the gas station and the pay phone around noon, only to discover that the station was closed and boarded up. The plywood was spray painted with graffiti, though of a much less imaginative kind than that of urban "artists."

They both pulled in close to the phone booth, which stood near the highway, and Michael went to check it out. It was the right number, he told her.

Andrea looked around. There wasn't a house or building of any kind in sight. It seemed a very strange place for Val to have made a call—especially at night. She herself would certainly have sought out a phone in a safer environment.

Again, it was exactly the kind of place a kidnapper might choose—isolated.

She shot a glance at Michael, who was studying the map again. Was she a product of the "TV movie" syndrome he'd accused her of? She didn't think so, but as a colleague had once remarked, the whole of society was infected by that mentality.

Then a sudden thought occurred to her. If Michael and Nick had made up that call from Val, how could Michael have known that they'd find a phone here? So apparently someone *had* called—but was it Val, or the men who might have kidnapped her?

"According to the map, there's a town just a couple of miles away," Michael said, refolding the map. "Let's go there and see if we can find out anything."

Watsonville turned out to be a collection of about two dozen shabby-looking houses and mobile homes that had long ago clustered around an intersection. Right at the intersection was a small general store that Andrea decided might have been there long enough to have once sold buggy whips. There were gas pumps out front—and a telephone booth, as well.

The store's hours were prominently displayed on a sign in the dirty window—7:00 a.m. To Midnight. And there were two tall mercury vapor lamps that would certainly illuminate the whole place, and probably the neighboring houses, as well.

Taking in the scene, Andrea considered it further proof that Val hadn't made that call. She couldn't know this area all that well, but if she wanted to call Nick, she would surely have sought out a place like this.

Michael came over to her car when they had pulled into the lot. "Not exactly a hot spot for tourism, is it? I wonder if they even have motels around here. I'll go in and see what I can find out."

He wasn't gone long, and when he returned, he lowered himself into the passenger seat of her car. "There are two motels in the area, but they cater mostly to hunters and she doesn't think either of them is open now. One is about twenty miles in that direction." He pointed toward the intersecting road. "And the other is roughly the same distance back the way we came and then left on Route 137."

"Did you ask her if she'd seen any strangers lately?"

"They haven't seen Val, if that's what you mean. And I'm sure they'd remember her."

He unfolded his map again. "She also said there are some cottages near a lake that are rented out in the summer. The owner lives there year-round, so they're worth checking out, too. Ahh, there it is."

He marked the approximate location of the motels and the cottages and they divided up the territory. Then they went their separate ways, after making plans to meet at a convenient intersection. But Andrea drove only a few miles before pulling off and heading back to the store. Michael had asked about Val, but she could ask about the two men.

Andrea decided that if she discovered any evidence that the two men were in the area, she would tell Michael about them. She certainly had her doubts about his and Nick's roles in this, but if the men had been seen here, then her kidnapping scenario couldn't be dismissed so lightly.

When she walked into the store, a very obese woman looked up from some papers she had spread out on the counter, and two older men followed her with their eyes. But she saw no sign of recognition and concluded with relief that Michael had told the truth.

She greeted the woman and proceeded to gather up some junk food to fortify herself for the day's travels and hopefully to make the woman more talkative. After paying for it, she launched into her story.

"I'm looking for my sister—my twin. She and her husband had a fight and she left. I'm really worried about her and I think she could be somewhere in this area. Her husband was abusing her, and I'm afraid that he or some of his drinking buddies might be out looking for her. Have you seen any strangers around here in the past few days?"

The woman regarded her silently for a long moment and Andrea could feel the eyes of the two men on her, as well.

"Wasn't you with that guy who was in here just a little while ago?" the woman asked cautiously.

"Yes, I was. But I'm not sure I can trust him, either. He's a friend of my sister's husband, too."

"Well, I don't rightly know what's going on here, but I'll tell you what I told him. There *was* a couple of guys in here. I don't recollect which day it was. They had accents—like maybe they was from New York. But they didn't ask about a woman. They just bought some food."

Andrea struggled to contain her anger with Michael and asked the woman to describe the two men. The descriptions fit the man who'd met Val at the restaurant and the one who'd been driving the Blazer.

"Did you happen to see what they were driving?"

"It was a black Chevy Blazer. Looked like New York plates when they pulled out—just like the ones on your friend's Cherokee. They sort of talked like him, too—except more, if you know what I mean."

She did. Michael's accent was definitely New York, but not as strong as some she'd heard.

"Could my sister have been with them?"

"Nope. It was just the two of them. I can be sure of that, because they was parked right out front."

"And you told the man I was with about them?"

"Sure did. I guess you were right not to trust him. My daughter's married to a guy who gives her trouble, but she won't leave him because of the kids. Your sister got any kids?"

Andrea said she didn't and refrained from pointing out that the children would be better off without a father than with an abusive one. It was an old, sad story—and one she'd heard many times.

"Is there anyplace she could be staying around here? Michael—the man I was with—said there are a couple of motels."

"Yeah, but they're not the kind of place for a lady. Mostly hunters stay there—and sometimes loggers. There's some cabins down at the lake, but they're not much, either. Unless she's at one of the hunting camps, I don't know where else she could be."

Andrea thanked the woman and got her name and phone number. She told Andrea that she would keep an eye out for her sister and for the two men.

"How much food did they buy?" she asked out of curiosity.

"Not a lot. Bread and milk and pop was about all."

Andrea sat in her car, thinking. If they hadn't bought much food, that meant they either already had a supply or they weren't planning to stay long. She thought about those hunting camps the woman had mentioned. Was it possible that they were using one of them? With a four-wheel drive, they could go just about anywhere, and she guessed that most of the camps were pretty isolated.

Michael had lied to her again. Now there could be no doubt about it. She tried not to feel hurt, telling herself that she'd suspected it all along. But it still stung—far too much.

She set out to find the motel she'd decided to check, no longer holding out much hope at all of finding Val there. If she was with those men, they surely wouldn't be holding her captive at a rural motel. It *had* to be one of those hunting camps—but how on earth could she find them? Here and there, she saw dirt roads that weren't on the map, most of them leading off into the thick woods. Maybe there were cabins farther back, but there was no way to know even if she had time and the little Miata could handle the terrain.

An image of Val being held captive in some isolated cabin deep in the woods swam before her, making her shudder with terror for her sister. Michael had been right—*she'd* always been the leader, the one who got them into and out of various scrapes. And now Val was out there somewhere, completely on her own.

She found the motel, a small white frame place with about ten units and an office in front. No one was working and there were no cars in the parking lot. On the far side of the large lot was a house, so she went there. The pleasant older man who came to the door affirmed that he was the owner, but told her that he'd had no guests since hunting season. She asked about Val and the two men, but he hadn't seen them.

She continued driving around the area. In a town called Sawyer, which, with perhaps a hundred or so houses, was the biggest place in the region, she checked gas stations and a supermarket. But no one recalled having seen either Val or the two men. And as she drove along the nearly deserted roads, she kept watching for her sister's Volvo or the men's Blazer. But it was rapidly becoming all too apparent just how easy it was for them to vanish in this huge wilderness.

And yet she was certain they must be here somewhere. Their purchases at the store seemed incongruous with someone just passing through. One look at the map confirmed that no one would be passing through this area—"off the beaten track" scarcely described it.

Once again, she thought about the police. But she knew that she still had nothing to offer them as proof that Val had been kidnapped. No one had seen Val with the men except for the trucker, and he'd seen nothing that would point to her having been taken against her will.

Finally she drove to the intersection where she'd agreed to meet Michael, mulling over how to handle the situation. If she told him now that she knew he'd lied, that would certainly end their supposed "cooperation" and leave her completely on her own.

She thought about what he'd actually said when he came out of the store and it occurred to her that he hadn't actually *lied*. She'd asked about strangers and he'd said that no one had seen Val. Very clever, she thought bitterly. Michael Borelli was obviously a master of deception.

And yet she continued to want to trust him. How could she feel this way, when she knew he wasn't honest with her?

When she reached the intersection, his Cherokee was there. As she pulled in behind it, she could see that it was empty. A chill shot through her. Could something have happened to him?

Thick woods grew close to the intersection on all sides and the hilly contours of the land prevented her from seeing any distance. She glanced at the clock and saw that she was a bit early. Maybe he'd just gone for a walk. She was feeling the need to stretch her own legs after spending so much time in her small car.

But Michael's absence continued to make her uneasy. What if the two men had found him? Just because the woman at the store had told him about them didn't mean that Michael had any reason to connect them with Val. Maybe that's why he hadn't mentioned them, and maybe they'd...

Stop it, she told herself. *You're making excuses for him and you're also making a bad situation even worse by thinking that he's disappeared, too.*

She was still debating the wisdom of going for a walk herself when she heard a car approaching and glanced into the rearview mirror apprehensively. Then she breathed a sigh of relief when she saw the state-police car pull in behind her.

"Any problems here?" the young officer asked as he walked up to the side of her car and she rolled down the window.

Andrea had to choke back a bubble of near-hysterical laughter at his question. Anything wrong? *No, officer, not here. My sister has disappeared. I don't trust my brother-in-law. And for some reason, I want to trust a man I barely know who's probably lying to me. Everything's just fine here, thank you.*

"No," she told him. "I'm just waiting for a friend. That's his Cherokee. He must have gone for a walk."

The officer walked over and glanced into Michael's vehicle. She got out of her car, wondering if there was some way she could get information from him without revealing her true reason for being here. The story she'd been using seemed to have worked well so far, but she had that innate fear of lying to the police that most people have.

"We've been looking for my twin sister," she told him. "She had a fight with her husband and took off. We think she's somewhere in this area, but we haven't seen her. I'm a little worried because her husband or some of his friends might be looking for her, too. They drink a lot," she added. "I've been trying to talk her into leaving him."

The officer shook his head sympathetically. "They almost never do—or else they go right back. What's she driving?"

"My sister has a dark green Volvo, and the others would probably be driving a black Blazer."

"I haven't seen a green Volvo, and I'd probably remember that. There aren't many of them around here. But a black Blazer?" He shrugged. "Lots of them around. Is she from around here?"

"She lives in Centre Valley, but I think she could be up here—maybe at one of the hunting camps. I was told she knows some people who own one, but I don't know exactly where it is."

"That's a problem. There are a lot of them around here— probably a dozen or more."

Andrea was silently congratulating herself on her ability to lie convincingly so far. Then, just as he was about to ask her another question she probably didn't want to answer, his gaze suddenly moved off to a point behind her.

"That must be your friend coming now."

Andrea turned to see Michael approaching on the intersecting road. She took a wicked satisfaction in knowing that he just might be very nervous right now, seeing her with a cop. Surely it was some sort of test of his honesty.

But if it was a test, he passed it easily. His expression was nothing more than slightly quizzical as he walked up to them, glancing at his watch and then grinning at her.

"I hope you didn't report me missing. I got here early and decided to stretch my legs."

Michael introduced himself to the officer, and then, in response to her question, said that he'd "struck out." The two men began to talk, and before long Michael had told him that he was a former NYPD detective and a private investigator who was here because he was a "friend of the family."

In spite of her other concerns at the moment, Andrea was intrigued by the interaction between the two men. She'd heard about "police culture" and how they tended to stick together and have a "them against us" mentality. One of her faculty colleagues worked as a consultant to several urban police forces, devising trainings to change that mind-set in order to facilitate community policing strategies.

She watched and listened to them now, thinking that she was at an even greater disadvantage than she'd imagined. Michael's occupation as a former cop, combined with Nick's statement that Val had left following an argument, would make it difficult to persuade the police to listen to her side of the story.

Finally the officer turned back to her. "Good luck finding your sister, and I hope when you do, you can talk some sense into her. There's a shelter for battered women in Centre Valley and they have some good counselors there. Maybe they can get her to go see one."

"Thank you. I'll certainly try." Andrea carefully avoided looking at Michael as the officer turned to say goodbye to him.

As the policeman drove away, Michael stood there staring after him. When he finally turned back to her, she expected some questions. But instead, he looked almost wistful.

"Once a cop, always a cop," he remarked, shaking his head.

"Do you regret leaving the force?" she asked, suddenly certain that he did.

He regarded her silently for a moment, then nodded slowly. "Yeah, I regret it—except when I look at my bank balance."

"Could you go back?"

"No, I can't do that. What did you tell him about Val?"

She repeated her story. "I had to explain what we were doing here, and I thought he might have seen her."

Michael regarded her through narrowed eyes. "You don't believe that, do you?"

"Believe what?"

"That Nick abused her."

"No, of course not! I told you, I had to give him some explanation."

"I just wondered. You seem ready to believe *anything* where Nick is concerned."

"That's because I know he's lying—or at least he's not telling the whole truth." She paused. "And neither are you, Michael."

"Oh?" His eyes narrowed again.

"You didn't tell me about the two men the woman at the store saw. I went back there to get something to eat."

"Yeah, she mentioned something about two guys she didn't know who'd been in the other day."

"One of them fit the description of the man Val met at the restaurant, Michael."

"If you recall, I fit that description, too."

"And the other one fit the description of someone who was waiting outside the restaurant at the time. *And* they were driving a black Blazer, which is what the other man was driving then."

"Why didn't you tell me this before, Andy? You never mentioned the other man or the Blazer."

"I didn't tell you because I didn't trust you," she said defiantly.

"I'm having a real problem dealing with this, Andrea. You tell me you think that Val's been kidnapped, and then you *don't* tell me about the other guy and the Blazer. What the hell's going on here?"

"That's exactly what I'd like to know!"

He ignored her implied question. "Is there anything else you haven't told me?"

"Only that the man Val met had a New York accent, and so did the men who came into the store. And the woman at the store said the Blazer had New York plates."

"Is that it?"

"Yes."

"Do you know how far we are from the New York border right now?"

"No."

"Less than fifty miles. I saw a couple of cars with New York plates today."

"But those men had city accents, Michael!"

"Well, that sure narrows it down to eight or nine million people."

"Stop it! You're being deliberately obtuse."

"No, I'm being *rational*—which you're not. You're determined to 'save' Val this time—to make up for the accident. And because of that, you're just not seeing things clearly."

Andrea felt like exploding. She couldn't take any more of his calm, reasonable tone, and his rational explanation of her behavior. So she turned and got into her car, then pulled out with a squeal of tires.

Damn him! How dare he say she wasn't being logical! She seethed and fumed about it as she roared down the highway. Then, finally, she redirected her anger at herself for letting him get to her. It was entirely possible that that had been his objective all along—to make her angry so she wouldn't think straight.

So think clearly now, she told herself. Either Michael was right and she was irrational, or Michael and Nick were lying. And if they were not telling the truth, what was the reason behind it?

Michael seemed bent on convincing her that Nick wasn't hiding anything—and that suggested to her that he *was*. Everything seemed to hinge on her finding out about Nick's past. But how could she do that?

On the other hand, Michael and Nick had shared that past—and she just might be able to find out something about Michael. She thought about how, twice now, something had crept into his voice when he'd talked about his police career.

If she couldn't yet think of a way to find out about Nick's past, she could probably find out about his friend's.

"SAM, IT'S ANDREA."

"Hi, Andy. You finally home? Word had it that you decided to turn into a beach bum."

"No, I'm in Centre Valley, where my sister lives, and I'm calling to ask a favor—or maybe several."

"Ask away."

"Do you have any way of checking on someone for me—a former detective in New York."

"Maybe. Who is it and what do you need to know?"

"His name is Michael Borelli. I think he left the force about five or six years ago. He's a private investigator now."

"Uh-huh. What do you want to know about him?"

"Well, it's a little bit complicated, but mainly I'd like to know why he left."

"So would a lot of other people."

"What do you mean? Did you know him?"

"Yeah. We worked a triple homicide together. I heard he'd gone private. And what I meant was that no one really knew why he quit. The story he put out was that he wanted more money, but guys I know who were close to him thought there must be something else."

"Could he have been forced to leave?"

"No chance of that. Borelli was a rising star—one of the youngest guys ever to get a detective's shield. A lot of people thought he was on his way to becoming chief of detectives. That's what made it so strange. Why are you curious about him?"

"I've just met him. He's an old friend of my sister's husband."

"Hey, Andy, this is an old detective you're talking to, remember? If you've got the hots for him, just say so."

Andrea smiled. Sam McLaughlin was a neighbor and a faculty colleague. He'd retired from the NYPD two years ago and now taught in the Administration of Justice Department.

"It's really complicated, Sam," she said, ignoring his remark about her interest in Michael. "My sister has disappeared. Her husband says she left after an argument. He called Michael to come and look for her."

"And you think someone's lying?" he asked shrewdly.

"I'm not sure at this point. All I know is that I don't have any proof, so I can't go to the police."

"Hmmpphh! Well, if you're worried about Borelli being involved in anything, forget about it—unless he's changed one helluva lot since his days on the force. He was a good cop—the best. A real straight arrow. Now tell me why you think someone's lying."

She told him the whole story, omitting the "feeling" she got on vacation that had brought her here. And as she talked, she wondered why she hadn't thought to call Sam before this. Not only was he an experienced cop, but he knew her.

"Andy," he said when she'd finished, "are you sure that you're not overreacting here? It sounds to me like your sister just took off to think things over for a while. From your description, that scene in the restaurant doesn't prove much.

If the place was crowded, the guy could have described her to this cashier when he said he was waiting for someone.

"Could be you're having trouble accepting that she might be having an affair."

It was not what Andrea wanted to hear—but she had to admit that maybe it was something she *needed* to hear. And Sam didn't even know the story of her estrangement from her twin. If he heard that, he'd probably tell her just what Michael had said—that she was on a "rescue mission" to atone for past mistakes.

She sighed. "Maybe you're right, Sam."

"Well, like I said, I sure can't see Borelli getting mixed up in anything that smells bad—even if her husband *is* his friend."

Andrea had intended to ask him to run a criminal check on Nick, but she decided against that now. Sam would probably do it for her, but he'd also think she was crazy.

And he just might be right. She hung up. Before she could talk herself out of it, she picked up the phone again.

"Michael, it's Andy. I'm just calling to let you know that I'm going home tomorrow."

In the brief silence that followed, she found herself holding her breath, hoping that he might want to see her again. Now that Sam had confirmed her feelings about Michael's trustworthiness, she didn't want it to end here.

"Let's have dinner tonight. I'd like to see you before you leave."

"I'd like that, too," she said, trying to adopt his casual tone.

After they'd made the arrangements, she put down the phone with a smile. Getting involved in this hadn't been a complete disaster, after all. It had brought Michael Borelli into her life. Now it was time to concentrate on *him,* and let her twin work out her own problems.

VALERIE Lockwood DeSantis felt numb—almost too out of it to consider the danger of her present situation. She'd been sitting on the hard cot for hours now, staring at nothing. Not that there was much to look at in any event. The upstairs of the cabin was sparsely furnished with rows of cots and three battered old dressers.

It smelled of wood smoke and old cigars, reminding her of the hunting camp her grandfather had belonged to, which she'd visited often in the summer as a child. Those memories might have soothed her if she'd been capable of feeling anything.

On the floor below, she could hear the two men moving around and talking sporadically, but their voices were too low for her to make out the words even if she'd been interested, which she wasn't. She'd already heard more than she wanted to hear.

She shivered, not so much from the lingering frost in the big room as from the deeper chill of her thoughts. In her mind, she could hear Andy's words, spoken over two years ago.

"Do you like him?" she'd asked her twin, trying not to sound too eager.

"He seems very nice," Andy had replied, and only someone who knew her as well as Val did could have detected that slightly false note.

"You're jealous!" she cried, wickedly pleased that her twin envied her for having found Nick. "You're jealous because I've found someone and you haven't!"

"That isn't it, Val."

"Then what is it?" Val had demanded, knowing full well that she should have ended the conversation. Or maybe that was only hindsight. She'd been flying high, still convinced that finally Andy envied *her*.

"There's something about him that...bothers me," Andy had said, slowly and reluctantly, which was out of character for her. Then, when she'd obviously seen the look on Val's face, she'd shrugged.

"It's probably nothing. I'm tired from the trip, that's all. I'm very happy for you, Val."

Remembering what followed, Val shivered again, recalling the sudden chill she'd felt then, on what should have been the happiest day of her life. They had both stared at each other, thinking about another time.

"Tell me!" Val had insisted, slightly nervous but ready to defend the man she loved.

"I just felt *something*, that's all. I told you it's probably because I'm tired."

"But what did you feel?" Val had demanded, unable to let it go.

"I...don't know. It's hard to explain. Just something *dark*. What do you know about his past? You haven't known him long."

"I've known him long enough. I was right. You're just jealous because for once I got the man I wanted!"

But she hadn't been right—and Andy *had*. Nick wasn't the man she thought he was. And now, with perfect hindsight, she could remember the times when he'd been silent and brooding, when he'd seemed almost fearful. That was right after she'd met him, when he'd come to town and bought the business and the farm from the Jensens, who were retiring.

Val had worked part-time for the Jensens, filling in over the busy seasons in addition to keeping their books and the accounts of some other businesses in town. She loved plants and had a true green thumb.

But the Jensens had been letting the business slide as they grew older and their energies waned. Then Nick had come, full of ideas and eager to reestablish the business and expand it. He told her that he'd had a lot of different jobs, but the one he'd liked best was working in his cousin's land-scaping business.

He'd asked her to come to work for him full-time, and she'd immediately accepted. They'd both worked really hard, and from the first, he'd treated her more as a partner than as an employee, listening carefully to all her suggestions and praising her business sense.

They'd become lovers quickly, and just barely two months after that, Nick had proposed to her in the green-house, amidst the beautiful colors and fragrances they both loved.

They'd been so happy. As the months passed, she saw no more of those brooding silences or occasionally fearful looks, and so she forgot about them—just as she had ignored Andy's warning. It was very easy to do when her life had become such a wonderful fairy tale.

Sitting here now, she realized that that's just what it had been, too—a dream. She was dimly aware of the fact that she wasn't giving Nick a chance to defend himself. But how could he explain such a thing? What possible reason could there be that would leave their love intact?

Val became aware of the voices below again. It sounded as if they were arguing, although they still weren't talking loudly enough for her to make out the words. She thought they were probably going to kill her, but it didn't seem to matter. She had no life left. The one she'd thought she had had been destroyed.

In a curious, detached manner, she wondered if Andy would know about her death. She'd still be in the Caribbean. Did distance even matter in such things?

A single tear trickled down her cheek. She didn't want to die without making things right with her sister. She thought about how Nick had encouraged her to heal the rift with Andy and had suggested that she invite her for the holidays. But she hadn't done it—and now it was too late.

She knew Nick thought she was being childish to continue her fight with Andy, but how could she have explained to him that it was more than the accident? She couldn't admit to him that she envied her twin and always had, and how it was really that jealousy that had caused the schism between them. The accident had been only a catalyst or maybe the final straw. It was so complicated that she had trouble explaining it to herself.

Long before the accident, she'd known that there was a big difference between them, and she knew that others saw it, too. Andy was always so sure of herself, always the one to take charge. Even though they looked alike, it was always Andy who was the more popular of the two. Then finally she'd found someone who wanted *her*. Nick had told her that he liked Andy, but that Val was the woman he loved.

She hugged herself tightly, wondering what he'd *really* meant when he said that. Probably he'd meant that she wouldn't ask too many questions, that she'd just be glad to have someone love her.

Chapter Five

"I think it's time for *both* of us to give up, Andy. I'm leaving tomorrow, too. We're not going to find Val because she doesn't *want* to be found at this point. And since Nick heard from her, we know she's okay. They need to work it out between themselves. I'm sorry I ever let him talk me into this."

But as he spoke those words, Michael's eyes were conveying something else—that out of this mess they'd found each other.

Across a candlelit table, amidst sparkling crystal and silver, they both acknowledged silently that this was not an ending, but a start.

No, she thought—not really a beginning, either. This had been sneaking up on them from the first time they saw each other. But they'd both been too busy involving themselves in other people's lives to see it clearly.

But now they were here together, talking about themselves—behaving like any couple out on a first date exploring a relationship to come. Fitting each revelation into the knowledge they'd already gained about each other. Leaving gaps in the conversation that quickly filled up with the subliminal whispers of desire.

Andy felt such a welcome sense of relief and pleasure in knowing that she'd been right about Michael. He was solid and real, and most importantly, he was a man who was totally comfortable with himself. No macho posturing.

She thought briefly about Sam's revelations. Whatever had led Michael to give up the police work he loved, he obviously had done it without regret—or at least, he'd made peace with himself over it.

"Why did you let Nick talk you into coming here?" she asked curiously, recalling Sam's statement that Michael would set limits even on an old friendship. Sam, of course, had been referring to the possibility that something criminal was involved, but she saw Michael as being someone who would always set limits—a very healthy thing and something she should have done where Val was concerned.

He sipped at his cappuccino before answering, his expression thoughtful. "That's not so easy to explain, although you might understand it better than most people would. Nick and I have known each other all our lives. I'm the elder by not quite two years, but when you're a kid that can seem like a very big difference. I became a sort of big brother and protector to him back then, and I guess I've never given up that role. So he calls and I come running. It's always been that way."

She smiled. She *did* understand and she liked him all the more for having the same problem she herself had. "Have you told him that you're leaving?"

He nodded. "Nick understands. The whole purpose of my coming here was to find Val and make sure she was okay. He knew I wasn't going to try to talk her into coming back."

Andrea thought that it would be a sad irony if the breakup of her twin's marriage was the price of meeting Michael. "I hope they do get back together," she said. "Val's been so happy with him. That's why I just can't see her..."

Michael reached across the small table and took her hand. "Let it go, Andy. You're not responsible for her happiness."

She laughed. "You sound more like a psychologist than I do. I think you missed your calling, Michael."

"No thanks. As it is, I have more than enough of people's problems to deal with in my work."

They left the restaurant and decided to go for a walk on campus. It was a cold, clear night, and with the students gone, the walkways beneath the huge, bare-branched elms were empty.

Their hands brushed lightly and Michael took hers. She could feel his warmth even through her gloves. They talked more—about their very different childhoods and about their careers. But the conversation seemed less spontaneous now, as though their minds were elsewhere.

At least, Andrea knew that *her* thoughts were elsewhere. She was wondering if they would see each other again and how they'd work it out, given the distance between them.

It isn't so far, she thought—only an hour and a half. Then, almost as though he'd been reading her mind, he mentioned that he'd been thinking of opening an office in southern Connecticut—probably Stamford. He had enough business in that area to start with, and he might even move up there himself. Maybe it was time, he said, to get out of the city. After all, he'd never lived anywhere else.

Michael said all this casually, but even though she wasn't looking at him at the moment, Andrea could feel his gaze upon her questioningly.

"You might find it difficult to give up the city," she said, thinking of friends who'd left and then gone back.

"Well, I might keep a small apartment there. I can justify it businesswise."

He drove her back to the motel, where they sat in the car for a moment, watching two drunken couples trying to negotiate the outside stairs to the second floor.

"I'm surprised you get any sleep here," he said with a chuckle.

"So far the rooms on both sides of me have been unoccupied. I just hope that continues tonight."

He walked her to her door. "I'd like to see you again, Andy. We may not have met under the best of circumstances, but..." His dark eyes gleamed as they bored into her, filling her with a heat that did everything but curl her toes.

"I'd like to see you again, too, Michael."

"There, uh, isn't anyone else in my life."

"And there's no one in mine, either." She smiled.

A heart-stopping moment of hesitation came—a nervousness on both their parts. Then their eyes met—and Andrea's world began to spin out of control.

At first, he merely leaned toward her slowly and his lips brushed hers so lightly that the kiss might have been only imaginary. But a small sound escaped from her as her lips parted. It was answered quickly by a low, satisfied murmur from him—and then they were in each other's arms, bodies struggling to overcome the impediments of clothing as a spark flared into brilliance.

Andrea clung to him, arched against him. Her fingers laced through his thick, dark hair. A sweet, hot wildness raced through her as she returned his kisses and felt his powerful hunger. The absurd thought came to her that they'd waited too long already and that was why things felt so out of control.

Then, to her surprise, Michael drew back slowly, releasing her as if by a very difficult act of sheer will. He smiled at her. "Well, I guess we can safely say that we both want to see each other again. I'll be in touch, Andy."

Then he took her key from her trembling hand, inserted it into the lock and pushed open the door. She thought for a moment that he would come in with her, and when his glance went from her to the bed, she was sure of it and began to feel the first, faint stirrings of caution. But once again he surprised her.

"Good night, Andy." He kissed her one last time and was gone, the echoes of his husky voice following her as she closed the door.

VALERIE LISTENED, straining to catch the words that floated up from downstairs. They were arguing again, but they were still keeping their voices too low for her to hear more than occasional words.

She *had* heard Nick's name being mentioned several times, and some talk about money. Now one of them said something about "making a deal" with Nick, followed by more murmurs she couldn't hear, and then the figure of a "half million."

Half a million dollars? They didn't have that kind of money.

Nick *couldn't* have promised them that much! There was no way he could raise it. The figure bounced around in her head as she backed away from the door, then somehow blended into the memory of a recent conversation with Nick.

"How does it feel to be worth a million dollars?" Nick had teased her after the insurance agent left.

"I'm only worth that much if I'm dead," she'd reminded him, laughing.

Valerie stuffed a fist into her mouth to stifle the cry that was welling up in her. *That* was the deal—they would kill her and then split the insurance money with Nick. The whole thing had probably been planned that way from the beginning. Maybe that's why they'd shown up now, claiming to be seeking revenge after all this time.

Yes, she thought with mounting horror. She could see it all now. Nick was tired of her, so he'd figured out a way to get rid of her and the burden of their financial problems at the same time.

He wouldn't do that, whispered the voice of her heart, the one that remembered his love, his patience, his gentleness.

Yes, he would, replied the cold voice of logic. *He's killed before. He's a murderer.* Andy had felt that, even if, at the time, she didn't know exactly what it was.

Ever since they'd brought her here to the cabin, Valerie had been afflicted with a numbness, a despair so deep that she was very nearly paralyzed. But now something else was growing in her—determination. At first, she was surprised to find it there. And then she began to make her plans.

She crept back to the door and listened again. She couldn't open it because the hinges squeaked badly. When she'd opened it earlier to go to the bathroom, the younger one had come running up right away, then waited until she returned to this room.

Their voices were muffled as before, but she could still hear enough to guess that they were probably drinking heavily. She'd smelled it on the breath of the younger one earlier. It was the first time they'd been drinking that much, so this might be her only chance to escape.

She returned to the bed and climbed in, pulling the heavy covers over her in case they came up to check on her. Below, the voices continued intermittently, then died away. Finally she heard footsteps on the stairs.

She listened fearfully as the steps stopped outside the door and the knob turned. In the light that spilled in from the hallway, she saw that it was the younger one. He'd confined himself to some suggestive remarks up to this point, but she began to worry about the effects of the alcohol.

He stood in the doorway, swaying slightly. She didn't move, trying to pretend she was asleep even as she calculated her chances of being able to overpower him in his drunken state.

The seconds ticked away in a terrible silence. Then he took a few steps into the room and nearly fell before bracing himself against a dresser. Finally he turned and went out again, closing the door behind him. She listened carefully as his steps faded away down the stairs. He hadn't put a chair against the door tonight.

There was nothing but silence in the cabin. Even the generator was off. She couldn't hear its distant hum. But still she waited, fearing that he might remember the chair and come back. Then, after a half hour had passed and she still heard nothing, she got quietly out of bed and went to the door, opening it just a crack to satisfy herself that the chair wasn't there. Breathing a sigh of relief, she fumbled in the darkness until she found her boots and her coat.

The squeaking hinge was very loud in the huge silence of the cabin, but she tried to ignore it as she went down the hallway to the bathroom, where she used the toilet, flushed it and washed her hands. If they'd heard the door squeaking, they'd just assume she'd gone to the bathroom. Or so she hoped, counting on the effects of the alcohol to make them less likely to check on her. On her way past the big bedroom, she pulled the door shut again.

There was, she thought with a small satisfaction, some benefit to being considered timid and passive. Even in their current drunken state, they'd probably be a whole lot more cautious if Andy had been their captive.

She paused at the top of the stairs to listen, but the only sound she could hear was muffled snoring. Then the generator came on again. She knew they were both sleeping in the downstairs bedroom, which was toward the back and not far from the generator.

It seemed to take her forever to get down the stairs, trying to avoid making any sound and expecting one of them to appear at any moment. The front door was locked, and in the darkness it took her a few precious seconds to realize that she needed to turn the key, which very fortunately was still in the lock. Their drunken carelessness was her salvation.

Then she was outside in the cold, still night air, almost unable to believe that she'd gotten this far. A spotlight mounted on the corner of the cabin provided a little circle of light, but was quickly swallowed up by the darkness.

Their Blazer was parked at the side of the cabin and she went to it first, hoping that they might have left the keys in it. But the ignition was empty. She knew better than to waste her time checking her Volvo, because she'd seen the younger one returning with the key after he'd pulled it into the woods.

The spare key, she thought. But it would make noise to get the hubcap off, and also take precious moments to get the car out of the woods behind the cabin. Her kidnapper's bedroom was on that side, too. If they heard her, they would surely catch her before she could get to safety.

She set off down the driveway at a rapid pace, ignoring the chill that was already creeping through her coat and boots. They were fashionable clothes, not intended to be worn for a long time outdoors. She wished that she had her scarf at least, but in the darkness, she'd overlooked it.

When they'd come here, the distance from the highway hadn't seemed very great, but now, as she hurried along the deeply rutted road that was frozen in some places and muddy in others, it seemed to go on forever.

Finally she reached the highway, and after a moment's hesitation turned right. They'd come from that direction and she remembered that there'd been a few houses not too far away.

Once on the highway, she began to walk more rapidly and that helped to keep her warm. But it also gave her time to think about her situation. Where could she go? She wanted so desperately to go home, but that meant confronting Nick. Tears welled up in her eyes, but she wiped them away angrily. Then the despair that had held her in its grip came flooding back—but this time, she pushed that away, too.

She had some money with her, but was reluctant to use her credit or banking cards. Somewhere, she'd read a story about someone being traced that way—or maybe Michael had mentioned it. When he learned that she'd escaped, Nick would probably check on that.

Nick. She stifled another cry. She couldn't afford to think about him now, about the nightmare her life had become. Instead, she thought about Andy. Would she be back from the Caribbean yet?

No, she couldn't go running to her sister—at least, not yet. She had to sort this out for herself. What she needed was a safe place to think and plan. This was *her* problem, and she was the one who had to deal with it.

When she first set out on the road, she'd turned every few minutes to see if any cars were coming. But none had passed in either direction. Then suddenly she saw light streaming past her and realized that someone was coming up behind her.

She froze for just a moment, then ran off the road into the woods. It could be her captors. They might have awakened and discovered that she was gone. Why hadn't she thought to let the air out of their tires?

She crouched in the woods, hoping that whoever was coming hadn't seen her. Then she heard the distinctive rumble of a big engine and saw, as the lights came closer, that it was a truck—an eighteen wheeler. And it was slowing down. There was the sound of gears shifting and the whoosh of air brakes.

The driver rolled to a stop just a short distance from her. A door opened and then another and she heard voices—a man and a woman.

"It must have been a deer, Teddy," the woman's voice said sleepily.

"It wasn't an animal, I'm telling you. It was a woman," the man replied as he began to shine a flashlight around. "Hey! Where are you? Do you need help?"

"What would anyone be doing out here? Did you pass a car anywhere?" the woman asked, yawning.

"No, but the car could be up ahead."

Something in their voices, perhaps the very ordinariness of them, together with the fact that it was a couple, made the decision for Valerie. She stood up.

DISBELIEF TURNED QUICKLY to anger when Andrea saw Michael's Cherokee parked beside the hangar. She felt betrayed by Michael and her own foolish heart.

When he had left her at the motel the night before with a kiss and a promise, Andrea had been certain that he was right about leaving. Val and Nick needed to work out their own problems. But this morning, she had been tormented by the thought that she was abandoning her twin. She simply could not let go of the feeling that had brought her here.

All through breakfast she had battled with her feelings about what to do. She could not leave without satisfying herself that she'd done her best to help her sister. The only question left was what more she could do to find Val.

And that had led her to the airport. When she'd been out here before to rent a car, she'd noticed the small charter-service sign. She knew that she could drive around forever in that rural vastness to the north, trying to find either the men in the Blazer or her sister. But in a small plane, the territory could be covered in a few hours.

She stared at Michael's vehicle, wondering if it was even remotely possible that he had awakened to the same thought. But even if he had, why would he pursue it—unless he knew or suspected that Val had not taken off on her own? After all, he'd stated very emphatically that this was none of their business.

A tall, slim woman not much older than Andrea herself was inside the hangar, seated at an overflowing desk in one corner and talking on the phone as she sorted through various papers. Andrea looked around the cavernous space and saw no one else. A twin-engine Cessna took up most of the space in the hangar. Its engine cowling was open and it appeared to be undergoing some maintenance. She hoped that the smaller, single-engine model parked outside was available—and a pilot, as well. The woman hung up and turned to her.

"I'd like to hire a plane and a pilot for a few hours," Andrea announced.

"Where do you want to go?"

"I'd like to just fly over the area north of here."

"You mean just fly around?" The woman frowned.

"Yes. I'm looking for someone and I thought maybe I could spot her car. It's too big an area to search from the ground."

It didn't take the look on the woman's face to tell Andrea just how foolish she sounded, so she smiled disarmingly.

"I know that must sound strange, but the person I'm looking for is my twin sister. She had a fight with her husband and took off. I have reason to believe that she could be staying at one of the hunting camps up there, but I don't know which one. I'm worried about her."

The woman nodded and Andrea thought she detected a softening of her attitude. Recalling Dolly and the woman in the general store, Andrea decided that when she was dealing with females, she gained a sympathetic audience.

"Is there a pilot and a plane available?" she asked hopefully.

"There's the Cessna outside—and you're looking at the only pilot available at the moment. My father owns the business, but he left with the other plane before I got here. He must have had a charter, too, and I don't know how long he'll be gone. I'd guess not too many hours, since he didn't file a flight plan."

Andrea thought privately that that was a safe bet. She knew exactly where her father had gone. "Will you have to wait until he gets back?"

"No, I'll just put on the answering machine. We don't really have much charter passenger business. Mostly we give flight lessons and we also have contracts with a couple of regional banks to provide check transit."

She switched on the machine, then scribbled a quick note that Andrea assumed was for her father. The two of them walked out onto the tarmac. The woman introduced herself as Carole Peterson, then asked Andrea if she'd flown in a small plane before.

"Yes, I have a friend at home in Connecticut who has a private license. I've even thought about taking lessons myself."

"I've been flying since I was twelve," Carole told her. "I'm an only child and flying has always been Dad's life. Mom kept pushing for me to become a nurse or a teacher, but here I am."

They started toward the Cessna, but then Andrea stopped, her attention once again caught by Michael's vehicle.

"You said that your father didn't file a flight plan. If he was taking someone to New York, would he have filed one?" By now, she was becoming all too accustomed to

Michael's deviousness and she wondered if he, in fact, *had* gone back home for the day.

"Oh, sure. He'd file one if he intended to land anywhere else." She nodded toward the Cherokee. "That must belong to his passenger. He didn't fill out the paperwork yet. He probably intends to do that when he gets back. Why?"

"I know who his passenger is—and I don't want him to know about me," Andrea told her. "It's complicated."

"He's a friend of my sister's husband and he's been looking for her, too. But he told me last night that he was giving up the search and going back to New York."

"Looks like he must have changed his mind," Carole observed.

"Yes, I suppose he must have. I didn't think of chartering a plane myself until this morning." She wanted to believe that was the case with Michael, but she couldn't. "Is there someplace I could hide my car so he won't see it when he comes back?"

"Sure. Just drive it over to that garage. I'll open the door for you and you can put it inside."

A few minutes later, they were taxiing down the runway, with Andrea's car hidden in the garage, which also contained Carole's father's antique Ford. Once they were airborne and headed northwest, Carole turned to her.

"Dad might see us if he's up here, too. The air space around here isn't exactly crowded."

"Can you try to spot him first and stay far enough away so that he won't be able to identify the plane?" Andrea asked, knowing that the big numbers painted on the side would be visible from some distance.

"We can try. We'll both have to keep an eye out. Why are you so worried about this guy seeing you?"

Andrea hesitated, then finally told Carole the whole story. "I was ready to give up and go home. But then I decided to make one last attempt to find Val."

"Jeez," Carole said. "I guess I can see why you haven't gone to the police, but you really should."

"They won't believe me." Andrea sighed. "Nick will tell them that she left on her own and Michael will back him up."

"Look, you can tell me to butt out if you want, but I might be able to help you."

"At this point, I'd welcome any help I can get," Andrea told her.

"Well, I've been dating this guy who's just been promoted to criminal investigator for the state police. I'll be seeing him tonight. If you like, you can come meet him and talk to him about it."

"Thanks, I might take you up on the offer," Andrea said.

The small plane had been headed north for some time now. Below them were open fields and tree-covered mountains spotted with snow. Carole told her to start looking for the camps and also keep an eye out for other planes. They were silent for a time, both of them craning their necks as they scanned both the ground and the skies.

Suddenly Carole began to bank sharply and drop altitude. "Two o'clock. I think that's Dad."

Andrea had been watching the ground, but she quickly looked up at the angle Carole had indicated and saw a plane some distance away. It was too far away to see clearly, which also meant that they couldn't be seen, either. Carole put the plane in a long, low curve as they both watched it get smaller and smaller.

"It looks like they're heading back," she told Andrea.

"Are you sure that was your father?"

"About ninety percent sure."

"Do you think he saw you?"

"I doubt it. He wouldn't be expecting me to be here and he couldn't have read the numbers from that distance, unless he had his glasses out. And speaking of them, maybe you ought to get that pair in the back."

Andrea retrieved the binoculars from the small storage space behind the seat and trained them on the increasingly rugged terrain below them. During the course of the next hour, they found eight isolated cabins—but no cars at any of them. Then Andrea spotted the boarded-up gas station where the pay phone was located. And from her bird's-eye vantage point, she could also see the tiny village with the general store. She asked Carole to make another low sweep of the immediate area.

As Carole obligingly dropped altitude, Andrea scanned the thickly forested mountain below them. It was mostly evergreens, which made it even more difficult. Then suddenly she saw something—a faint break in the forest that could be a road. She followed it with the glasses as Carole began to circle away.

"Go around again," she said. "I thought I saw a road down there."

The land beneath them tilted and spun as Carole maneuvered the plane expertly. Andrea struggled to keep the glasses trained on the road, which was very difficult to see except at just the right angle.

"There!" she cried in triumph. "I think I saw a cabin!"

"Let's get some altitude," Carole suggested as she began to climb steeply.

The cabin was just barely visible, nestled as it was in the midst of the thick pine forest. And as Andrea trained the glasses on it, she thought she saw wisps of smoke rising from the stone chimney. She asked Carole to take the plane lower.

"I will, but we probably shouldn't go down too low. If they're there, we might scare them away."

"Right," Andrea said, glad that Carole had thought of that.

They made a wide circle around the area where the cabin was located. Andrea was nearly certain now that she saw traces of smoke—and something else. There were no vehicles parked in the open space in front of the cabin, but she caught a glimpse of something in the trees not far away— something dark that looked like a vehicle.

"How can I pinpoint that spot, so I can find it from the ground?" Andrea asked.

"No problem. That's Route 132 down there. Just let me get my bearings and I can mark the map for you when we get back. But you're not going to go there yourself, are you?"

"Not if we can get your friend to check it out," Andrea said.

"This isn't his jurisdiction, but he can call the barracks up here and have them check it."

They returned to Centre Valley, and as they taxied up to the hangar, Andrea saw with relief that Michael's Cherokee was gone. She wondered if he'd spotted the cabin.

"Carole, can you make up some story for your father— maybe tell him that I'm interested in flying lessons? I don't really want anyone else to know about this."

"I could," she said reluctantly, "but you can trust Dad— and we can find out if they saw anything."

Andrea nodded, realizing belatedly that it was unfair to ask Carole to lie to her father. It was a sad reflection on her own state of mind that she'd made such a request.

They went inside, where Carole gave her father an abbreviated version of the story, then asked about his passenger.

"That was him, all right." He nodded. "Michael Borelli. Got his charge slip right here, and he told me pretty much the same story—except that he didn't mention the possibility that she might have been kidnapped."

"Did you find anything?" Andrea asked.

"Nope. We saw six or seven cabins, but no sign of life at any of them." He gave Andrea a stern look that reminded her of her own father.

"You'll have to pardon me for saying this, young lady, but what you should be doing is going to the police."

"We're going to talk to Ted tonight, Dad," Carole assured him.

"Good, but I have to say that I can't see Borelli being mixed up in any kidnapping. He seemed like a real straight guy to me. He used to be a cop himself."

"I'm not sure that he *is* mixed up in anything," Andrea told him, thinking that here was yet another testimonial to Michael Borelli's character. It seemed she was the only one around who didn't believe him—the supreme irony, since she really wanted to trust him.

She left after paying for the flight and making arrangements to meet Carole and her friend that evening at a jazz place in town. But all the way back to her motel, that cabin continued to haunt her. She was sure she'd seen smoke, and nearly as certain that a vehicle was hidden in the woods nearby.

It was five hours until she would be meeting with Carole and her friend, and probably the next morning before he could have someone check on the cabin. It seemed an unacceptably long period of time.

She began to wonder if perhaps she should go up there now, just to confirm that someone was there. She could do that and still be back in time to meet them.

The idea seemed to acquire an urgency, possibly because she was tired of feeling frustrated and more than ever aware of the passage of time and what that could mean to Val's safety. She knew that there was some risk involved, but she decided that it was worth it. If she established that someone was there—and especially if she saw either Val's car or the Blazer—then her case to the police would be even stronger.

She was about to leave when she decided to check her answering machine again. She'd been checking it regularly, even though she knew it was unlikely that Val would call her. So she was totally unprepared for the familiar sound of her twin's voice following the beeps.

"Andy, it's Val." There was a pause and Andrea heard her choke back a sob. "Andy, I'm in trouble. You were right about Nick. Don't call him. I don't know what to do. I . . ."

And there the message ended. Andrea was so stunned that she forgot to punch out the code to save it, and the machine erased it as it reset. She dropped the receiver back into its cradle as a chill engulfed her.

She'd heard no other voices in the background, but the fact that Val's message had been cut off suggested that someone had deliberately done it. Or perhaps she'd just regretted making the call.

"You were right about Nick." Val's sad admission tormented her. It was a confession her sister hadn't wanted to make—and one Andrea didn't want to hear, either. Not only did she feel Val's pain at such a discovery, but she also felt the hurt of knowing how Michael had deceived her. Whatever was going on here, it had to involve them both.

Chapter Six

Andrea checked out of the motel and headed north. Snow was beginning to fall—big fat flakes that didn't seem threatening, despite a low, leaden sky.

How she wished that Val had said where she was calling from. But of course she couldn't know that Andrea was in town. She wondered if she should leave a message on her machine to let Val know that she was here in case she called again. But that was leaving an open invitation to burglars.

She spotted a convenience store up ahead and pulled in next to the outside pay phone. A burglary would be a small price to pay to let Val know she was close by.

It took her several tries before she got it right, since she wasn't accustomed to changing her message by remote, but when it was done, the message said that she was "visiting her sister in Pennsylvania" and would be checking her messages regularly.

By the time she reached the area where the cabin was located, the light had dimmed considerably and the snow was falling more thickly, making the road slushy. She missed the narrow, unmarked road on her first try, then turned around and went back, cruising slowly on the deserted rural highway until she found it.

She turned in, trying to recall exactly how the road had appeared from the air. It had seemed to be fairly straight, but she could see now that it was, in fact, a series of dips and rises. Knowing that her headlights could be visible for some distance, she cut back to her parking lights and crept along slowly through the increasingly heavy snow. And then, when she had gone as far as she dared, she started to look for a place to turn around. There was no place to hide her car, so the only precaution she could take was to turn around so that she was facing back toward the highway and could get away faster.

The night was cold and raw and the snowflakes stung her face as she set out, carrying her flashlight but keeping it trained on the road at her feet. The road was still slightly muddy in places and frozen solid in others. She was picking her way gingerly through a muddy spot when she saw something—and stopped. Then she squatted down to get a better look.

It looked like the imprint of a woman's high-heeled shoe or boot. And now she saw that there were several more prints—leading away from the cabin. There might well have been more, but they'd been obliterated by tire marks.

She drew in her breath sharply, thinking about that phone call. Had Val been here—and escaped? And had she then been recaptured? She knew that Val had been wearing dressy boots, thanks to Beth's description, and how likely was it that any other woman would have been walking along this private road?

She continued up a small hill, scanning with the flashlight for more prints. And then suddenly the cabin lay just ahead! She switched the flashlight off quickly, praying that she hadn't been seen.

Lights were on inside, and in the utter stillness, she could hear the very faint sound of some kind of engine. Fearing that someone was coming, she scrambled into the woods beside the road and strained to see better.

In the darkness beside the cabin, she could just barely make out the shape of a dark, boxy vehicle, but it wasn't moving, even though that barely audible sound continued. The longer she stared at the dark shape, the more certain she became that it was the Blazer. But what was that sound?

Then she realized that she hadn't seen any utility poles along the road and knew it must be a generator. The lights inside the cabin were definitely electric.

She returned to the road and began to move toward the cabin, not daring to use her flashlight now. Then, when she was less than a hundred feet from the cabin, she left the road and made her way along the edge of the tree line toward the vehicle. It was, indeed, a black Blazer, with New York plates.

She turned to stare at a lighted window, knowing she should get out—and quickly—but irrationally impelled to see the men for herself. There were no curtains at the window, so she approached it at an oblique angle, then froze as a shadow moved inside and a man's face appeared.

She was sure he couldn't see her out there, especially since it was snowing and she was dressed in dark clothing, but she still held her breath until he turned away again. He was older, a big, heavy man with a full head of gray hair—undoubtedly the man the truck driver had described to Dolly.

She could hear a faint murmur of voices and assumed that the younger one must be there, as well. But was Val inside?

Enough snow had fallen by now to create an ambient light that made it easier for her to find her way around the outside of the cabin. None of the windows was curtained, and as she moved cautiously from one to the next, she had a good view of the entire downstairs, which was mostly open. There was only one bedroom on the lower level, and in the light spilling in from the hallway, she determined that it was empty. Pressing her face against another darkened window, she confirmed that it was a bathroom inside.

As she peeked into the kitchen window, a man suddenly walked in and went to the refrigerator. It was a close call. If he'd turned in her direction, he would almost certainly have seen her. He did, indeed, bear a slight resemblance to Michael, and she froze for a moment before backing away from the window.

The upstairs windows were all dark. She stared at them, wondering if Val could be up there. Her fears summoned up an image of her twin, tied up and tossed onto a bed. Andrea was not unaware of the danger she herself was in, but that knowledge was simply overridden by her determination to find her twin.

There was a small back porch to the cabin. Half of it was completely enclosed, but the other half was open and supported by a sturdy post. Above the enclosed portion was a window.

As she stood there uncertainly, a sudden noise startled her. The generator had come on again, and from the sound, she guessed that it must be housed in the part of the porch that was enclosed. If it stayed on for a while, it should provide good cover for her.

Before she could give in to her fears, Andrea swung herself up over the banister and grabbed the post, finding it sturdy. Ignoring the snow and the penetrating cold, she pulled off her jacket and shinnied up the post to the porch roof, then crawled carefully along the angled roof, where the snow was just thick enough to be slippery.

She felt a surge of frustration as she reached the window. There was only the faintest of light from the stairwell, which was just barely visible off to her left. She muttered a curse as she realized that she'd left her flashlight in her jacket pocket. But as she stood there shivering, wondering if she should go back for it, her eyes gradually adjusted to the dim light in the room.

It seemed to be mostly one big open space, filled with narrow beds and several dressers. There was no sign of Val. She knew that there was a small portion of the upstairs she couldn't see from this angle, however, and tried the window, only to find it locked.

Then she heard a door open below her and footsteps on the porch. She froze. Had they heard her up here? The generator was still running and she hadn't made much noise. But her jacket was down there! She'd dropped it in a heap just below the porch railing. She held her breath, waiting for an exclamation that would tell her she'd been discovered. If the man saw the jacket, he'd guess immediately where she was!

The seconds ticked away slowly. She could feel his presence just below her. A trace of cigarette smoke tickled her nose, the odor more threatening than annoying now. She shivered, both from the cold wind and from the wet snow that had settled on her.

And then the porch floor creaked beneath his weight and the door opened and closed again. She exhaled in a soft sigh and began to crawl over to the post. Leaning out over the edge of the roof, she saw her jacket. It was already nearly covered by the snow. From his vantage point on the porch, it would have been invisible.

The generator shut off just as she was shinnying down the post, trying to keep an eye on the back door, which had a window in it. As quietly as possible, she let herself down onto the railing, then jumped to the ground, grabbed her jacket—and ran.

When she was safely out of sight of the cabin, she stopped long enough to put on her jacket, then switched on the flashlight and hurried along the road to her car. But when she reached the highway, she stopped, uncertain what to do now.

Her little sports car wasn't very good in snow. Returning to Centre Valley now seemed impossible. The snow was coming down thick and fast. She kept seeing those prints in the mud and knew Val *was* here somewhere. She wished that she'd taken the time to find out if the Volvo was at the cabin. She realized the car was the proof she needed to get the police involved. If it was there, where was it hidden? Unless that vehicle she'd thought she'd seen from the air had been Val's car, not the Blazer....

Well, it was too late—she couldn't go back. If she did, she might very well get stuck in the snow. What she needed to do was to find a place to stay for the night—and to check her machine again in case Val had called back.

Finally she started out, heading toward the motel she'd checked when she'd been up here with Michael. The owner lived in a house next to it and had seemed nice, so perhaps she could persuade him to give her a room.

Her car slipped and slid as she inched along through the storm, scanning the radio dial for a station with a weather report. There weren't many stations coming in and the few that did had either interminable sports reports or country music that set her teeth on edge. She switched it off.

The motel was dark, but lights were burning in the house next door, so Andrea pulled in beside a big pickup and hurried up to the front door.

The same man she'd spoken to before came to answer and she told him that she desperately needed a place to stay. He glanced past her and snorted.

"I guess them little things don't do too well in the snow."

She admitted that was true, then asked how much snow was expected.

"They're calling for about four or five inches tonight—but that's just for starters. The main storm isn't supposed to hit until sometime tomorrow." He chuckled. "When those guys won't say how much is coming, you can bet it's going to be bad. Lot of wind, too." He stepped back and ushered her inside.

"Come on in till I get the keys. It's gonna be cold for a while, though. There's electric heaters in the rooms and I keep them on just enough to keep the pipes from freezing."

Andrea waited in the small foyer, her stomach growling as she caught a pleasant smell from the kitchen. She wondered if the motel had any vending machines, since she knew there were no restaurants nearby. He came back a moment later with a ring of keys and led her across to the motel.

"I'll give you the room right next to the office. That should be warmer. Some of us get together every Thursday to play some poker in there."

Another truck pulled in as he was unlocking the door. "That'll be them coming now," he said. "A little snow won't stop them."

He turned on the light to reveal a Spartan but clean-looking room that still held a faint trace of tobacco smoke. "You want some chili? The wife makes the best around and I always have her fix a big pot in case the boys get hungry."

Andrea smiled. "Thank you. That would be wonderful. Is there a phone I can use?" She'd noticed there wasn't one in the room.

"There's a pay phone, but it's outside. You can use the one in the office if you want."

By the time she followed him back to the office, another truck had driven up and a group of five men were gathered there, all of whom stared at her curiously. She explained that she would be making a long-distance call and would use her credit card, and he gestured to a battered desk in the corner.

"Help yourself. I'll get the chili and some coffee."

She punched in her home number and credit-card number and waited impatiently after hitting the code to activate her machine. There were no messages. The men had seated themselves at a big green baize-covered table and were talking, trying a bit too hard to ignore her.

She heard one of them remark that it was a "damned shame" that they hadn't had this snow last month during hunting season, and it occurred to her that these men just might know who owned the cabin where she'd seen the two men.

She was about to ask them when her host returned with a pot of chili, followed by his wife who was carrying a pot of coffee. There was a tiny kitchen in one corner of the office and she began to ladle out the food. Her husband turned to Andrea.

"You still lookin' for your sister—a twin, wasn't it?"

"Yes, I am—and I think I know where she's staying, although she isn't there now. It's a cabin—a hunting camp, I guess." She told them where it was.

Her host nodded. "That'd be one of those gangs from the city—Philadelphia, I think. They don't mix much. Got themselves about two hundred acres of good deer country and don't let no one else hunt on it, neither. There's a couple of others like that, too."

"That bunch is from New York," another man said. "I thought I seen one of them the other day. Drives a black Blazer with New York plates. I wondered what he was doing up here now, with hunting season over."

"Charlie says he thinks they hunt out of season, but he hasn't caught them at it yet," a third man put it.

"Could your sister know them?" her host asked.

"She must," Andrea lied, then thanked her host and hostess for the use of the phone and for the food and left quickly, carrying the steaming bowl of chili and a mug of coffee back to her room.

The food was good and the coffee rich and strong. She ate at a small, wobbly table as the men's voices floated through the thin walls. They were still complaining about "outsiders" who came in and bought up all the best hunting land.

So the men actually *owned* that cabin. She'd assumed that they'd broken in and, in the absence of any evidence that Val was there, she could at least cause them trouble over that. Now it appeared that she'd lost her only weapon against them.

Belatedly she realized that she should have called Carole to let her know that she wouldn't be able to make their meeting tonight, but she hated to disrupt the poker game, which was now in progress.

However, her chief concern at the moment was finding Val. If she wasn't at the cabin, where *was* she?

MICHAEL COULD SEE Nick nervously turning to look toward the cordless phone on the table beside him, even as he clicked his way restlessly through the channels. He finally settled on a basketball game just when Michael was about to grab the remote away from him.

The promised call hadn't come. Michael had done his level best to convince his old friend that there could be many reasons for it, and not all of them meant disaster. But he knew that Nick didn't believe him.

He got up to get them more beer and paused to look out the window. The snow had begun earlier, a heavy, wet fall that clung to tree branches and filled the night world with a beautiful, ghostly light. The forecast was for a brief letup tomorrow morning, to be followed by more later in the day.

That meant he probably wouldn't be able to get into the air again tomorrow, to go back over the area in the hope that he'd missed something the first time around. He'd even gone out and bought a more powerful pair of binoculars.

He wondered if Andy had gotten home safely. Since the storm was moving west to east she should be fine. He'd called her motel earlier and had found out that she hadn't checked out until afternoon, but she should still be well away from the storm.

And far away from everything else, too, he thought gratefully, even though he already missed her.

He'd called her home earlier, allowing enough time for her to get back to Connecticut, but he'd gotten only her machine and hadn't bothered to leave a message. He glanced up at the kitchen clock, then at the phone, thinking that maybe he should call her again. But at that moment, Nick came into the kitchen and started going over the whole situation again.

ANDREA AWOKE EARLY, after a night of tossing and turning in which she was following her fleeing sister into the darkness, her legs strangely heavy and unresponsive as she tried to run.

She got up and went to the window to peek out through the blinds. The snow had dwindled to a few fat flakes, but it lay heavily on everything in sight. She showered and dressed quickly, then went to the office to call home again, still hoping to find another message from Val.

But there were none. Her host had thoughtfully left coffee for her to make a pot, and as she did it, she considered her options. It seemed to her that the only thing she could do now was to try to find out if anyone had seen Val.

If her sister had been at the cabin and escaped on foot, she would surely have gone to the nearest house for help. As Andrea recalled, there were several along the highway a few miles from the road that led up to the cabin. The little village of Watsonville wasn't too much farther away. She could go back to the general store and check there, in case Val might have gotten a ride from someone.

There was no sign of life at the house next door this early in the morning, so she left some money for her lodging and a note saying that she might return, then went out to scrape the snow off her car.

The road had been plowed, but the parking lot at the motel hadn't, so it took her some time and a lot of maneuvering to persuade the little car to make its way to the highway.

She drove to the town of Sawyer, where she filled her stomach at a fast-food restaurant, thinking ruefully that she was becoming a junk-food addict. Both there and at a twenty-four convenience store, she inquired about Val, but got negative responses. The clerk at the store was kind enough to call several other employees at home, but they hadn't seen Val, either. So she drove on toward the village of Watsonville, which, in any event, seemed to be the more likely place that her sister would go.

As she stopped at an intersection, Andrea was stunned to see a black Blazer approaching on the other road. Immediately she noticed the New York plates. They drove past, and although she didn't get a good look at them, she was sure that there were two men inside.

They were headed away from the cabin. Could they be out searching for Val—or was she back at the cabin?

Knowing the risk she was taking, Andrea nevertheless turned in that direction, keeping an eye on the rearview mirror in case the men turned around. She doubted very much that they could have seen her and they couldn't have recognized her car, but she was still wary.

Then she saw the two houses clustered together that would have been the logical place for Val to have gone if she'd escaped. So she pulled into the driveway of the first one, where a woman was shoveling snow.

She hadn't seen Val, and neither had the older couple in the house next door. Not certain just when Val might have escaped—if she had at all—Andrea inquired if they'd been home most of the time during the past day or so. From their responses, she guessed that one or the other of the two families had been there the entire time.

Still watching her rearview mirror for any sign of the Blazer, Andrea continued on to the road that led up to the cabin. Then, after one final check, she turned and started up the road, staying in the wide tracks of the Blazer and wishing that she, too, had a four-wheel drive. If she got stuck here, she'd be in very big trouble.

But she didn't—that is, not until she reached the cabin and tried to turn around to make a quick getaway. Then the back wheels began to spin, and after a fruitless effort to free them, she got out and saw that she'd managed to turn around in a muddy area that was now even worse, thanks to the heavy, mushy snow.

She stared at the cabin. Since no one had come out, she could safely assume that it was unoccupied—unless Val was in there, tied up. She marched boldly up to the door, even though her heart was pounding wildly in her throat.

To her surprise, it wasn't locked. She pushed it open, fearing that at any moment someone would leap out at her. Warm air and the smell of wood smoke and coffee rushed out at her—that was all.

"Val!" her voice boomed out in the silence, but there was no response.

Most of the downstairs was one big room, filled with old but serviceable furnishings. Off a hallway was a bedroom fitted with twin beds, both of them unmade. Men's clothing was scattered about and there was shaving gear and other items in the bathroom across the hall.

In the kitchen, she found dirty dishes in the sink and a well-stocked refrigerator. Behind the kitchen was a small room containing a generator, as well as a stack of firewood for the big fireplace in the living room.

Finally she went upstairs, after going first to a window to make sure that the men weren't returning yet. Up there, it was completely open, except for a short hallway and a door that led to what she assumed must be another bathroom.

Beds were scattered about the big space, together with several old dressers. One of the beds was unmade—and on the one next to it lay a scarf!

Andrea made a strangled sound as she stared at it. The big, square paisley-print scarf was identical to one she herself owned, bought from one of her favorite catalogs. She picked it up and caught the scent of one of her own perfumes. Tears stung her eyes at this poignant proof of the powerful link between Val and her that survived even after their closeness had vanished. Even apart and with little contact, they had chosen the same things.

She took the scarf and searched the room for any other evidence of her twin, but found nothing. There were used towels in the bathroom, but nothing else. It didn't really matter, though; she knew that Val had been here—and that, somehow, she'd escaped.

Andrea turned her attention to the problem of getting out of here before her sister's captors returned. They were almost certainly out looking for her, so she probably had some time. But that meant little if she couldn't get her car freed.

She went back downstairs to look for a shovel or a cardboard box she could break up and use beneath the wheels for traction. But what she found instead set her on a different course of action.

Hanging on a hook inside a large pantry closet in the kitchen was a set of keys—Volvo keys attached to a large pewter flower. Val's car! It was here somewhere. It seemed unlikely that they would have abandoned it elsewhere, since it might be found.

Remembering the vehicle she thought she'd spotted from the air, hidden in the woods, Andrea left the cabin. She found it a few moments later, pulled beneath a canopy of snow-laden pines off to one side of the cabin. In fact, when she'd been prowling around out here last evening, she'd been very close to it.

The engine turned over right away, and she spared a moment to thank Nick for that. Val had said that he was a real stickler about maintaining cars. While it warmed up, she scraped off the snow, hoping that she'd have less trouble getting it out than trying to move her car.

The heavier Volvo moved easily through the snow. Back on the main road, Andrea turned toward the village with the general store. She wanted to check there to see if anyone had sighted Val, but she was also well aware of the danger now that she was driving her twin's car. She smiled grimly, wondering what the two men would think when they returned to the cabin and discovered the Volvo gone and a Miata in its place.

Snow had begun to fall again by the time she left the cabin and it seemed to be growing heavier by the moment. The wind whipped around her as she got out of the car, already feeling much colder than it had earlier.

The same woman, alone in the store at the moment, greeted her in surprise. "Still looking for your sister, are you?"

Andrea acknowledged that she was, but unfortunately the woman hadn't seen her. "Has anyone else been in asking about her?"

The woman shook her head. "Those two strangers were in again yesterday, though—the ones with the black Blazer. They bought some more groceries. Someone said they've got a hunting camp around here somewhere."

She looked toward the dirty windows at the front of the store. "Looks like we're in for a big one now. Every time I turn on the radio, they say we're going to get more snow. A lot of wind, too. You'd best be careful out there."

"How much are they predicting now?" Andrea asked.

"Could be two feet or more, and that wind will mean a lot of drifting, too."

Andrea bought some snacks and frozen dinners, as well as a cup of coffee, then told the woman she'd be staying at the Eagle Motel. "If you see my sister or hear anything about her, could you call me there?"

"Sure, but I thought they were closed."

"They are, but they were kind enough to give me a room." Andrea thanked her and started toward the door, then stopped.

"Is there anyone around here who might take in roomers?"

"Well, there's Annie Duncan. She puts up hunters and sometimes takes in folks who're in town to visit family. But she's gone to Florida to spend the winter with one of her daughters."

Andrea thanked her and left, disappointed that her sudden inspiration had come to nothing. She was nearly blown off her feet by a gust of wind and stinging snow as she tried to balance her coffee and her other purchases and get the car door open.

She drove back to the motel, determined now to call the police. She had proof that Val had been at the cabin, even though she knew that the two men, if questioned, would probably claim that she'd been there voluntarily.

The snow was piling up fast and the road was already covered. She began to fear that there would be little, if anything, the police could do until the storm was over. If only she could be sure that Val was safe somewhere.

She realized that she wasn't giving her twin much credit for being able to manage on her own and that brought back her conversation with Michael about their roles as protectors of Nick and Val.

An image of Michael Borelli came into her mind. How could she have allowed herself to be deceived by him? Even now, she wanted to find some way to excuse his behavior, to believe that he was innocent of any involvement.

When she reached the motel, she saw that the pickup was gone and the lot had been plowed, although the snow was piling up rapidly again. She assumed they must have gone shopping before the roads became impassable. At first, she thought that she'd just have to wait in the car for them to return, but then she noticed a white envelope tucked into the metal scrollwork of the storm door at the house.

Her name was written on the envelope and there were keys and a brief note inside, telling her to make herself at home and confirming that they had, in fact, gone shopping.

She returned to the car and then pulled it around to the side of the motel, as far from the road as she could. Deciding that it would soon be unrecognizable under a blanket of snow in any event, she left it there and made her way through the blizzard to the motel office.

As she put the frozen dinners she'd bought into the tiny freezer compartment of the office refrigerator, Andrea reflected that she'd made the acquaintance of some very kind people and was being given a glimpse of a life-style she'd all but forgotten. The area of Connecticut where she lived was rural, but deceptively so. She couldn't imagine any motel owner there simply leaving keys for her, secure in the knowledge that no one would take them.

It was, she thought, the first truly pleasant thought she'd had in days. She could only hope that Val had found some equally kind people who'd helped he..

That thought sent her to the phone to check her machine again, but there were still no calls. She sat down and put herself into her twin's situation.

Assume that she'd escaped and somehow found someone to help her. Once she was safe, surely her first call would be to her or their mother. And if she'd called their mother, then certainly she would have called Andrea and left an urgent message.

But what if she'd called Nick—despite her warning to Andrea *not* to call him? It wasn't out of the question. Whatever Val had found out, she would have a difficult time believing it. And if she'd called Nick, could he be up here already, or might he have somehow contacted her captors?

She made a sound of disgust. She hated knowing so little. She couldn't assume that Nick—or Michael—were in collusion with the men who'd kidnapped Val. But she couldn't eliminate that possibility, either.

She picked up the phone again, thinking that she could at least find out if Nick was home, then put it down again quickly as she remembered the caller-identification device that Michael had attached to his phone. She didn't want them to have any idea where she was, and even if she said nothing, they might well guess who was calling. In all likelihood, Michael had been checking to see if she'd arrived home yet.

She was about to leave the office when she froze! The black Blazer was pulling into the lot! She doubted that they'd seen her yet in the office, but they might have spotted the Volvo.

Chapter Seven

The two men got out of the Blazer and started toward the office. Andrea backed into a shadowy corner. There were no lights on in the office and the miniblinds that covered the window and the glass portion of the door were slightly slanted, making it impossible for them to have a clear view of the interior.

They wouldn't expect her—or rather, Val—to be here in the office, but she had no doubt that they'd identified the car and would be convinced that Val was here somewhere.

She jumped nervously as one of them rattled the doorknob, trying to open it, then began to pound on it impatiently. The light, both outside and inside, was dim. It was already late afternoon and darkness was hastened by the thickly falling snow.

The older one continued to pound on the door, while the younger one stepped to the window and cupped his hands around his eyes to try to peer inside. Andrea forced herself to remain totally still, knowing that any movement might catch his eye.

Finally the pounding stopped and the two of them stood there for a moment, their backs turned as they faced the lot. She could hear their voices, but couldn't distinguish the words. Then they started toward the house.

She left her corner and went to the phone at the desk, her fingers trembling as she picked up the receiver and dialed 911, only to have the phone respond with a squealing sound, followed by a droning recording that informed her she'd called a nonexistent number. She scanned the dim office, looking for a telephone directory—and then the office was flooded with light! She cried out involuntarily, then tried to stifle the sound. But it was too late. The outside lights had come on, as well—all of them apparently on a timer—and the two men were now starting back to the office!

This time, she knew they'd seen her. She gave up her search for the phone directory and instead looked for the timer. It was mounted on the wall behind the desk and she switched it off, bringing darkness once again.

There was no more pounding at the door; instead, one of the panes shattered as they tried to gain access to the office. The lock required a key to open it from either side, but she'd left it in the door and knew she couldn't get it now. Instead, she looked around desperately for a means of escape.

Then she spotted a door. Certain that it must be only a closet or a storage space, since there was no matching door in her room on the other side of the wall, Andrea nevertheless tried it.

It opened into a long, narrow storage room and she stepped inside, then pressed the button on the knob to lock it—just as more glass shattered out in the office.

She was trapped! The lock on the storage-room door wasn't that strong. She glanced around, seeking things she could pile up against the door—and then she saw what could be her salvation! High in the end wall was a small window, opening out to the far side of the motel.

The window was too high for her to reach from the floor, so she dragged some small but heavy cartons of cleaning supplies over to the wall beneath it, then climbed up and unlocked the window, which swung outward on a hinge. The opening wasn't large, but she thought she could squeeze through if she got rid of her heavy jacket first. So she unzipped it, tore it off and threw it out the window just as she heard them trying the knob to the door.

The flimsy metal hinge gave way as she pushed against it, creating a larger opening by freeing the window to swing all the way up. Sliding through the opening, Andrea let herself drop to the ground below, a distance of some seven or eight feet.

Her fall was somewhat cushioned by the snow, but pain still shot through first her ankle and then her knees as she tumbled to the ground. Her knitted cap had snagged on the window latch, but she didn't stop to retrieve it as she grabbed up her jacket and began to run for the rear of the motel.

Her only hope lay in getting to the car before they realized she'd escaped, and the shortest route would have been to go around the front, but that also made it more likely that they'd spot her. So she ran clumsily through the snow, ignoring the cold because she couldn't stop to put on her jacket.

When she had finally reached the corner, she peered out cautiously. The Volvo was only about twenty yards away, covered now with snow. Just as she started toward it, she heard a loud crash and knew that they must have broken through into the storage room.

The inside of the Volvo felt like a snowy cocoon with all the windows covered. She started the engine and switched on the wipers. They moved enough snow from the windshield for her to see the two men come running out of the office toward her.

She put the car into gear and started toward the highway. They continued to run toward her, jumping out of the way only at the last possible moment. Instinctively she braked and the car fishtailed. There was a dull thump and a cry, and she knew she must have hit one of them, although she couldn't see what had happened because of the snow-covered windows.

Then there was a noise at the door on the passenger side and she realized that one of them was trying to get in. Fortunately the door was locked. She stepped on the gas and the car shot forward, sliding a bit until it gained purchase in the snow.

When she reached the highway, she rolled down the driver's side window and pushed away the snow. No traffic was in sight, so she pulled out. But she wasn't going to be able to make a speedy getaway; the snow was already too deep. So she kept her speed slow and steady, knowing that she didn't dare risk getting stuck. They were sure to be following her.

The nearest town was about ten miles away. She hadn't seen a police station during her previous visits there, but she figured she should be safe enough if she pulled into a gas station or any other public place. Then she could call the police from there.

The highway was completely deserted. She kept glancing into the rearview mirror, even though she could see nothing because of the snow covering the windshield. Then suddenly it seemed to her that the snow had grown brighter. Was it the headlights of a car—probably the Blazer? They could certainly make better time than she was.

She turned her head to look directly at the rear windshield, certain now that something was back there. And just as she turned back to the road ahead, an old car pulled out from a side road directly into her path!

She pumped the brakes, just as she'd been taught to do all those years ago when her father had instructed her in the intricacies of winter driving. The car slewed a bit, but remained under her control.

Unfortunately the same could not be said for the other car. The driver had apparently given it too much gas as he pulled out onto the highway, perhaps realizing his mistake at the last moment. The old sedan began to slide. Andrea swung the Volvo around in a desperate attempt to avoid a collision. Her last thought, as metal struck metal with a resounding crash, was that in her desperation to escape from the two men, she'd forgotten to put on her seat belt.

MICHAEL'S FIRST THOUGHT, when he answered the door, was that the guy who stood there was a cop. He wasn't in uniform and he wasn't driving a marked car, but Michael knew he was right.

"I'm looking for Nick DeSantis," he announced.

"He isn't here at the moment," Michael told him. "I'm Michael Borelli, a friend of his. Can I help you?"

The guy sized him up for a couple of seconds. "Maybe you can. I'm a criminal investigator with the state police, but I'm not really here on official business. Do you know Andrea Lockwood, his sister-in-law?"

Michael's face must have shown the sudden fear he felt, because the guy was peering at him intently. "Sure. I know her. What's this about?"

"Mind if I come in?"

Michael showed him into the living room, his thoughts spinning. Why was he asking about Andy? Had she stayed around, after all, and gone to the police? What had he meant about not being here on official business? At least that must mean that she hadn't been hurt or...

"Like I said, this isn't exactly official. The woman I'm dating is kind of worried about her. She was supposed to meet us last night and she never showed up. Carole, my girlfriend, checked at the motel where she was staying, but they didn't have anyone by that name registered. I already went over there with the description Carole gave me and they told me she checked out yesterday."

"How does Carole know her?" Michael asked curiously as he tried to think how to handle this.

"Carole works for her dad. He owns Valley Flying Service. It's a charter service and flying school out at the airport. Carole's a pilot and Andrea Lockwood hired her yesterday to fly her up north. She said she was looking for a cabin where her twin sister might be staying. I understand the sister's married to Nick DeSantis."

Michael spared only a moment to admire Andy's ingenuity, then began to wonder if she'd spotted something he'd missed and had then gone off on her own to pursue it.

"She seemed to think her sister was in some kind of trouble," the cop said.

Michael nodded. "Yeah, I know she thought that, but I persuaded her she was wrong. Nick and Val are having some problems and she took off. Nick and I go way back. I used to be with the NYPD and now I'm private." Michael got out his wallet and showed him his P.I. license.

"Nick called me and asked me to try to find Val because he's worried about her and wants to be sure she's okay. I flew up there myself yesterday to search for her.

"Look, there's a lot of complicated history between the two of them—Andy and Val, I mean. And Andy isn't always rational when it comes to her sister. My guess is that she drove back up there again to look for Val, even though I told her to forget about it because she'd called yesterday and talked to Nick. She's okay, but she wants some time to think things through."

"So you don't think Andrea's in any trouble, then?"

Michael shook his head, even though that was exactly what he *was* thinking. "She probably got caught in the snowstorm and decided to stay over up there—or maybe she went on home to Connecticut."

The cop looked relieved and Michael guessed that he hadn't really wanted to come here to begin with and had just done so on his girlfriend's insistence. They swapped war stories for a couple of minutes and then he left.

Michael took the stairs two at a time, threw clothes into his suitcase, grabbed his guns and ran back downstairs to the kitchen to leave a note for Nick.

Then he paused for a moment, wondering if Andy *could* have gone home. It was too much to hope for, but he decided to call Connecticut just in case.

After her message had played, he hung up with a frown. She'd changed it—probably by remote, since she wasn't likely to have left a message stating that she was in Pennsylvania if she'd, in fact, gone home.

But why that particular message, he wondered. She was far too smart to leave a message that was an open invitation to burglary—unless she wanted to let Val know that she was here and not home. Could it mean that Val had contacted her and she wanted to let her know where she was? Michael was still thinking about the implications of *that* when he heard Nick's truck pulling up outside.

He told him what had happened and what he thought *might* have transpired, as well. Nick, of course, wanted to go with him, but Michael persuaded him to stay home, reminding him that he needed to be near the phone. Then, before Nick could change his mind, Michael stowed his gear and took off as the snow began to fall once more.

The flakes grew steadily worse as he drove north, staying at a slow, steady speed despite his desire to go faster. He wondered what he was going to find. Double trouble, he thought unhappily, thinking that his life would be a whole lot less complicated right now if he'd never met Andrea Lockwood.

MICHAEL ARRIVED at the motel after several hours spent wrestling the Cherokee through snowdrifts and around various stalled vehicles.

He had decided to go first to the motel that Andrea had visited when they were up here together. He recalled that she'd told him it was closed, but that the owner lived next door, and it seemed likely that if she were in the area, this was where she would go to seek shelter.

The Eagle Motel was dark however, and his gut twisted with fear as he pulled into the driveway of the house next door, stopping behind a pickup. There were no other vehicles in sight.

A weather-beaten middle-aged man came to the door before Michael had reached the front porch. He looked at him warily. Michael introduced himself and said that he was looking for a woman friend whom he thought might have come here seeking a place to stay.

"Her name's Andrea Lockwood," he told the man. "Tall, good-looking redhead."

The man continued to stare at him suspiciously, which Michael thought did not bode well. "Why're you looking for her?" the man demanded.

Michael started to unzip his jacket and get out his P.I.'s license, hoping that would allay the man's suspicions. But the man backed quickly into the house and picked up a shotgun, then leveled both barrels at Michael.

"Hey, calm down! I was just getting some ID. I'm a private investigator—and Andy's a friend of mine. It's kind of complicated, but I'm here because I'm afraid she might be in some kind of trouble."

He withdrew the case containing his license and extended it to the man, at the same time readying himself to grab the shotgun, if necessary.

The man peered closely at the license and then back at Michael. A short, rather stout woman appeared behind him, frowning with concern. Both of them stared at Michael for a long moment, and then he set aside the shotgun and motioned for him to come in.

"She was here—but she's gone." He turned to his wife. "Why don't you make some coffee, Martha? I'll take him over to the office and show him."

Michael waited impatiently as the man pulled on his boots and jacket. He'd already guessed that it was best to let the guy tell his story in his own way, even though his stomach was churning with fear. Damn Andrea for getting involved in this and for getting under his skin.

They made their way across the parking lot, where the snow had already drifted to a depth of two feet in places. Even before they had reached the motel office, Michael saw that the glass panes in the upper half of the door had been broken and replaced—apparently quite recently—with plywood.

They entered the office and he closed the door behind them, then gestured to it. "That's how whoever it was broke in. Miss Lockwood must have been in here. We were out shopping, but I'd left her a note and the keys in case she came back."

"When was this?" Michael asked.

"Yesterday afternoon. We left about three and got back about five-thirty."

"But if she wasn't around when you left, how can you be sure she was here at all?" Michael asked, still clinging to a hope that Andy was safe at home... anywhere but here.

But even as he asked the question, he got his answer. The man picked up a knit ski cap. Michael stared at it, feeling the tight knot in his stomach grow even harder and colder.

"That's Andy's."

"Yep. She left some food in the freezer, too. I found the cap in there, caught on the window latch."

He showed Michael the storage room, where several cartons had been piled beneath a high window. "I figure she escaped by climbing out there."

They returned to the office and he gestured to the parking lot. "I could still see some tire tracks out there when we got back. Hard to be sure, but it looked like two sets. Funny thing is, though, neither set looked like that little car of hers."

"Did you call the police?" Michael asked, wondering if Andy had managed to escape or if they'd taken her and the car.

"Sure, but they're pretty busy right now, what with the storm. All we got are the state police, and they're stretched pretty thin. They just took the information and said they'd send someone over as soon as they could. I gave them a description of her car, too."

He frowned. "I called them a little while ago, but they haven't spotted her car. I just can't see how she could have gotten very far in the snow in that little thing.

"I'd sure as hell like to know what's going on here. She came here a couple of days ago, saying she was looking for her twin. She told me she thought her sister might be in trouble, but it looks like she might have found some herself."

"Did she say anything about where her sister might be?"

The man scratched his head. "Yeah, come to think of it, she did. For some reason, she seemed to think she might be staying at a hunting camp about twenty miles from here that's owned by some guys from New York. I had some fellows here playing poker, and one of them said he thought he'd seen one of them the other day."

"Was he driving a black Blazer?" Michael asked.

The man nodded. "That's the one. Tire tracks I saw out there looked like they could have come from a Blazer, too."

"Where is this camp?" Michael asked as fear grabbed his gut. If Andy had found them—or they'd somehow found her...

ANDREA OPENED her eyes, then closed them again quickly as waves of nausea engulfed her. Everything ached—even her teeth. The accident! A car had pulled out in front of her and caught her off-guard because she'd thought someone was behind her—the kidnappers!

She opened her eyes again, ignoring the headache and pain. She was in the upstairs of the cabin, lying on the same bed Val must have used.

Slowly she pulled herself into a sitting position. The room spun for a few moments, then settled down. She moved her arms and legs and wriggled her toes and fingers, then felt her face. Everything seemed to be in working order, except that she had a definite lump on her head.

Then she became aware of voices downstairs. Before she could try to understand what they were saying, she heard one of them start up the stairs. She tried to get to her feet, but her legs were wobbly and she sat down again, just as the younger of the two men reached the top of the stairs and stared at her. She returned his look defiantly, although she was seeing two of him at the moment.

"You aren't her!" he said accusingly.

"No, I'm not," she said with grim satisfaction. "I'm her twin. Where is she?"

He swore, and for a moment Andrea was sure he was going to hit her. But instead, he turned and called down the stairs. "She's awake, Dad. They're twins! I told you she looked different."

Andrea might have enjoyed his befuddlement and the look on the other man's face when he joined them—if only the circumstances weren't so heavily weighed against her at the moment. About the only good thing she could think of was that his words made it clear that Val had indeed escaped.

"Where is my sister?" she demanded when they said nothing. "I know you kidnapped her. Where is she?"

"What're you doing here?" the older man demanded.

"I think that's pretty obvious," she stated coldly. "You brought me here—after you tried to kidnap me at the motel."

"Who knows that you're up here nosing around?" the younger man asked, still staring at her dangerously.

It was a loaded question—and one that could tell her something she needed to know. "Michael knows—and Nick, too, I suppose."

"Michael?" The younger one asked, exchanging a look with his father that seemed puzzled. "Who's he?"

"Michael Borelli." She watched them carefully, praying that they didn't know him.

"Borelli," the older man said in a musing tone. Then he gave his son a sharp look. "That's the—"

"Shut up, Dad," the younger one said, then took his father's arm and led him back downstairs.

Andrea heard them talking, but once again couldn't make out the words. She got to her feet, swaying, and made her way over to the top of the stairs. But before she could hear anything, another wave of nausea came over her and she turned to the bathroom instead. She threw up into the toilet and then sat there, too weak to get up at the moment.

As she sat there on the cold bathroom floor, she heard the voices below her raised in argument. But the only word she could hear clearly was "cop." Were they talking about Michael? It seemed to her that they hadn't immediately recognized his name, and then the father had. Did that mean that Michael was innocent? But he'd lied to her, so he must know something.

Unfortunately the effort required to come up with some guesses was beyond her at that moment. She dragged herself to her feet and went back to the bed.

ANDREA AWOKE to a sound, which she belatedly identified as a door slamming. She felt better—at least, until she tried to get out of bed too quickly. Then she stood there swaying and waiting for the dizziness to pass.

It was very quiet downstairs. Could they have left? She made her way carefully over to the window. It was still snowing and the world beyond the window was a landscape of whites and grays and the dark pines.

There was no sign of the men—or of their Blazer. Val's Volvo was parked in front of the cabin, so covered in snow that she could just barely identify it. Her Miata was hopefully there, as well, buried in the drifting snow.

She wondered where they were. There were no tracks in the snow to indicate that they'd left in the Blazer, and in any event, she doubted that even it could get through the drifts.

She went to the bathroom, listening carefully for any sounds on the first floor. But the cabin remained silent. She felt hungry, which she took as a good sign. Then she wondered just how long she'd been here. Time had gotten away from her. When she looked at her watch, which also showed the date, she frowned, then began to do some mental calculations.

The accident had happened yesterday. She'd now been here twenty-four hours—or nearly that. Her stomach growled, reminding her that she hadn't eaten for that time.

She didn't really want to confront her captors again, but her hunger compelled her to the stairs, which she took very slowly and carefully, fearing a return of the dizziness. When she finally reached the first floor, she still saw no sign of them and her curiosity outweighed her hunger for the moment.

Just as she reached a window, she saw them trudging through the snow, heading away from the cabin. Then she began to understand. They must have left the Blazer down at the end of the road, next to the highway.

She was surprised that they would just leave her here—at least, until she realized that they had no reason to fear she would leave. How could she?

But where were they going? Had they gone out again to search for Val—or were they leaving for good? They'd definitely been arguing earlier, and she wondered if they might have given up their scheme—whatever it was.

She went into the kitchen and found it well stocked. Obviously they intended to stay for a while. She heated some soup and made herself a sandwich, then carried it into the living room and sat down before the fire.

Her thoughts kept spinning around and around. Where was Val and what had she learned about Nick? Again and again, she went over what she'd learned, and still nothing made sense.

And what about Michael's role in all this? His name *had* meant something—at least to the father. She was convinced that her mention of him had come as a shock to them.

She decided it was pointless to think any more about it. Instead, she began to wonder if she could get out of here. She was definitely feeling better now, even though the muscle aches and pains were as bad as before.

She finished her meal and went again to look out the window. To her dismay, the storm had regained its former strength. Even as she stood there, the wind began to howl and shriek along the eaves of the cabin. The Miata was completely invisible; she wasn't even sure where it was. But the blowing snow had partially uncovered the Volvo and she saw now that the damage to the front and side wasn't as bad as she'd feared. Obviously it could be driven, since they had brought it in here.

Should she dig out the Volvo and try to get away? The road was mostly downhill from here and perhaps it wasn't drifted as bad in the woods.

Then she wondered about the keys. Would they have left them? She began to search for them, and when she didn't find them, went back upstairs to get her purse, thinking that they might have put them there. The keys to the Miata were there, but the Volvo keys were nowhere to be found. She thought wryly that they must have had less faith in her little car than she did.

The Volvo keys just might be in the car itself, she thought, and decided that it was time to brave the outdoors. And that was when she realized that both her boots and her jacket were gone!

Angry and now more determined than ever, she searched the cabin for something to wear. She found a pair of boots in the little room in back where the generator was housed. They were far too big, but they fit well enough after she stuffed some old newspapers in the toes. And in a small closet under the eaves upstairs, she found an old hunting jacket in that red-and-black plaid she could remember her grandfather wearing. It was heavy and musty smelling and too big, but it would be warm. With it was a matching hat with ear flaps. That left only gloves and she knew she had an extra pair in the suitcase that was, she hoped, still in the trunk of her car.

As she was lacing up the boots, her gaze fell on the gun case in the corner beneath the stairs. It surprised her that she hadn't noticed it before. Through the glass doors, she could see three guns inside.

Andrea's father and grandfather had both been hunters, and so she had some familiarity with guns. She went over to the case and discovered that it was locked. She was about to give up on the idea of arming herself when she began to think about the very real possibility that her captors could return—and the certainty that they weren't going to be very happy if they found her trying to escape.

So she picked up a heavy piece of firewood and rammed it through the glass, then carefully broke out the remaining shards of glass and took out one of the guns. It was a shotgun, and a box of shells lay beneath it on the floor of the cabinet. She'd seen her father load such a weapon many times and after fumbling about for a few seconds, managed to break it open and push two of the large shells into the chambers.

As she stepped out onto the porch, the wind nearly blew off her cap. She secured the strap beneath her chin and trudged through the snow to the Volvo, carrying the shovel she'd found on the porch. Within a few moments, she'd cleared away enough of the snow to see that the keys weren't in the car. So she left it for the moment and began to poke around in the huge drifts to find the Miata, then uncovered its trunk and dragged her suitcase up onto the porch to get her extra gloves.

Now what do I do? she asked herself, staring balefully at the Volvo. And then a thought came to her. It was a very long shot, to be sure, but perhaps the only one she had. She went back inside to get the screwdriver she'd seen in a kitchen drawer.

It took a while, but she finally managed to pry off the right rear hubcap—and there was a key! Feeling more elated than she had any right to be, she began to push the snow off the car.

Their father had always kept a spare key taped to the inside of the right rear hubcap. After she and Val had gotten their licenses, they'd had more than one occasion to need it. She herself had adopted the same habit, until concern about possible car theft had caused her to remove it. But Val lived in an area where she didn't have to worry quite so much.

From the cabin, the road sloped downhill into the woods, and even though the snow was in places up to the Volvo's bumper, it plowed through the light powder. She was able to move along quite steadily for a time—especially once she reached the woods, where the snow hadn't drifted so much.

Travel was nearly all downhill for the first part of her journey, but then she saw her first big problem ahead. The road entered a deep cut that appeared to be filled with a great deal of drifted snow, and beyond it lay a fairly short but very steep uphill grade.

There was nothing to do but gun the engine and hope that the momentum would carry her through the drift and up the hill. It nearly worked, but the car faltered as it struggled to reach the crest on the far side of the cut.

After spinning the wheels until she could smell rubber burning, Andrea gave up. The snow was so deep that she could just barely get the door open. She'd brought along the shovel, but it didn't take long for her to realize that she couldn't possibly dig her way out before dark. Already the light was fading, helped along by the thickly falling snow. So she picked up the shotgun and set out on foot, making very slow progress through the deep snow.

MICHAEL FOUND THE ROAD that led to the cabin, but not before he'd had to dig the Cherokee out of snowdrifts twice. Plows appeared to be in short supply, or maybe they'd just given up in view of the fact that the wind was pushing the snow back onto the road as fast as it could be removed.

When he'd first set out from the motel nearly two hours ago, the snow had actually seemed to be letting up, but for some time now it had been falling thickly once again and powerful gusts of wind were constantly buffeting his sturdy vehicle.

He stopped in the middle of the highway and stared at the road that led to the cabin. There were no tracks visible, but it did look as though something had been parked at the end near the highway not too long ago.

He downshifted and turned into the road, unzipping his jacket as he went and taking out the nine-millimeter automatic to lay it on the seat beside him. He had no idea what he might find at the cabin and refused to let himself think about it now. But a vision of Andy with her long-legged stride and her windblown auburn hair persisted in tormenting him.

The Cherokee made slow but relatively steady progress through the snow, slipping occasionally before finding purchase and edging forward again. An unnatural twilight had settled over the land, but he didn't turn on his lights, hoping to preserve the element of surprise. Inside the cabin, they might not hear the engine, but they would certainly see any lights.

Ahead of him, the road dropped into a ravine—and in it sat Val's car. He came to a stop, knowing he couldn't hope to get past it on the narrow road and trying to figure out why it was there. Judging from the amount of snow on the hood and windshield, it hadn't been there very long.

Michael picked up his gun and stepped cautiously out into the howling blizzard, wondering who had left the car there and where they might be now.

Chapter Eight

Andrea froze! Through the gathering darkness and the falling snow, she saw movement in the woods. Then she realized that it wasn't there, but on the road. Ahead of her, the road curved as it spiraled downhill and what she'd glimpsed was a dark, boxy vehicle—coming toward her. Her captors were returning!

She scrambled quickly up the steep bank on the left side of the road and hid in the shelter of snow-covered pines, the shotgun cradled in her arms as she watched the road below. Long seconds passed and she saw nothing, but a portion of the road was hidden from her view.

Her fingers were nearly numb with cold, but she fumbled loose the chin strap on her borrowed cap and then lifted the thick earflaps. Any hope that she was wrong vanished as she now heard the sound of an engine.

Then she saw it, approaching slowly and without lights—a familiar dark, boxy shape. They'd come back, and within a few seconds they would see the Volvo and know that she'd tried to escape.

She held her breath, hoping that they would see the stuck car and assume that she'd gone back to the cabin, then go there themselves, giving her the time she needed to reach the highway.

She shifted her gaze to the bank she'd just climbed. Already her footprints were nearly gone in swirls of blowing snow. She could only hope that she was hidden, as well—despite her red-and-black plaid jacket. At least her borrowed clothes weren't the florescent orange that hunters wore nowadays.

The vehicle rolled to a stop at the crest of the hill above the ravine where the Volvo had stalled. A man got out, and even from this distance and in the fading light, she could tell it was the younger one—and that he was carrying a gun. She clutched the shotgun more tightly and waited to see what he would do.

He began to circle the car warily, half-crouched, the gun aimed at the car. Then, after he had circled it at a distance, he moved quickly, flinging open the passenger door, and pointed the gun inside. Andrea winced, imagining her fate if she'd been in there. There was no doubt in her mind now that they intended to kill her, and that freed her from her fear-induced paralysis.

Slipping and sliding, she began to make her way through the woods, away from her captors and toward the highway. If they'd managed to get back here, there must surely be other traffic on the road. There *had* to be; it was her only hope.

MICHAEL STOOD THERE, frowning. The most likely scenario was that they'd given up and returned to the cabin. But he was troubled by the fact that it was Val's car sitting here and not the Blazer. Why wouldn't they have taken it instead?

He circled the Volvo again, this time searching for footprints in the blowing, drifting snow and wondering if it could possibly have been Val or Andy in the vehicle—or both of them.

Then he saw the first footprints and gave up on that speculation. The prints were too large for a woman's boots. They led him over to the edge of the road, and there they stopped. He peered up the steep bank alongside the road and was finally able to make out some shallow depressions leading up the hillside.

He revised his previous scenario, deciding that he or they must have seen him coming and had then taken off into the woods. Torn for a moment between his desire to find out if the women were at the cabin and his need to know where the men were, he finally started up the bank.

Tracking his quarry was much easier once he was in the woods where the wind was somewhat broken by the trees. He saw more bootprints and began to follow them, his eyes searching the dark woods ahead.

Then he stopped as he caught a glimpse of someone up ahead in an old plaid hunting jacket and cap. And before the figure was lost to view, he saw that he was carrying a shot-gun.

The strange twilight was rapidly giving way to darkness as Michael began to trail the figure, wishing now that he'd brought his rifle instead of the nine millimeter. Still, he knew he had the advantage of surprise at this point. The guy up ahead had paused to look back a couple of times and it was clear that he hadn't spotted Michael in his dark clothing.

ANDREA CAST A QUICK look behind her. She couldn't see anyone following her, although it was nearly dark and he'd been wearing dark clothing. They must have gone on to the cabin. Perhaps she could risk returning to the road, where she could make better time.

She angled back toward the road, then stood at the top of a short hill, looking down at it. Returning to the road would leave her more exposed, but it would also mean she could get to the highway faster. Her head had begun to throb again and she was worried about a recurrence of that earlier dizziness and blurred vision. She decided to take her chances on the road.

She started carefully down the slope, maintaining her grip on the shotgun with one hand as she clutched at branches and trunks to help her descend. The last part of the slope was very steep and treeless and her feet began to slide. As she struggled to remain upright, the shotgun slid away and tumbled down the slope, ending up in the ditch at the bottom. Her headache was growing worse and she could feel the nausea begin to well up inside her.

"No!" she said aloud, commanding her body to obey as she sat down to slide the rest of the way to the road.

When she reached the bottom, she grabbed for the shotgun and at the same time cast a quick glance back up the road. Then, out of the corner of her eye, she saw movement on the hillside above her and swung around, pointing the shotgun in that direction.

"Drop it!" a male voice commanded. "I've got better range and better accuracy."

She could just barely make out the figure standing on the edge of the slope above her, once again crouched in the stance of a shooter. She didn't know if he was telling the truth about range, but she didn't doubt the part about accuracy, and his professional stance further undermined her confidence.

"Drop it!" he ordered again.

Andrea hesitated, then laid the shotgun down and started to get to her feet, fighting the waves of dizziness. Something about his voice, she thought. It sounded different. But with the howling wind, she couldn't be sure.

"Stay down!" he ordered as she began to rise to her feet. "Don't move!"

"Michael," she said softly as he began to descend the slope and she got a better look at him. She recognized the jacket now, and his somewhat larger size.

For one brief moment, she felt elated. But the moment spun quickly away into a bleakness that nearly overwhelmed her. Michael was one of them. Why else would he be here?

He nearly made it down the slope, but then he lost his footing and began to fall. She lunged for the shotgun and brought it up. He went into a roll, then sat up with his gun still aimed at her. They were about fifty feet apart in the dim light.

Suddenly his gun wavered slightly as he got to his feet. "Andy?" he asked, his voice uncertain. "Andy, it's Michael!"

She kept the shotgun trained on him and choked back a sob. She wanted desperately to respond to the gentleness she could hear in his voice—a kindness she knew must be calculated to make her believe in him. And why not? It had worked before. But not this time.

He'd lowered his gun, but she kept the shotgun trained on him. "Put it down, Michael!"

"Andy! What the hell's wrong with you?" Instead of dropping the gun, he unzipped his jacket and slid it into his shoulder holster as he struggled through the snow toward her. "Andy, it's me—Michael! You're safe now."

"Stop right there, Michael!" she commanded, struggling to hold the heavy gun steady as another wave of dizziness rolled over her. "Start walking—back up to your Cherokee. Then you can drive us both to the nearest police station."

Her tone sounded firm, but an inner voice was whispering that she couldn't shoot him—not even to save herself.

"Andy, I don't know what happened, but you can't believe that I'd hurt you."

His voice was low and soothing—the sound of someone well-trained in handling volatile situations. Of course, he'd been conditioned that way; he'd been a cop. She knew that, and yet she still wanted to believe him—trust in him.

As he walked toward her, she unconsciously backed up—and then it was too late! The snow beneath her foot gave way and she fell backward into the ditch, still clutching the shotgun. The dizziness washed over her again, creating two images, both of which were now kneeling at her side, and prying the gun from her grasp.

"Andy, honey, you're safe now," he said in that same soothing tone as he tried to reach out and fold her into his arms.

"I think I'm going to be sick," she muttered, then pushed away from him and promptly threw up in the snow.

He knelt beside her and handed her a small mound of snow. "Here. Take this to rinse out your mouth. Can you walk?"

She nodded, but when she tried to stand, she swayed against him and his arms gripped her waist firmly. "I have a concussion."

He made a sound of disgust. "Then what the hell are you doing out here? Is there anyone at the cabin?"

She started to shake her head, then stopped as the pain grew worse. "Not now. They left."

"Good. Then we'll go there." He bent to pick up the shotgun, then wrapped a steadying arm around her shoulders and began to lead her back up the road.

Andrea went with him because she had no choice. She wasn't at all certain that she'd be able to walk without the support of his arm across her shoulders and his body pressed against hers. But she could feel the hardness of the gun under his jacket—not to mention her weapon he was now carrying in his other hand.

As they made their way slowly to his vehicle, she kept waiting for him to offer an explanation for his presence here, or to speak some more false words of reassurance. But he remained silent until they reached the Cherokee.

"You get inside and stay warm, while I see if I can dig my way past the Volvo," he told her, helping her into the passenger side and then going around to start the engine before getting a shovel from the rear. When he was only a few yards away, he had vanished almost completely into the swirling snow and the darkness.

The heater poured blessed warmth over her. Jazz played softly on the CD. Andrea sank back into the seat and closed her eyes, wondering if she'd ever truly feel warm again and wondering why she continued to believe in this man who'd betrayed her trust.

There's an irony here, she thought sleepily. *I felt something wrong in Nick. I sensed danger for Val. But nothing warned me about Michael.*

She yawned as the warmth finally began to seep into her, for some reason bringing with it a memory of Michael's kiss. How she wanted him to be innocent in all this—and yet how could he be? He'd already lied to her, and if he were not guilty, he wouldn't even be here now. He had to have come because he knew where Val had been taken.

But if he'd known, then why had he hired a plane to search the area?

Too tired to sort it all out, she dozed, then snapped awake as a blast of cold air struck her and Michael climbed in beside her, his shoulder brushing against hers as he settled into the seat.

"I think we can get past now," he said as he put the Cherokee into gear.

And they did, though not without considerable maneuvering. Michael had to dig some more while she slid into the driver's seat and rocked the vehicle back and forth.

Her legs felt rubbery as she climbed out at the cabin, but she waved off his offer of assistance, determined not to appear weak in front of him. Rather to her surprise, he said nothing, but instead waited for her at the door as she made her slow way up the steps and across the porch.

After the overheated interior of the Cherokee, the cabin felt chilled, though still far warmer than the outdoors. She staggered over to the couch and collapsed.

"Is there more firewood?" he asked, staring at the smoldering embers in the fireplace.

She nodded, then realized that she couldn't hear the generator. "There's a generator, too," she told him. "But it must have stopped after I left."

The last thing she heard before she dropped off into oblivion was a coughing, sputtering sound, and then the smooth hum of the generator.

"WHAT'S YOUR NAME?"

Andrea roused herself, though not very much. "What?"

"Tell me your name."

She opened one eye. She was lying on the sofa with several blankets tucked snugly around her and a pillow beneath her head. Michael was hovering over her, his dark brows knitted into a frown. She liked having him there and the warm and snug feeling of safety.

Safe? she thought. *Am* I safe with him?

"I know my name—and so do you." Why was he asking such a dumb question? Surely he didn't think she was Val!

The frown disappeared and a smile took its place. "I still want you to tell me. You said you had a concussion."

"Andrea Lockwood," she stated succinctly. "And there's nothing wrong with my brain."

"I'm not prepared to swear to that." He grinned. "How about some soup?"

By now, she had awakened enough to notice the delicious aroma and her stomach began to growl nosily, reminding her that she'd lost her last meal. Michael chuckled.

"You know, I think that was a first. I don't ever recall having a woman throw up when I appeared."

She grimaced and pushed the blankets aside, thinking that it was kind of him not to remind her that she'd also threatened him with a shotgun. She curled up in the corner of the sofa and he handed her the bowl of soup. He sat down on the other end of the sofa, with the blankets piled between them. He'd removed his jacket—but not the shoulder holster and gun.

He saw her staring at the gun. "They could come back, Andy, although I doubt it'll be anytime soon. It's still snowing. When you've finished eating, you can tell me what happened."

But she said nothing even after she'd emptied her bowl. She had no intention of telling him anything until he explained his presence here—and a few other things, as well.

"Okay," he said after the silence had gone on for a few minutes. "I'll tell you what I know and maybe you'll be moved to fill in the gaps. Your pilot friend sent her state-trooper boyfriend out to talk to Nick, after you didn't show up to meet them. Nick wasn't there—but I was. So I know that you hired her to fly over this area, and I guess you must have spotted something from the air and came back up to investigate.

"The guy at the motel said you were interested in this cabin, that you thought Val was here. Then apparently someone came after you at the motel and you managed to escape. Or maybe you didn't. That's where things get a little hazy. Since I give you credit for being very bright most of the time, it's kind of hard for me to believe that you came out here on your own in the middle of a storm."

She still said nothing, even though he'd explained how he'd come to be here—and for once, it actually sounded like the truth. He sighed, settling back into the corner of the sofa as he gazed at her steadily. With the fire crackling away and the wind howling outside and the heap of blankets piled between them, the entire scene had a powerful intimacy that had her thinking again about his kisses.

"Okay, so let me speculate a bit further, since you seem to have lost your voice. The Miata is buried in a snowdrift outside, the Volvo has been in an accident and you have a bump on your head.

"You came here in the Miata before the snow got too bad, then couldn't get out. The Volvo must have been here, so you took it back to the motel. They must have spotted it and thought Val was there. You escaped out that window, then apparently had an accident. But that still doesn't explain how you ended up back here and I'm getting tired of talking to myself."

"If Mr. Roberts at the motel knew that someone was after me, why didn't he call the police?" she demanded. "He must have guessed that it was the men who were staying here."

"He did, but in case you hadn't noticed, there's a blizzard out there. They're calling it the 'Storm of the Century.' There aren't many police around here to begin with, and they're pretty busy at the moment."

"So he told you instead," she said, thinking once again that he had a real talent for convincing people of his trustworthiness—everyone but *her,* that is.

"Right. He told me because he was worried about you and knew I was, too." He paused, glaring at her.

"Dammit, Andy, tell me what happened! I need to know what I'm dealing with here."

"*You're* the private eye," she replied scornfully. "I'm just a college professor."

"Right—a professor who insisted on sticking her nose into something she should have stayed out of. Sometimes you can be a real pain in the—"

"You seem to forget that it's *my* sister we're talking about here. Who *are* those men—and why did they kidnap Val?"

"I'm not sure they *did* kidnap her. She could have taken off on her own."

"Stop lying to me, Michael! You and Nick have been deceitful from the beginning! If Val wasn't kidnapped, then how did she end up *here,* along with her car and scarf?"

"Then where is she now?"

"I don't know. I think she must have escaped."

"Or maybe she just left of her own free will."

"Right," she said sarcastically. "She just walked off into a blizzard, leaving her car behind. I told you before, my brain is working just fine."

"Your mind is working on one track. You've convinced yourself that Val was kidnapped and you're seeing everything through that filter.

"Think about this. Suppose that Val *does* have a lover. I know that you don't want to believe that, but it happens. So she comes here with him. He's probably one of the owners of this place. Then she has a fight with him, or maybe she decides she doesn't want him, after all. So she leaves. She could have left before the storm. Or maybe he had the keys and wouldn't give them to her. Or maybe she was somewhere else with him and just walked off.

"Then he sees the Volvo at the motel and sees you, and because he's the possessive type he wants her back. Nick's pretty possessive himself, so Val must go for that type."

"And I suppose that he just happened to bring his father with him? Get real, Michael! If you're going to make up stories, at least do me the courtesy of making them believable."

"Look, it could be that his father was already here. Maybe he came to do some hunting."

"I hate to disillusion you, city boy, but hunting season's over," she said scornfully, even as she recalled what the men at the motel had said about them hunting out of season.

Michael shrugged. "So he was just here, period. I have a cabin up in the Adirondacks and I go there just to get away. I don't even hunt."

"Michael, they broke down the office door to get me!"

"Like I said, maybe he's the possessive type. Some men get crazy when they think a woman's going to leave them. You want to know how many homicides I worked on where some guy killed his wife or girlfriend just because she wanted out? You still haven't told me what happened after they found you at the motel."

She told him about the accident and their discovery that she wasn't Val.

"So they brought you here. Under the circumstances, it wasn't a bad idea. You'd been in an accident and the nearest hospital's probably miles away over bad roads.

"Besides, they didn't threaten you in any way, did they? And taking your car keys wasn't such a bad idea, either. You were in no shape to drive and you were safe enough here. The place has enough firewood and food to last at least a week."

"So where did they go?"

"Who knows? Maybe back to New York. This storm is tracking northeast, toward New England, so they could be out of it pretty quickly. Maybe Dad talked some sense into his lovelorn son. That's probably what they were arguing about before they left."

Andrea sat staring into the fire. He was wrong about all this. She was certain about that, but she couldn't find any way to prove that to him. Even if she told him about Val's call, he would only say that she had been referring to Nick's supposed affair.

She really hated the fact that his explanation made all too much sense, but as she went over it again, she could see that it did. There wasn't one fact she knew that couldn't be twisted around to fit his explanation.

Could she really have been so wrong about all this? Had she really come charging into this because she thought she saw a way to end the estrangement with her twin? She knew, better than most people, how easily one can delude oneself into believing something.

Not that she'd wanted to think that Nick and Val were having marital problems, but she knew she could have subconsciously seen her opportunity to "rescue" her sister and thereby make up for her failure the last time.

"Well, what are we going to do?" she asked as Michael got up to look out the window.

"We're going to wait out the storm," he said matter-of-factly.

"You got in here," she reminded him. "So you should be able to get out again."

"Maybe, but I doubt it. From the looks of it, at least another couple of inches has come down since we got here. And the wind has really picked up. The weather report I heard earlier said we could get thirty inches or more.

"Anyway," he said, turning back to her. "There's no place we can go even if we could get out of here. We sure aren't going to be able to get all the way back to Centre Valley, and this place is more comfortable than the motel."

"I want to find Val," she said stubbornly. "I *have* to find her."

He gestured to the door. "Go right ahead. I'm staying put. Did she call you, by the way?"

The sudden question caught her off-guard. "Why do you ask?"

"Because you changed the message on your machine to say that you were in Pennsylvania. I thought you might have done it because Val had left a message."

"I changed it because I thought she might call and I wanted to let her know I was here," she replied, thinking that he wasn't the only one who could shade the truth. "Why did you call me?"

"I wanted to see if you'd gotten home safely, and then I called again after that state trooper came by."

"'Got home safely'?" she mimicked. "You just wanted to make sure that I was out of the way."

"It amounts to the same thing, doesn't it?" he challenged with a smile. "It couldn't possibly have had anything to do with the fact that I care about you. And of course, that didn't have anything to do with my coming up here in the middle of a damned blizzard to look for you."

He had walked over to stand in front of her, leaning forward to make his point. She stared fixedly at his gun, trying to ignore the soft curls of warmth that were unfolding themselves inside her.

"Will you please get rid of that gun? It makes you look like some gangster."

He chuckled and slid the strap from his shoulder, then laid the holster and gun down on the table. "Do I have your word that you won't try to blow me away? I don't think I'm ever going to forget you aiming that shotgun at me. Have you ever fired a shotgun, by they way?"

"No."

"Well, just in case you get the urge sometime in the future, let me warn you about them—espccially models like that one. They have a hell of a kick to them. If you'd fired it, you'd probably have a dislocated shoulder to go with your concussion."

"Thank you for the information," she responded dryly. "I'll keep that in mind."

"So," he said, arching one dark brow, "what do you suggest we do to keep ourselves out of trouble while we're holed up here? Do you happen to play poker?"

"I'm afraid not," she said, trying to keep her own voice as casual and teasing as his was. But it wasn't working for either of them.

He had begun to flip idly through a stack of sports magazines on the table. She stood there, feeling their isolation even more strongly as she avoided looking at him. But it did no good. She could *feel* him even when she wasn't looking at him. Everything that was Michael Borelli seemed to be invading her very pores, sliding through her like liquid fire.

"I could always teach you how to play poker," he suggested, breaking the silence that had become unbearable.

She flicked her gaze to his—a mistake, because now they were both caught up in the web of sensuality that was being spun around them, a very fragile web filled with uncertainty and desire in an unstable mixture that could not coexist for long. She looked away.

"If there's hot water, I'm going to take a shower."

She walked away, feeling his eyes on her, caressing her body.

STANDING BENEATH a welcome torrent of hot water, Andrea found that she could think more clearly. She doubted, however, that the water had much to do with it.

She began to edge away from her willingness to accept Michael's version of the situation. First of all, there was the eagerness of both Michael and Nick to get rid of her. If Michael was telling the truth, why should they care about her presence?

He would undoubtedly say that Nick feared she would be adding fuel to an already blazing fire because of her stormy relationship with her twin and her dislike of him.

Then there was the question of Michael's miniarsenal, plus the statement he'd made earlier when he'd explained away his gun-toting by saying that the two men might return. Why would he feel threatened by Val's lover and his father?

But if she put that question to him, he would simply embellish on his theory that Val's supposed lover was hotheaded and unpredictable and he was just playing it safe.

The water began to cool and she got out of the shower with a sound of disgust. Things had apparently reached the impossible point where she could lie for him, instead of forcing him to do it himself.

Still, in the back of her mind lingered the possibility that Michael might just be telling the truth, and when this was all over, she was going to look like a world-class fool. And if that happened, it would take every ounce of willpower she possessed not to strangle her troublemaking twin—definitely not an action that would win her trust and affection again.

But she continued to think about Val's brief call. She knew she might be dwelling too much on it, but how could she do otherwise, when it was the first time in all these years that Val had actually reached out to her?

Val had said she was "right about Nick." But if what she'd meant was that he had betrayed their marriage, would she have used that phrase? Andrea had never said that Nick would be unfaithful to her. What she'd said was that there was something dark and dangerous in his past.

You're nit-picking, she told herself—playing a game of semantics. *You can't expect Val to be precise when she's so upset.*

She dressed and opened the bathroom door to be greeted by mouth-watering aromas. Following her nose to the kitchen, she found Michael busy cooking.

Not only was he bright and funny and sexy, but he could cook, she thought wryly. Every woman's dream. She herself was one of those people who had long ago perfected a few carefully chosen recipes and had stuck with them. Clearly Michael was good at improvisation—and probably in more ways than one.

"Don't get your hopes up," he said, turning from the stove. "This needs to simmer overnight. If you're hungry now, you'll have to settle for a sandwich or an omelet."

She thought he probably made perfect omelets, too. "You're a good cook," she observed.

"My mother didn't believe in just teaching her daughters how to cook. Somewhere along the line, she went from being a traditional Italian mother to becoming a feminist. Or maybe I should say that she somehow manages to combine the two.

"I only know how to cook Italian, so it's a good thing that our hosts are also Italian."

"How do you know they are?" she asked casually, thinking she'd caught him at last.

"Look at what they brought with them," he replied evenly, although for just a moment she thought he seemed disconcerted.

But she had to admit that he was right. She'd checked the supplies earlier, but had paid more attention to quantity than to individual items.

He asked her if she wanted an omelet, then made her one that was indeed picture perfect as well as delicious. Michael Borelli was truly a man of many talents—*too* many talents.

"No more dizziness or nausea?" he asked as she finished it off quickly.

"No. I feel fine now—just a little tired."

"Good. It must have been a mild one, then." He picked up her empty plate and plunged it into a sinkful of suds. "There's not a lot of oil left for the generator, so I suggest that we both sleep near the fireplace and turn it off for the night. You can have the sofa and I'll drag out a mattress from the bedroom.''

''Fine,'' she said, avoiding his gaze and trying to ignore the subliminal conversation. ''How long do you think we'll have to stay here?''

''That's hard to say. If we end up with as much snow as they were predicting and the wind continues, it could be a couple of days. We're going to have to walk out to the highway.''

She sighed and he turned to her with a lazy grin. ''Like I said before, I can always teach you how to play poker.''

Chapter Nine

"I suppose you're going to say that it was just beginner's luck," Andrea said as she gathered together her pile of chips.

"Of course not," he responded dryly. "It was your brilliant playing, thanks to my excellent teaching."

"The wind has died down," she said, getting up to look out the window. "And it's not snowing as hard, either."

"Is my company that terrible?" he teased.

She wasn't about to take that bait—especially since he knew perfectly well that she didn't find his company unpleasant. The sensual tension between them was growing by the minute, it seemed, and had by now reached the point where she tried to avoid eye contact as much as possible.

The truth is, she told herself, *that you're living every woman's fantasy—snowbound with a very handsome and very desirable man. Unfortunately he might also be a very lying one.*

They'd talked for several hours the previous night before going to sleep—about everything. And as she lay there later, watching his sleeping face in the firelight only a few feet away, Andrea forced herself to face up to the fact that she was falling for him—and hard.

But she wondered how *he* felt. She didn't doubt that he wanted her, but how did he *feel* about her? She knew she wasn't the only one who had mixed emotions. For all his teasing, he was hesitant, too.

She belatedly responded to his teasing remark about her not enjoying his company. "You seem to forget why we're here, Michael. Val's out there somewhere—and she needs help."

"If she needed help, she would have called you."

"She *did* call me. She left a message on my machine."

She'd expected some sort of rise out of him, but he merely nodded. "I thought as much when I found out you'd changed your message. What did she say?"

She walked back over to the table and sat down across from him. "She said she was in trouble, and she said I was right about Nick—that she couldn't trust him. She told me not to call him."

"Of course she doesn't trust him at this point. She thinks he was having an affair. Didn't she say anything about where she was or where she was going?"

"No. It was just a short message." She didn't tell him that she thought Val had regretted her impulse to call. "But I don't think she was referring to his having an affair."

"Why not?"

"Because she didn't just say that she couldn't trust him. She also said I was right about him."

"So?"

"So, I never said that he wouldn't be faithful to her. What I told her was that I'd sensed something dark in his past."

Michael heaved a sigh. "Twilight Zone time."

She smacked the table with her palm, startling him. "Stop it, Michael! Don't try to make me out to be some sort of weirdo! I don't make any claims to being psychic. All I know is what I felt. And if Val mentioned it, it's because she found out something that made her believe I was right." She leaned forward, fixing him with a hard stare.

"There are three possibilities here. Either you're right and Val took off on her own, or I'm right and someone kidnapped her and Nick has lied to you, or she was kidnapped and both of you are lying."

"Andy, you're making something very simple into something far too complex."

"You said that before."

He shrugged. "Give me high marks for consistency, then."

She continued to lean toward him, pinning him with her gaze. "I'm going to find out the truth sooner or later, Michael. Have you thought about that? When I find Val, I'll also find out what *really* happened."

He met her gaze, but for the first time she saw signs of uneasiness in him. She could actually feel it as he finally shifted his gaze away from her.

"And that matters to you," she said, pressing her point. "I know it does."

He said nothing as he got up and went to the kitchen. She started to follow him, then decided to let him think *that* over for a while. She knew she was making a pretty big assumption when she'd implied that he cared enough about her to be concerned about what she thought of him, but she was sure she was right.

But if Michael had any worries about her discovering that he'd lied, he showed no inclination to tell her the truth. After a brief hiatus—just long enough to make them think the storm might have passed on—both the wind and the snow returned as heavily as before. Michael spent much of the time pacing around the cabin like a caged panther, then doing push-ups and flipping through sports magazines.

She found an old Robert Ludlum paperback and tried to read instead of thinking about Michael. But it didn't work. Finally, late in the afternoon, the snow had once again let up and she began to dress for the outdoors. He stopped his pacing and looked at her questioningly.

"I'm going to dig out my car."

"You might have asked me to do it for you," he observed.

"I'd be grateful for your help," she replied coolly.

Just getting the front door open required his strength, because the wind had blown snow across the porch and up against it. When he finally got it open, they stepped out into thigh-high drifts. The little Miata was nothing more than a slight bump in the snow. She would never have known it was there if she hadn't remembered where she'd left it.

When she paused after digging for quite a while, he stopped, too, giving her a concerned look. "Why don't you go back inside and let me finish? In case you've forgotten, you have a concussion."

"I'm fine," she responded as she resumed her digging, even though she was developing a headache.

The wind made the digging twice as difficult. The snow was light and powdery, and no sooner had she moved a shovelful than part of it would be blown back again. Still, they both continued their labors because, however worthless they were, at least they weren't locked in the cabin together.

Finally patches of bright blue became visible and she began to sweep the remaining snow off with her gloved hands while Michael started to shovel the area behind the car, telling her that he'd clear the exhaust pipe so she could start the engine and let it run for a time.

With the driver's side now clear, Andrea opened the door and reached in to get the brush she kept to clear snow. Her headache had gotten worse and when she straightened up again, a wave of dizziness came over her. She staggered backward and lost her footing, falling into the deep snow beside the car.

"Andy!" She heard Michael's sharp cry as she sank into the cold whiteness. She was reminded of that earlier scene as two images hovered over her, both their faces blurred.

He knelt beside her and slid an arm beneath her shoulders, drawing her up against his chest. Even through the bulky layers of clothing, she could feel his strength and warmth.

"Come on, you've had enough. I never should have allowed you to come out here in the first place."

"You're not my keeper," she protested with as much anger as she could muster under the circumstances.

"Maybe not—but it sure looks like you could use one," he replied as he helped her to her feet, then swept her into his arms when she swayed against him.

Struggling through the snow, he carried her up onto the porch and back inside the cabin, where he deposited her on the sofa in front of the fire and began to pull off her boots.

She let him remove the boots and then the jacket, wondering what it was about this man that made her *want* to let him do things for her. It had to be something unique to Michael, because she'd never felt that way before.

"I'd suggest some brandy to warm you up, but you really shouldn't have any alcohol. How about some coffee?"

She shook her head. "I don't want anything. Thank you."

He smiled, that gentle half smile that did all but curl her cold toes. Then he reached out to smooth tendrils of hair from her cheeks.

"You were right, you know," he said softly. "I *do* care what you think about me."

But before she could pursue that confession, he got up quickly and announced that he was going back outside to finish the job.

The dizziness subsided and warmth began to seep back into her body. She could feel the cool touch of his fingers against her cheek and touched the spot absently as she thought about him.

It seemed so unlikely that she could fall for someone like Michael, even if it weren't for the lies. The men in her life had always lived mostly in their minds, while Michael was clearly oriented toward action. Surely it had to be nothing more than chemistry, augmented by being snowbound here in this isolated spot with him.

"ANDY."

"Mmmpphh!" She made a halfhearted attempt to bat away the hand that was stroking her cheek.

"Wake up. I want to know that you're okay."

She opened her eyes and stared straight into Michael's face only inches away.

"What time is it?" she asked huskily, caught again in that silken web of intimacy that had snared them both.

"Nearly ten. You've been sleeping for four hours. How do you feel?"

"Better," she said, then sniffed. "And hungry."

"Spaghetti bolognaise is on the menu. Would madame like to be served here or in the kitchen?"

She pushed aside the blanket and sat up, then stood carefully, still fearful that the dizziness might return. He wrapped an arm around her waist.

"I'm fine," she protested—and it would have been true if he hadn't touched her.

"Too bad." He smiled.

Her mouth curved in a smile, too, and his dark gaze focused on that movement. She felt her breath catch in her suddenly constricted throat.

They stared at each other in a charged silence broken only by the soft cracklings and hissings of the fire. His hand slid very slowly up from her waist to curve about her neck. His eyes were still on her mouth and she noticed that he had very thick, dark lashes that curled slightly at the tips—a soft touch to a face that was uncompromisingly male.

Their kiss was long and slow and tentative, a soft melding that held out the promise of much more as one moment filled up and then spilled into the next.

She didn't really know who moved first, but suddenly they were on the sofa and his hard body was pressing against her and she was arching to him hungrily, wanting it all. His warm breath fanned against the sensitive skin of her neck as he traced the outline of an ear with his tongue, drawing a strangled, urgent sound from her.

The languorous heat of passion roared through her, building to an all-consuming blaze. She wanted it to continue, but was afraid. He was the wrong man in the wrong place at the wrong time.

Then the decision was out of her hands when Michael suddenly moved away from her. He got up and walked over to the hearth, running a hand through the black hair she'd mussed up. His back was to her and his voice was low and husky.

"I want you, Andy. But talk about the wrong woman at a bad time..." He shook his head as he continued to stare into the fire.

She was stunned to hear him echo her own thoughts, then perversely wanted him even more because he'd spoken them. "Yes," she agreed in her own husky voice.

She got up and went to the kitchen. He didn't join her, and after she had eaten she returned to the living room to find him sitting on the floor, still staring into the fire. She complimented him on his cooking and he merely nodded without turning to her. His silence and stillness unnerved her, but he was still there more than an hour later when she fell asleep again.

THE UNACCUSTOMED brightness in the room startled Andrea when she opened her eyes. She blinked a few times before she realized that if the sun was out, the storm must be over at long last. Still, as she lay there she could hear the wind whistling and howling around the walls of the cabin.

Drawn by the aroma of coffee, she got up and went to the kitchen, expecting to find Michael there. But he was nowhere in sight. Filled with a sudden fear that he'd gone, she ran to the front window, then saw that his Cherokee was still there, completely cleared of snow. Her Miata was nearly half-buried again.

The day was extraordinarily beautiful, with deep blue skies and brilliant white snow as far as the eye could see. Here and there, the wind whipped it up, blowing it into swirling, glittering diamonds.

She had just returned to the kitchen to make some toast when she heard him come in. A moment later, he was standing in the kitchen doorway, bringing with him a cold, fresh scent as he shook the snow from his hair. Their eyes met and slid away too quickly.

"I think I've found our way out," he announced. "There's a snowmobile in the shed. It won't start, but I think I can fix it."

"Oh," she said, thinking that her captors must have tried to leave on it before giving up and walking. That explained where they'd been when she couldn't find them. She told him about that.

"They probably didn't have any tools with them, but I do. I always carry a toolbox in the Cherokee."

"Have you ever driven one?" she asked. She certainly hadn't and they weren't exactly commonplace in Manhattan.

He nodded. "I have one up at my cabin. If you don't want to come along, you can wait here until I get a plow."

"No, I'll go with you," she said quickly. It wasn't likely that the men would come back, but she didn't want to risk it. Besides, it could be quite a while until they could get a plow up here.

"HANG ON TO MY WAIST—and don't worry. I promise to take it easy."

She climbed onto the seat behind him and wrapped her arms around his waist. The truth was that this felt more like an adventure than an act of desperation. Although it was bitterly cold and the wind only added to the chill, the day was beautiful and a dazzling world of white beckoned.

True to his word, Michael kept his speed down as they skimmed over the snow, sending up clouds of white powder that sparkled in the sun. It was so bright that she had to squint. She'd insisted that Michael take the goggles he'd found in the shed, since he was driving and also bearing the full force of the wind.

"You okay?" he asked, turning around briefly.

She nodded. She was more than fine, actually—she was thoroughly enjoying herself. She might have had her doubts about this with anyone else driving, but Michael was one of those rare people who inspired trust in whatever he did.

Trust! She couldn't seem to avoid that word when it came to him. It was at the core of everything—the nine-hundred-pound gorilla that sat there between them.

They came to the nearly buried Volvo, and as Michael maneuvered past it her thoughts turned again to Val. The first thing Andrea intended to do when they got to town was call home to see if her sister might have left a message.

But as they passed the car and proceeded smoothly down the road, her twin's problems seemed almost remote. It was as though, with the passing of the storm, other dangers had cleared, as well. Wherever she was, Val must surely be safe.

Finally they made it to the highway, only to encounter even higher drifts now that they were out in the open. The wind was much worse, too, as it blew across the open fields on the other side of the road. Michael turned to say something to her and she pressed closer to hear, but his words were carried off by the wind and the noise of the snowmobile.

Suddenly a shot rang out! For one brief moment, Andrea thought it was a sound from the snowmobile. Only when she felt Michael's body stiffen and saw him turn his head sharply did she realize what she'd heard.

She turned, too, and saw the other snowmobile some distance behind them, barely visible through the blowing snow. Then another dark blur materialized beside it and she realized there were two of them.

Even as she stared, unable to quite believe that the nightmare had come back on this beautiful day, the figure on the closest snowmobile raised a rifle. She screamed, but Michael had apparently already seen it, because he suddenly veered off the road and up the bank into the woods. Then he stopped briefly and pulled his gun out from beneath his jacket, handing it to her.

"Hold on to this for me in case I need it fast. I'm going to head back to the cabin."

Before she could respond, they were off again. In the last moment before they were hidden from view by the snow-covered pines, she saw the two men begin to climb the bank awkwardly in their snowmobiles.

Michael set out on a zigzag course, maneuvering the snowmobile with an ease that she knew was deceptive. She kept looking back and trying to avoid thinking about just how vulnerable she was. Several times she saw them briefly, but they didn't appear to be gaining. Obviously they lacked Michael's expertise with the snowmobiles, since they should have had the advantage of extra speed.

Then, just as she was beginning to believe they'd gotten away, the snowmobile struck something and she felt herself flying through the air!

She fought her way out of the snowdrift, calling Michael's name, panicked because she couldn't see him. The snowmobile lay on its side not far away, its motor still running, but Michael was nowhere to be seen.

She called him again, and then saw a mound of snow begin to move and finally resolve itself into human form. She struggled over to him. "What happened? Are you hurt?"

"The only thing that's hurt is my pride," he muttered as he sat up and brushed the snow off. "Where's my gun?"

She'd dropped it. He got up to right the snowmobile while she began to dig through the snow where she'd landed. She was sure that she'd held on to it even as she tumbled in the snow.

Michael joined her and the two of them pawed through the snow on their hands and knees, both of them casting regular looks over their shoulders to see if they were still being pursued.

"Forget about it," Michael said after a few minutes. "Let's get going before they show up."

"Wait! I found it!" She held it up triumphantly, only to have Michael grab it from her and push her down into the snow again, then begin to drag her toward the snowmobile.

Gunshots echoed in the cold air as they both crouched beside the snowmobile. "Don't move!" he ordered and ran in a crouch to a nearby tree. Another shot rang out. Hiding behind the thick trunk, Michael waited. She saw him examining the gun. Then she heard the snowmobiles approaching. They sounded very close.

Michael leaped out from behind the tree, firing even as he moved. A volley of shots assaulted her ears, and it took her a moment to realize that they were all coming from his gun.

In the silence that followed, the sound of the snowmobiles dwindled away.

"They're gone," he said, leaving the shelter of the tree and coming back to her. Then, when she said nothing, he knelt down beside her. "Are you okay, Andy?"

She shook her head. She wasn't okay. The sound of those shots was still ringing in her ears and she could still see him spinning out from behind the tree, firing. She saw it, heard it—and yet didn't believe it.

"Andy," he said gently. "We're safe now. They've gone. I had to let them get close because this gun doesn't have that great a range."

She nodded and got up. For once, he didn't understand. She wasn't frightened now; she was horrified. There was a difference.

Fortunately the snowmobile was undamaged and they both climbed on it, then set out again. Andrea kept turning to watch for their pursuers, but there was no sign of them. She didn't believe for one minute that they'd given up, but at least they appeared to have done so for the moment.

She had no idea how close to the cabin they were and was therefore surprised when they crested a hill and she saw it just a short distance ahead. Instead of stopping at the front, Michael drove around to the rear, then cut the engine.

Andrea climbed off, her ears straining to catch the sounds of the other snowmobiles. But all was silent, except for the ticking of the cooling engine. Still, she started nervously when Michael wrapped an arm around her and drew her to him.

"We're safe now," he said soothingly, his voice close to her ear. "Even if they follow us here, I can hold them off, and I don't think they will because they know that."

When she still said nothing, he let her go, then gestured to the snowmobile. "Do you think you could help me get this thing inside? I had to break the lock on the shed to get it out and I don't want to take the chance that they might show up and take or disable it. And by the way, in case you hadn't noticed, it's starting to snow again."

Surprised, she lifted her head and stared at the gray sky. A few flakes were falling, settling lazily to a land that had already seen too many of them. When had the sun vanished?

Together they dragged the snowmobile through the doorway into the small room that held the firewood and the generator, then braced it against the door in case the men returned and had keys. Michael restarted the generator and they both carried firewood into the living room. He set about building the fire, while she went to make coffee. When she carried it into the living room, he was standing at a window.

"I think we're safe for now. If they were going to chase us back here, we'd have heard from them by now."

She stared at the rifle he must have gotten out of the Cherokee and the handgun that lay beside it, together with boxes of ammunition. *When this is over,* she thought, *I never want to see a gun again.* Then she thought about the two men.

"Where could they have come from?" she asked.

"Isn't there another cabin not far from here—one that's visible from the road?"

Andrea frowned, trying to remember. "Yes, I think you're right. There was a sign. Something Sportsmen Rod and Gun Club. Do you think that's where they've been staying?"

"They could be. They were probably on their way back here and either got stuck or realized they wouldn't be able to get back up here."

Andrea settled down in front of the fire, suppressing a shiver. Michael picked up his coffee and lowered himself down beside her.

"There wasn't anything I could do to protect you," he said quietly. "If you'd been able to run the snowmobile, I would have changed places with you. But as it was, I knew our only hope of getting away was to head for the woods and pray I could outmaneuver them. We couldn't have outrun them on the highway."

"You were very good."

"There's a group of us who have these crazy races up near my cabin. We go out before winter and mark off a course—a sort of obstacle course through the woods. The object isn't really to go as fast as you can, but to finish the course without crashing."

"And do you always win?" she asked, smiling.

"Actually, no. I usually finish last. The others are local guys and I don't get up there all that often."

They both lapsed into silence. Andrea decided to wait. He knew as well as she did that his explanation no longer worked. The only question now was whether he had been lying to her, or had himself been deceived by Nick.

The episode had also renewed her fears for Val. Kidnapping was one thing; attempted murder was quite another. Admittedly the distinction could be a fine one, but she still felt it keenly and hoped that wherever her sister was, she was well beyond their reach. She was still lost in her thoughts when Michael's voice—which was deadly quiet—intruded.

"I've been lying to you, Andy—but you know that already."

She merely nodded as a knot tightened in her stomach that was part dread of what he would say and part anger and sadness that he'd lied.

"The only excuse I have to offer is that I promised Nick I wouldn't tell you. It seemed an easy enough promise at the time, because I hadn't met you."

He got slowly to his feet and rested his hand on the stone mantel, his head bent as he stared into the fire. "It's a long story, but bear with me because I want you to know it all. I told you that Nick and I grew up together. It was a tough neighborhood, and since I was older than him and pretty tough myself, I always protected him. He was like a kid brother to me.

"I had decided that I wanted to be a cop by the time I was twelve—maybe even before that. My dad was a dockworker, but two of his brothers and a cousin were all cops.

"Nick never seemed to know what he wanted to do. It used to bug me because I was so sure of my future and he wasn't, and I had this idea that we should both become cops.

"After high school, we began to drift apart. I went to Fordham on a scholarship and moved into an apartment up there with some guys. He got a job and stayed at home in Brooklyn. We still saw each other regularly, but our lives weren't as . . . connected.

"After college, I went through the police academy, while Nick was going through a series of nothing-type jobs. He was still hanging around with some guys from the old neighborhood and my folks told me they thought he was headed for trouble. I talked to him about it, but he wasn't listening. I'd become a cop, and I probably came across pretty strong.

"By the time I made detective, we were only seeing each other a couple of times a year, going out to a bar and mostly reliving old times. I worried about him, but there didn't seem to be much I could do because he wouldn't let me help him.

"Then he got a job through some family connections with a big landscaping firm up in Westchester and I could tell he really liked it. Things seemed to be looking up for him. He was going to move up to Westchester and that would have gotten him away from the guys he was hanging around with.

They were bad news. I'd found that out because I was assigned to the precinct in our old neighborhood.

"But then his dad died suddenly and his mother was one of those women who just couldn't cope on her own, so he stayed in Brooklyn."

He paused and the silence went on for so long that Andrea thought he'd changed his mind about telling her everything, but finally he began to speak again in a voice that was now tautly controlled—a cop's voice, she realized.

"One day, I was on my way back to the station house when I heard a report over the radio about gunshots. Since I was less than a block away, I went to investigate."

He paused again, shaking his head and his voice changed to a sad, musing sort of tone. "It wasn't my call. I could have ignored it, but I didn't.

"Anyway, I pulled up out front, and a woman told me that she'd heard shots in the apartment above hers. Hotshot that I was, I didn't even wait for backup. I just went up alone, banged on the door, announced myself and kicked it open. A real Rambo type.

"A guy came running out of the bedroom and fired at me. I shot him point-blank—right through the heart. Then I looked into the bedroom.

"There were two bodies on the floor, a man and a woman—and a guy kneeling next to the female. It was Nick. He was white as a ghost and shaking all over. He told me that he'd come here with his buddy who said he needed to talk to the guy about a job. But when they got there, his friend whipped out a gun and accused the guy of fooling around with his girlfriend.

"Nick was pretty confused about what happened next, but apparently the woman was hiding in the bedroom and the guy ran in there and Nick's buddy shot them both. The woman was still alive, but she died later in the hospital.

"As Nick was telling me this, I could hear the sirens. I believed him, but I also knew the law. He was an accessory to murder and he was going to do some hard time."

Andrea interrupted for the first time. "But Nick wasn't the one who shot them. Why would he—?"

"In New York, and in most states, if you're with someone who commits a crime, you're an accessory. Accessory to murder carries a pretty heavy sentence—at least five years.

"A good defense attorney might have been able to get Nick off, but I didn't want to chance it. The D.A. could easily have found witnesses who would testify that this guy was Nick's buddy, and then make the case that Nick should have known what was happening.

"Anyway, I knew Nick was guilty of nothing more than poor judgment and the penalty he was facing was far too stiff. There was a fire escape outside the bedroom window. I told him to get the hell out and then I ran downstairs to meet the officers and head them off so they wouldn't find him.

"A couple of people had seen two men come into the building, but I told them that the other one must have left before I got there. I knew the woman might contradict me because she was semiconscious when I arrived. But it was a risk I took. Then she died without talking—or at least without speaking to us. But it's possible that she talked to someone in her family—or maybe someone in the building gave the family Nick's description and they figured out who he was."

Finally he turned to face her. "The men who kidnapped Val are her father and brother. We couldn't figure out how they found Nick because he left New York right after that and never told anyone but me where he was. Since they apparently own this place, I guess they either must have seen him in Centre Valley, or they saw one of his ads in the newspaper. He said that they've been using one that shows a picture of Val and him. But it doesn't matter. The problem is that they found him—their name's Santini.''

Andrea had to swallow a few times to moisten her dry throat before she could speak. "You mean they intend to kill Val in revenge for the other woman's death?''

Michael shook his head. "No, they want money to keep quiet about what they know. They're scum, Andy. I did some checking up on them as soon as Nick called me. They've run a couple of businesses into the ground and both of them gamble. They figured Nick was now a successful businessman with a lot to lose, so they took Val sort of as insurance in case he balked at paying them off.''

Still stunned by his story, Andrea nevertheless felt anger welling up in her. "Why didn't Nick go to the police? He was just trying to protect himself, wasn't he? He put Val's life at risk to protect his reputation!''

"It isn't that simple, Andy. He was trying to protect Val, too. Think about what it would do to her if this all came out. Centre Valley is her home and she cares about the business as much as he does.

"Besides, the police don't really have a very good track record in this kind of thing. Kidnappings are very delicate matters. The kidnapper might not intend to kill the victim—in most cases, they don't. But the minute the police get involved, all bets are off. Most cops aren't that well-trained to handle kidnappings. I've had specialized training in hostage negotiations, and I have the added advantage of being in private practice.

"Anyway, Nick was trying to raise the money and I was searching for Val. Then, when he agreed to their demands, they got greedier. Nick couldn't raise any more money, so I had to get it myself. But then we didn't hear from them again—probably because Val had managed to escape.''

"You said that they didn't intend to murder Val—but they tried to kill *us!*"

"Yeah, I know. The game has changed. She got away and now they're getting desperate. They probably figure at this point that they've got nothing to lose. The people they owe money to back in Brooklyn are not nice. And you're a threat because you can identify them."

"They know about you, too," she said as she remembered how she'd flung his name at them.

"They do?"

She explained. "I wanted to see if they'd recognize your name. I didn't know if you were working with them."

He rubbed his neck, frowning. "Yeah, they'd probably remember my name. I talked to the father a couple of times. Maybe by now they've got it all figured out."

"I'm sorry, Michael."

He waved away her concern. "That's not important now. What we've got to do is get out of here as soon as possible and try to find Val before they do."

"But where can she be?"

"That's the million-dollar question. The last I talked to Nick, she still hadn't used her credit cards, so that tells me she's holed up around here somewhere, probably trying to decide what to do next."

"They must have told her what happened," Andrea said, as much to herself as to him. She felt such anguish for Val.

"Yeah—*their* version of it."

"What do you mean?"

"If they told her anything, you can be sure they made it sound like Nick's the one who killed their daughter and sister."

"Oh." Pain twisted inside her as she thought about Val hearing that the man she loved was a murderer. And she'd believe it, too—especially since Andrea had said there was something "dark" in Nick's past.

"We've got to find her and tell her the truth," she stated firmly.

"Wrong. *I've* got to find her. As soon as we get out of here, you're going back to Connecticut—or at least to Centre Valley. You're as much at risk as Val is, at this point."

"I'm not going, Michael. Val might not believe you—but she will listen to *me*."

Chapter Ten

Andrea awoke suddenly, certain that a strange sound had interrupted her uneasy sleep. She looked down from her bed on the sofa and saw that the mattress Michael had dragged out for himself was empty, the blankets flung aside hastily.

For a moment, she forgot the noise that had awakened her, and heard instead Michael's calm, controlled voice, describing what had happened all those years ago.

Then her thoughts were brought back to the present when she heard it again—a soft thud that seemed to be coming from somewhere outside. The men were back—and trying to break into the cabin. She sat up quickly and turned toward the front door. The chair Michael had braced under the knob was still in place.

The back door, she thought. They might be trying to force it open, pushing against the snowmobile. But where was Michael?

She flung back the covers and reached for the lamp switch, then remembered that the generator was off. The cabin was cool, even with the fire still burning, and she shivered as she got up and started toward the kitchen, straining to hear any sound and peering into the darkness beyond the reach of the fire's light.

She was halfway back down the hallway that led to the kitchen when something moved in the darkness ahead of her—and she was grabbed by two strong arms and a hand pressed against her mouth.

"Quiet!" Michael's voice whispered close to her ear. "I think we have company."

She sagged against him in relief as the thought came to her that now she could truly trust him. No more inner arguments. And no more denial of how she felt about him, either.

Then they both stiffened as they heard that same muffled thump again, coming this time from the front of the cabin. He whispered to her to stay where she was and took off toward the living room. She ignored his warning and went to the gun cabinet. He'd replaced the shotgun she'd taken and she now grabbed it again, then started to follow him.

"You don't listen very well," he observed mildly as he came toward her, a large, dark shadow at the edge of the firelight. "I think it was just snow falling off the roof, but I'm going outside to have a look around."

"I'll come with you."

"Right. Then there'll be *two* trigger-happy nuts prowling around in the dark. You stay here and barricade the door behind me."

He seemed surprised when she nodded, then hurriedly put on his boots and jacket and went out. She replaced the chair, certain he must be right about the snow, but still nervous. Peering out a window, she saw that the moon was out and, with the snow to reflect its light, it was actually much brighter outside than in.

The minutes tickled slowly by and she filled them with images of Michael being grabbed from behind or hit over the head. When the doorknob finally rattled, she let out a little sigh of relief.

"Michael?" she called as she approached the door.

"No, it's the Big Bad Wolf and I'm too cold to huff and puff."

She laughed and moved the chair. He came in in a rush of cold air and ran a hand through his hair to shake loose the snow.

"It was just the white stuff. I could see where it fell."

He crossed the room and pulled off his jacket and boots, then tossed a couple of logs onto the fire. "I noticed some brandy in the kitchen, but I guess you'd better not have any. Do you mind if I do?"

"I'll get it for you."

When she returned, he was sitting on the mattress and the fire was once more blazing brightly. Instead of going to her sofa bed, she sat down beside him.

"You quit the police force because of what happened, didn't you?"

He nodded. "I couldn't stay. For a couple of months, I tried to convince myself that I hadn't done anything wrong, but it didn't work. Personally what I did *was* right—I still believe that. But as a cop, I took the law into my own hands, and I couldn't live with that."

She told him about her neighbor and faculty colleague. "He said that everyone thought you were on your way to becoming chief of detectives."

"That was my goal, and I might have made it. But I like my work now—and it pays a lot better."

But it isn't the same, she thought, and it never will be—no matter how much money you make. He had paid a very high price for his sense of honor.

"I would have done the same thing," she said quietly. "I mean, I would have helped Nick as you did." But what she *didn't* say was that she wasn't so sure she would have given up a career she loved.

She thought about what she'd sensed in him from the beginning—that rocklike steadiness and trustworthiness that

had made it so difficult to accept that he was lying. Now she
understood it much better. What she'd really been feeling
was his integrity. It wasn't a quality she'd thought much
about before because she'd never known anyone who'd been
put to such a test.

"I'm sorry I didn't trust you before, Michael," she said,
following her thoughts.

He smiled. "You had good reason not to. I was lying to
you."

"Yes, but . . ." She stopped, not knowing how to explain
what she meant.

He reached over to take her hand. "I won't lie to you
again, Andy. I promise that."

They sat there quietly for a time, their hands comfort-
ably intertwined. Andrea thought that something very
powerful and enduring had been sneaking up on them ever
since they met. But until now, it hadn't really broken
through to her consciousness, caught up as she was in her
worries about Val and her ambivalence about his role in this.
There hadn't been much doubt that a physical attraction
existed—and had from the very beginning—but still she
wasn't prepared for the depth and breadth of feeling that
filled her now.

Accustomed as she was to analyzing human behavior,
Andrea was still unprepared for the force of her own feelings, and as yet unwilling to call it by its true name. But
there could no longer be any doubt in her mind that Michael Borelli had touched something in her that had never
been touched before. The feelings she'd tried so hard to keep
bottled up because of her doubts about him now flowed
unchecked through her—a deep, powerful stream.

"It's kind of scary, isn't it?" he asked suddenly, his voice
almost tentative. "Something's been happening to us while
I was keeping the truth from you and you were trying to get
beyond my lies."

She laughed, albeit nervously. "And you accuse *me* of being psychic? That's exactly what *I* was thinking."

He dropped her hand and slid an arm around her, drawing her close. She nestled her head against his shoulder and they both sat there in silence, listening to the crackling sounds of the fire even as heat of a very different sort began to steal through them.

They both seemed to be caught in the strange contentment of anticipation, lingering in this moment, drawing it out—knowing where it would inevitably go.

She laced her fingers through his, liking the square roughness of his hand, the contrast of his much darker skin against hers, the flesh-to-flesh contact that hinted of more to come. His thumb traced lazy circles against the fleshy pads of her palm, and the sensation was unbearably erotic, skittering through her with tiny little electrical shocks.

"You're not falling asleep on me, are you?" he teased lightly, his breath fanning against the top of her head.

She laughed softly. "No, Michael, I'm not falling asleep." She knew he didn't believe that. He could surely feel the soft, voluptuous heat in her, just as she could feel that subtle, distinctively male tension in him.

His lips pressed lightly against her brow, lingered and then moved slowly down across her cheek as he turned her face toward his, at the same time shifting so that she was half sitting in his lap. And then she seized his head in both hands and brought an end to his teasing kisses by meeting his lips with her own.

"I want you, Andy," he said huskily as he finally lifted his mouth from hers. "I want you so damned much. I know this isn't the time or place, but—"

"I want you, too, Michael—and I don't care about the time or place."

It took them a very long time to undress themselves and each other. They both had to savor every nuance of feeling, every subtle shading of sensation. Michael's warm, unhurried affection was a beautiful revelation to her, especially because she could feel just beneath it the raw, primitive force of his hunger.

When they were both naked to the waist, they held each other for a time, fingers gliding slowly over skin bathed in the heat and glow from the fire. The steady drumbeat of desire was growing more demanding now, throbbing through them both insistently. But with great delight, they both realized that each of them enjoyed holding it to a slower tempo, dwelling fully in each moment before falling into the next.

They managed this for a time even after all barriers had fallen away and the firelight flickered over his dark, hair-roughened angles and her paler, smooth curves. She was lying back on the mattress and he was propped on his elbow above her, his face and body shadowed and powerful.

His long, dark lashes hooded his eyes as his gaze traveled the length of her leisurely, despite the unmistakable evidence of his undeniably male need. He slid a hand beneath her foot and she gasped as his lips brushed against her toes and began a slow, meandering journey up her leg.

When he had reached the juncture of her thighs, he paused and lifted his gaze to meet hers, as though seeking permission to bestow that most intimate of kisses. She loved him all the more for that—for understanding that pleasure needed to be mutual. And then she gasped with nearly unbearable surprise as he bent to her again.

Both of them still wanted to take it slow, but their bodies now ignored them, clamoring for a satisfaction too long postponed. Passion whispered and then roared in their ears, drowning out all thought, whirling them off into a kaleidoscope of sensations.

His hard, unyielding maleness met her willing female softness and they rode the crest of the wave in a wild coupling, then slid slowly back down again to calmer and still deeper feelings that buffeted them gently with aftershocks.

Michael held her close, chuckling as he stroked her smooth skin. "Well, that takes care of lust. Maybe we should try making love sometime."

Andrea laughed at his teasing acknowledgment that, somehow, they had just managed both.

THE FIRST PALE LIGHT of dawn was outlining the windows when she awoke to a body that felt wonderfully decadent. And in that tentative light, she saw Michael in front of the fireplace, stark naked as he tended the fire.

Soft curls of heat unfolded themselves within her as she snuggled into the warmth of the blankets. She smiled sleepily as she admired the lean, hard contours of his body and felt that unique thrill of possessiveness. She was still smiling when he turned around.

He knelt beside her and traced a finger along her lips. "I like that smile. I haven't seen much of it, you know."

She kissed his fingers. "There hasn't been much to smile about." A nagging little voice reminded her that their problems were far from being over, but she ignored it. They had this time, and it was enough.

He slid into the enveloping warmth of the blankets, sending shivers through her as his cold body touched hers. But within seconds her shivers had started to turn to tremors of a very different sort.

They made love unhurriedly, newness giving way to the different pleasure of familiarity. But there were still things to be discovered about each other, new erotic pathways to be roamed along the way to ecstasy. The hunger and driving need were still there, though, undiminished in force.

Afterward they lay in each other's arms, bodies and blankets entangled as they stared silently into the fire. Reality was insinuating itself into the moment, clamoring for attention. But, oh, how she wanted to stay here—to shut out the dangers beyond the walls.

Finally Michael heaved a sigh. "We should get going soon. I think it'll be safer if we leave as early as possible."

She made a sound of protest and he hugged her tightly. "I know. I want to stay here, too, but I don't think they've given up. I'd rather you wait here while I go for help, but that could be putting you at just as much risk as if you come with me."

She nodded and sat up. Her hair was tangled and falling across her face and Michael began to comb it with his fingers as he stared at her.

"We'll find time for ourselves, Andy—when this is all over."

LESS THAN AN HOUR LATER, they were on their way, once again surrounded by a world of strange beauty. The difference this time, though, was that they both knew what danger could be awaiting them.

Both of them kept turning, scanning the area for any sign of the two men. Andrea expected at any moment to hear the sharp crack of a rifle. A spot between her shoulder blades felt tingly as she pressed against Michael and prayed that their pursuers were still sleeping.

The sun had just risen to greet the white world around them, brushing soft colors over the snow and starkly outlining the bare branches and the snow-encrusted pines. Not even the bitter cold could detract from the magnificence of the scene.

Andrea's thoughts turned back to Val. There had to be some way of finding her. This was a sparsely populated area and she didn't understand how her sister could have eluded them thus far. Michael continued to believe that Val must have broken into another cabin and was now trapped by the storm. Reluctantly Andrea decided that he must be right.

There was always the possibility that Val had called her again and left a message saying where she was. It was even possible that she'd called Nick, although Andrea doubted that.

She felt again her twin's anguish over what she'd probably learned about her husband. Surely Michael could convince her of the truth—but even the truth was less than pleasant. Val had painted a picture for herself of a perfect husband and Nick fell far short of that . . . even if he wasn't the murderer she probably believed him to be.

Then another thought struck her. Val had mentioned Michael several times during their infrequent conversations, and Andrea knew that she was very fond of him. How would she react to the news that the two of them were involved?

Not very well, she thought unhappily. When they were in their teens, and even before the accident, boys had always been more attracted to Andrea. Val had complained more than once that she'd always ended up with "second best." Now it seemed likely that she would view it that way again, despite the fact that Nick had put his troubled past behind him and become a very different man.

What a mess, she thought miserably. Perhaps she should just go back to Connecticut and leave this to Michael. But she knew she couldn't do that. Michael might need help convincing Val of the truth, and in any event, Val was likely to find out at some point that she'd been here.

They reached the highway without incident and both were pleased to see that a plow had come by. However, the road was still all but impassable for any vehicle other than a snowmobile, thanks to the heavy drifting.

They drove along without any problems now that the going was easier. Both of them turned to stare at the spot where they'd taken off into the woods yesterday to avoid their pursuers. Faint tracks were still visible along the bank.

Andrea wondered what might have happened if they hadn't encountered the men and been forced to return to the cabin.

There was no traffic at all and no signs of other snowmobiles, although they both kept turning to check behind them. Then, finally, as they came to a farm, they saw two snowmobiles in the field, heading straight toward them.

Michael unzipped his jacket to make his gun more accessible as they slowed down and stared at the two figures approaching them. But they both realized quickly that the riders were kids. Michael signaled them to stop, then asked if they'd seen anyone else on snowmobiles or in a black Blazer.

"I'm looking for two men," he said. "A guy about my age and an older, gray-haired man."

The youths shook their heads. They'd been out riding in the area for nearly an hour, but hadn't seen anyone. Michael thanked them and they continued on toward town.

Snowmobiles seemed to be the dominant form of transportation, together with oversize four-wheel-drive vehicles and pickups, nearly all of them with plows. Miniature mountains of snow were piling up everywhere as residents struggled to return to their normal lives.

They stopped at a gas station to fill up the tank, and once again Michael asked about their pursuers. No one had seen them, and Andrea let herself begin to hope that they might have left.

While Michael waited in line, she went in to the combination gas station and convenience store to get them some coffee. Several well-bundled people were ahead of her and she smiled, thinking of her own rather strange attire. She was still wearing the old plaid hunting jacket and the big boots and her hair was tucked up under the cap with earflaps.

The woman ahead of her paid for her items and turned, then smiled at Andrea. "Good morning. It's nice to be out again, isn't it, even if we have a lot of digging ahead of us."

"Yes, it is," Andrea agreed, thinking that the woman couldn't possibly know the half of it. She turned and watched as the tall, gray-haired woman left the store and climbed onto a bright purple snowmobile that had drawn both their attention when they pulled in.

After drinking their coffee and watching the townspeople going about their various chores, they got back onto the snowmobile and headed to the motel, where they found Dan Roberts plowing out the parking lot. He stopped when they appeared, then got out of his truck to greet them.

"I was real worried about you two," he told them. "Fact is, I was planning to call the police again and suggest that we try to get up to that cabin. Is that where you've been?"

They told him they had and he shook his head. "The police are real busy, though. A couple of local fools went ice fishing when it let up yesterday and they haven't been heard from since. And someone said that a couple of snowmobilers are missing, too. Most of the local search-and-rescue team are out with the police, looking for them." He shook his head again at such foolishness, then asked if Andrea had found her sister.

"No," she admitted. "But I just don't know where else we can look for her. I want to call my house now to see if she might have left a message."

He waved a hand toward the motel office. "Go right ahead. I take it that your cars are out at the cabin—or stuck somewhere?"

Michael spoke up. "My Cherokee, Andy's Miata and her sister's Volvo. Can you plow us out when you're finished here?"

"I can give it a try. The rest of this lot can wait. You say her car's out there, too?"

Both Andrea and Michael nodded.

"Did she take off with those guys from New York, then?"

"No," Andrea said. "I think she must have left the cabin on foot before the storm."

He frowned. "This is gettin' too complicated for me. Why don't you come over to the house and we'll warm our insides a bit? Martha made some carrot muffins. Every time it snows, she seems to get this urge to bake up a storm. You can make your call from there."

So they followed him into the house, which was fragrant with delicious baking smells. Andrea thought she could understand the woman's urge to bake at such a time. Coming in from the cold to such mouth-watering aromas was wonderful.

She called home, but the only messages were from friends, several of whom expressed concern about her being in Pennsylvania. Apparently the storm had largely missed Connecticut, but was making big news.

She hung up, disappointed. It began to seem more and more likely that Val had regretted her tentative reaching out to her twin.

And how is she going to react when she finds out that I'm here and that I know everything? Andrea wondered again.

Michael called Nick, choosing to accept the offer of the phone in the TV room for privacy. In the meantime, Martha plied her with carrot muffins and coffee cake while Dan began to ask more questions. Andrea skirted along the edges of the truth, hating the fact that she was lying to these people who'd been so kind.

Michael returned as she was telling her story and shook his head at her silent question.

"So you think they might have all gone back to New York?" Dan Roberts asked.

"We don't know," Michael said. "They might have gotten out before the worst of the storm."

After doing justice to their hostess's offerings, they set out for the cabin in Dan's truck. It took surprisingly little time for him to plow his way through to the Volvo. Michael suggested that they dig it out and she could then drive it back to the motel. The plow had been at work again on the highway and the wind had died down.

Dan left them there and continued slowly up the road. "What did Nick say?" Andrea asked the moment they were alone.

"He hasn't heard from Val—or from the Santinis, either. He wanted to come up here, but I convinced him to stay put in case Val calls."

"Did he check with the credit-card companies and the bank?"

"Yeah, and she still hasn't used them. But there's a couple of days' lag time with the plastic, so she could have used them by now."

"Do you really think that the Santinis gave up and left?"

"I don't know. Like I said, they're scum, but as far as I know, neither of them has a criminal record. So maybe they did think better of it and go home."

"Still, that doesn't mean they won't try again at some point," she said unhappily.

"Yeah, that's what Nick was saying, and it sure doesn't add to his peace of mind at the moment. He's going nuts worrying about Val."

As well he should, she thought self-righteously. If he'd told her the truth long ago, she'd have accepted it, and now she wouldn't be hiding somewhere thinking she'd married a murderer.

Michael's thoughts were apparently running along the same lines. "He always worried that Val would find out someday. I said he should tell her the truth, but he wouldn't. He was too afraid of losing her, and the more time passed, the less likely it seemed that she'd ever find out."

"What are we going to do to find Val?" she asked.

"Start checking all the other cabins in the immediate area of the one where we were. Dan should be able to tell us where they are. But we'll need another snowmobile in case we find her. Do you think you could handle one?"

"They don't look all that difficult—and you're not leaving me behind."

He paused in his digging and grinned at her. "What I should do is conk you on the head and leave you at the motel, but you were right when you said that it might take both of us to convince Val."

"She might not listen to *either* of us, Michael—especially if she knows about us."

"Why should that make a difference?"

"She's always thought that I attract the 'best' men. I know she likes you a lot—and now she thinks she's married to a murderer."

He shook his head. "This is so damned complicated it puts soap operas to shame. But there's no point lying to her about us, Andy. She'll find out soon enough."

THAT EVENING, they sat at the Roberts' kitchen table with the map that marked the location of the camps in the area. Although the camp they'd used sat on more than two hundred acres, its location on all that land was such that there were four other camps within five miles of the spot where the road met the highway. One was owned by several local men and Dan Roberts had already called them. They'd plowed it out and confirmed that no one was there.

Andrea stared at the map doubtfully. Despite Michael's continued insistence that Val must be at one of them, she just couldn't envision her sister walking all that distance.

"Are there signs for all of them?" she asked, seeming to recall that she'd seen some.

Dan nodded. "I think so. Most of them, anyway. And none of them is as far from the highway as the one you were at."

Andrea supposed that Val could have gone to one of them. After all, she didn't know the area and she would have been looking for a place to hide. But would she hide in a nearby cabin, knowing that the Santinis would be looking for her? On the other hand, what choice would she have had—unless someone had helped her?

Finally they said good-night to the Robertses and walked across the lot to their rooms. Both the snowmobile they'd taken from the cabin and one they'd borrowed from a friend of Dan's were mounted on a trailer he'd also lent them. Michael's Cherokee already had a trailer hitch, so they could drive to the roads that led back to the cabins, then use the snowmobiles to reach them.

Michael had teased her about Dan giving them separate rooms . . . and said they could sneak back and forth to see each other. "I'm going to take a nice, long bath," she announced as they reached the motel. "I'm not sure that I'll ever be warm all the way through again."

He arched a dark brow. "Oh? Well, after I take a shower, I'll come over and see if I can prove you wrong."

She was still in the tub when he appeared, and it didn't take him long to make his point.

"JANUARY THAW," Michael remarked as they stood in the motel parking lot the next morning. "Maybe we should have borrowed rowboats instead of snowmobiles."

The day was clear and sunny, and while the temperature was just barely above freezing, it was the kind of day that made one think about spring—despite the mountains of snow everywhere.

But Michael's teasing and the beauty of the day failed to lift Andrea's spirits. He had succeeded admirably in distracting her last night and this morning, but her thoughts had now returned to Val, and her instincts continued to tell her that they were wasting their time searching the other cabins.

Michael attached the trailer that held the two snowmobiles to his Cherokee and they set out on roads that were still several inches deep in snow that was rapidly turning to gray slush.

"Before we start checking the other cabins, I want to have a look at the one the Santinis were probably using," he told her.

She merely nodded, her mind preoccupied with Val and how they could convince her of the truth if they *did* find her.

When they reached the cabin in question, Michael pulled over to the side of the road as far as possible and stopped. The cabin was just barely visible through a thick screen of trees, perhaps a quarter mile from the road.

"There are tracks," she said, peering ahead at the road that led up to the cabin.

Michael nodded. They'd learned from Dan Roberts that this particular camp was owned by a group of men from Centre Valley, and it seemed unlikely that any of them would have been up here so soon after the storm.

"I'm going to walk up there. You stay here," he ordered in a tone intended to settle the matter.

"I'll wait exactly twenty minutes, and if you're not back I'm coming after you," she replied in the same manner as he got out of the Cherokee.

She sat there impatiently, watching until he disappeared from view into the woods. If Val *had* broken into one of the cabins, this was surely the most likely one, since it wasn't far from the other cabin and was close to the highway. And yet she was sure that her twin wasn't there.

She peered through the woods and caught sight of him briefly as he approached the cabin. Then he was lost to view again. When fifteen minutes had passed with no sign of him, she reached into the back seat and picked up his rifle.

She stared at it. As a teenager, she'd done some target shooting with a .22, but it was clear that this was a far more complicated gun. Nevertheless, it was still a rifle. If she had to, she could use it.

The minutes continued to tick slowly past. She worried that at any moment, she would hear gunshots. Images of the fate that might befall Michael tormented her, interspersed with equally terrifying thoughts about Val.

Twenty minutes. She got out of the Cherokee, cradling her rifle, and started toward the driveway—frightened but determined. But before she reached it, she suddenly saw Michael running toward her.

"What's wrong?" she asked, looking past him and fearing that the Santinis were pursuing him.

"This," he said, grabbing the rifle from her. "I knew you'd be a woman of your word."

"Well," she said, ignoring his taunt, "were they there?"

"Not now, but someone has definitely been there. From what I could see through the windows, they didn't leave anything behind. I think they put the snowmobiles back into the shed, too. There were tracks leading up to it."

She sighed with relief. "Then they must have gone."

"Maybe. Or they just want it to look that way in case anyone comes looking for them."

"They could have gone back to their own cabin," she suggested reluctantly.

"It would be impossible to tell with so many vehicles in and out, but I doubt they'd go back there. They have to think there's a good chance that the police are looking for them at this point."

"I just wish that I could be certain about *something*." She grimaced.

He slanted her an amused glance as they got back into the Cherokee. "Well, *I'm* sure about something—that whoever coined the phrase 'double trouble' had a certain pair of twins in mind. One of them pulls a disappearing act and the other one's busy playing Andy Oakley."

She glared at him. "You know, you have some very unpleasant sexist tendencies. And Val did *not* 'pull a disappearing act.' She was kidnapped."

"Yeah, but she escaped. *Then* she pulled a disappearing act."

"Well, what would you expect her to do? She thinks her husband's a murderer."

"If she loved Nick, she'd at least give him a chance to explain," he said stubbornly.

"That's true," she acknowledged. "But Val's still insecure, and besides, she thought Nick was having an affair. Or was that just a story he made up?"

"No, he didn't make it up—exactly. But it happened last fall. It involved some client who made a play for him and Val let her imagination carry it further."

"Like I said, she's insecure."

He reached over to grasp her hand. "Well, at least insecurity isn't one of *your* problems. And I'm not sexist. If I were, would I be falling for *you?*"

She smiled. "*Are* you falling for me, Michael?"

"I thought that was pretty obvious."

"It is. But even very secure people need a bit of reassurance from time to time."

He chuckled. "Okay, I get the point. So I'm guilty of that common male affliction of not being able to talk about my feelings."

She smiled. That wasn't entirely true—or maybe it was just that he could say quite a lot with very few words.

They had reached the road that led to the next cabin. Michael pulled into the narrow, unplowed road, then stopped, and they hauled the snowmobiles off the trailer. He gave her some quick instructions, and they set out.

The cabin was about a mile back, but they reached it easily. The windows were shuttered and snow had drifted nearly waist-high at the door. Still, they checked both doors and shouted Val's name. Michael examined the locks and said that there was no sign of a break-in.

Neither was there any evidence of Val's presence at the other cabins. Andrea hadn't really expected to find her, but she was still disappointed—and more worried than ever.

During the course of their journey, they stopped in the general store they'd visited before, but the storekeeper hadn't seen the Santinis again, and she hadn't seen Val, either. It wasn't until they were back on the road again that Andrea realized why the woman had been looking at them so strangely—and Michael had obviously noticed it, as well.

"I wonder if she could be lying," he remarked. "She was giving us some pretty strange looks."

"That's because I went back to see her after we split up that day. I didn't trust you, and I told her that."

"Thanks a lot," he replied with a grimace.

"I had good reason not to trust you then. You lied to me. They *had* been in there."

"I didn't lie. I told you she hadn't seen Val."

She rolled her eyes. "You shade the truth very carefully, Michael."

"I had to—and it won't happen again."

"Does Nick know that you've told me?"

He nodded. "Despite what I told him, he thinks you'll try to talk Val out of going back to him."

"That decision is hers to make. Besides, why would he think she'd even listen to me?"

"Out of habit. He said that she nearly walked out on their wedding after you told her what you'd felt."

Andrea was shocked. Val had given her every indication that she hadn't believed it and thought she was simply jealous. She thought now about all the times when Val had sounded so happy in her marriage. Was that nothing more than bravado—an attempt to prove that Andrea had been wrong, and all the while she'd secretly feared she was right? She resolved that, from now on, she would keep any "feelings" to herself.

They started back to the motel as dark clouds moved in to cover the blue sky and bring an abrupt halt to a beautiful day. Andrea drifted with her thoughts, back to the time of the accident—and the long, terrible months afterward.

The thought came upon her slowly, stealing into her mind and then chilling her very soul. And she knew that it had actually been there for some time, lurking in some dark corner. Was it possible that Val was dead? Could the Santinis have killed her—or could she have killed herself?

"No!" she cried, not even realizing that she'd spoken aloud until Michael turned to her sharply.

"No what?"

"I...was just wondering if she could be..." She couldn't finish as she sat there hugging herself miserably.

He pulled into the lot of the motel and quickly drew her into his arms. "Don't let yourself start thinking that, Andy. She's alive."

"Michael, maybe she *wanted* to die! She tried to kill herself once—about six months after the accident."

"I know. Nick told me."

Something in his tone made her draw back to stare at him. "Then you've thought about it, too, haven't you?"

He hesitated, then nodded slowly. "I *did* think about it, but I don't believe it. We know she escaped from them, Andy. If she wanted to die, would she have done that? And she called you."

Yes, she thought, it was a call for help. How many suicides do that? Many, if not most of them. And she hadn't been there to respond. Tears welled up in her eyes and began to trickle down her cheeks. Michael wiped them away gently.

"You'd know if she were dead, Andy."

"M-maybe." She wasn't so sure at this point.

"You'd know," he repeated, holding her tightly.

Chapter Eleven

"Got some news for you—maybe," Dan Roberts said. They were unloading the snowmobile they'd taken from the cabin.

Both Andrea and Michael turned to him quickly.

"There's another place I forgot about. It's one of those precut log places, built last summer. It's not really a hunting camp and I guess that's why I didn't think of it. Up on top of Rattlesnake Mountain."

The name meant nothing to either of them. Andrea waited patiently, having learned by now that Dan Roberts imparted his news in his own way.

"Anyway, Tom called me to say that when he was out plowing in Brush Valley, he looked up and saw smoke coming out of the chimney. We don't think it's very likely that the guy who owns it is up there. He's a professor down at the university and he just goes up there to write."

Andrea felt a surge of excitement. "Where is this?"

"Well, that's the thing, you see. By the road, it's not close to that camp you were at, but it's only a couple of miles over the mountain."

"Through the woods, you mean?" Michael said, and Andrea could hear the doubt in his voice that she herself felt. Val certainly wouldn't have taken off into the woods—not with the road there.

"Well, not exactly. You see, there's an old logging road. The guy who built the cabin improved it on his side. But it runs right over the top of the mountain and down the other side—to the camp you were at. The guys from New York improved it to get to their place from this side, too."

"I didn't notice any other road," Michael said, frowning. "Does it connect?"

"It must. Years ago, before those guys bought all that land, we used to use it sometimes."

"I think I know where it comes out at the cabin," Andrea said. "When I found Val's car, it was pulled into the woods beside the camp, and I remember that it looked like an old road."

Michael glanced from her to Dan Roberts. "What's the fastest way to get to that log cabin?"

"Well, I think you'd be better off taking the Brush Valley Road, then going up that side of the mountain on the snowmobiles."

They put the second snowmobile back onto the trailer and left after Dan had given them directions. Neither of them spoke for a long time. Finally Michael turned briefly to her.

"We shouldn't get our hopes up too much, Andy. It sounds like a long shot to me, even if someone *is* up there."

"I've just been thinking. If that logging road is the one I saw, Val could have thought it was the road out. The cabin sits at an angle to the real road, and she could have gotten mixed up—especially if she was scared to death. There was already some snow on the ground—enough to hide the fact that the road is in better shape."

Michael gave her a doubtful look, but said nothing as they drove through the valley and then started up a narrow, twisting mountain road that Dan Roberts had called the "Rattlesnake Pike."

The road that led up to the log cabin was unmarked, but Dan's directions had been good, and they found it without difficulty. They pulled into it a short distance and unloaded the snowmobiles.

"If someone's up there, they haven't gotten out yet," Michael remarked as they mounted the snowmobiles and started up the stretch of unbroken snow.

They were still a half mile from the cabin when they spotted it—and the smoke rising from its chimney. It sat on the very top of the mountain in the midst of a small clearing. Michael slowed down.

"I want you to wait here while I go on up to check it out."

"You think it could be the Santinis?" she asked, having managed to dismiss them from her thoughts for the moment.

"I don't think it's very likely, but I don't want to take any chances."

So she sat there impatiently, watching as he sped around the final curve and approached the log cabin. Before he had come to a stop, the door opened and a man came out. Andrea's slowly rising hopes sank quickly. Then she followed Michael. The man was tall and thin with light hair—definitely not one of the Santinis.

He turned out to be the owner, who had come up to write between semesters and was now trapped by the snowstorm. Obviously happy to see them, he invited them in to warm up.

"There's not much food left," he said ruefully. "But I've got plenty of coffee."

Michael told him their story and he frowned. "I didn't *see* anyone, but I heard a snowmobile back there."

"When?"

"Let's see," he said, scratching his head. "Time kind of got away from me. It was around noon or so the day after the storm started."

"Which day was that?" Michael asked. "It snowed twice."

"Right. We had a couple of inches Tuesday, and then it stopped. That's when I should have gotten out of here," he remarked ruefully. "Then it started again the next day—Wednesday. So it was Thursday I heard it."

"What kind of shape is that road in?" Michael asked.

"It's not too bad—or it wasn't before the storm. I've walked it all the way down to that other cabin a couple of times. It's not that far."

He made them coffee, but Michael took only a few sips before putting on his jacket again. "I'm going back there to have a look. You wait here and warm up, Andy."

She nodded distractedly, trying to rouse herself from the blue funk she'd fallen into after letting her hopes rise. She felt as though their last hope of finding Val had vanished.

Steve, their host, was talkative, the result, no doubt, of being trapped up here for so long. Andrea tried to keep up her end of the conversation, but her thoughts were on Val as she struggled to put everything into a time frame. Steve's remark about time getting away from him had struck a chord, reminding her of the gap in her own memory after the accident—a span of nearly twenty-four hours that included the time when Steve had heard the snowmobile.

Then she thought about how Michael had questioned her about the time of Val's call, to try to estimate when she'd escaped. But she hadn't been sure of that, either, because at that point she hadn't been checking her machine that often.

Why would the Santinis—or one of them, at any rate—have been up here on the mountain during the storm? They certainly couldn't have been looking for Val, who was long gone by then. And if they *were* looking for her, wouldn't they have come here to Steve's cabin?

That long lapse in her own memory taunted her. She'd awakened that one time and her captors had established that she wasn't Val. Then she'd fallen asleep again, and when she woke up the second time, they were leaving—presumably to resume their search for Val.

But what if they'd found Val in the meantime? The question pierced her with shards of ice because she knew now why Michael had gone back there. They could have found Val and killed her, then taken her body up here on the mountain, perhaps hoping it would look as though she'd lost her way and frozen to death in the snow.

Pain wrenched through her. She thought about Michael saying that Val couldn't be dead because she would know. But there was no comfort in those words. He didn't understand the ''feelings'' she had, how imprecise they were. What she'd felt on that beach could as easily have been a foreshadowing of death to come.

Steve asked her if she wanted more coffee and she shook her head, unable to speak. Instead, she got up and went to the window, waiting for Michael to return.

He was gone a long time and Steve expressed some concern. She told him that Michael was an expert snowmobiler and she was certain that everything was fine. What she *didn't* say was that he was gone so long because he was searching for Val's body.

Daylight was fading by the time she heard the familiar whine of the snowmobile and ran again to the window. But she felt little relief when she saw that he was still alone on the machine. The chances of his finding a body buried in snow were minimal at best.

Michael said nothing about his search when he came in and she didn't ask. That would have to wait until they were alone. After warming himself at the hearth and having another cup of coffee, Michael told her she could ride back down the mountain with him and Steve could take her snowmobile. If he noticed her silence, he said nothing.

They were less than halfway down the mountain when they met a truck with a plow making its way up. The driver turned out to be a local acquaintance of Steve's who had just heard that he might be trapped up here. Steve thanked them for their help and turned the snowmobile back to Andrea.

"Why did you go out there?" she asked when they had reached the Cherokee.

"Help me get these snowmobiles back on the trailer," he said, ignoring her question. "We have to get moving before the roads get icy."

She did as told and they climbed into the Cherokee. "You were looking for Val's body, weren't you?" she asked in a thin, taut voice.

Michael started the vehicle, then drew her clumsily into his arms. "I still think she's alive, Andy, but I wanted to be sure."

"You *can't* be sure. She could be there and you wouldn't see her because she's b-buried in the snow."

"Andy, you know it's unlikely that they could have found her when they'd already been out looking for her before. And if they *had* discovered her, I don't think they would have killed her."

She drew away from the comfort of his arms—and his words. "You said yourself they were getting desperate. And they tried to kill *us*."

He said nothing, and his silence was eloquent.

"What other reason could there be for them to be out on a snowmobile in the middle of the storm?" she demanded, hoping foolishly that he would have an answer.

"You said they were arguing. One of them might have taken off just to cool down."

She thought that rather unlikely, but she said nothing. Still, they hadn't killed *her* when they'd clearly had the chance. On the other hand, she wasn't the wife of someone they hated, someone they blamed for their daughter and sister's death. Michael had said that what they wanted was money, but she thought they must have wanted revenge just as much.

They made their way slowly down the winding mountain road. With the arrival of darkness, the temperature was falling fast and snow that had melted on the road was now turning to ice. Even with Michael's skilled driving, the Cherokee slid a few times, and the trailer only made it worse.

"I think we may have company," Michael said, breaking the long silence between them.

Andrea turned and saw headlights rounding the curve behind them. "You mean the Santinis?" she asked in confusion. "But how could they have found us?"

"The Cherokee was parked down there along the road for a couple of hours. They could have seen it and just waited for us. When we passed that last intersection, I saw something parked near it with the lights off. It looked like a Blazer."

Andrea faced forward again and fear crawled along her spine. They were on a narrow mountain road with a steep hill on one side and a sharp drop-off on the other. She turned around again and the vehicle behind them suddenly switched on its high beams. Caught in the sudden glare, she turned around again quickly.

"What are we going to do?"

"We don't have many choices," Michael said as he geared down for a steep descent with a curve at its end. "I don't think they'd be dumb enough to try anything now, but stay down just in case."

She slid down in the seat, praying that he was right but thinking about their desperation. Michael unzipped his jacket and got out his gun, placing it on the seat between them. The interior of the Cherokee was now lit brightly by the headlights of their pursuers. A moment later, there was a thump and the Cherokee jolted forward. Michael swore.

"They rammed us. I think they're going to try to run us off the road."

Andrea crouched low in the seat, recalling all the curves on the road as she felt the Cherokee slip again and again as it tried to gain purchase on the ice. They slid around a curve, and when they were on a straight stretch again, she felt another bump.

Michael cursed under his breath as the Blazer rammed them again. If there was someplace to pull over, he'd be glad to take his chances with the gun. But the narrow road didn't afford him that opportunity. He had no choice but to keep going, even though the trailer gave him a definite disadvantage.

Ahead of him was the next curve—a bad one. And he could see the dull sheen of ice reflected in his headlights. On the side they were on, the drop was probably at least a hundred feet—and now he saw that the guardrail was broken.

A desperate plan began to form in his mind—a possible way to use the trailer to his advantage. The lights of the Blazer shifted as it moved out to pull alongside. He knew what their plan was—they intended to force him over the edge. A death on icy roads that would be ruled an accident.

He spared one brief moment to glance at Andy, wanting to say something—wanting to tell her that he loved her. Then her eyes met his and he was sure she knew that already—and that she felt the same way.

The patch of ice was coming closer and the Blazer was now nearly alongside him. He hit the brakes, hoping his desperate scheme would work.

The sudden braking jackknifed the Cherokee and the trailer swung out just as he'd hoped, smashing into the side of the Blazer. The other driver tried to avoid the crash by jerking his wheel sharply—just as his tires hit the ice!

The next moments passed in sickening slow motion for both Andrea and Michael. The Cherokee began a slide toward the edge as Michael pumped the brakes and yelled for her to get out. Slightly behind them, the Blazer too lurched toward the edge, then rocked wildly as the careering trailer struck it again.

Then suddenly Michael had the Cherokee under control again, helped by the trailer that was now wedged against a snowbank at the edge of the road. And the lights of the Blazer were gone.

"Are you okay?" he asked, his voice shaky.

She managed to nod. In her mind, they were still sliding toward the darkness, even though she knew they were stopped on the road. "Where are they?"

"They went over the edge," Michael said grimly as he opened the door.

They both started back to the gap in the guardrail, then stopped as the darkness below them was suddenly illuminated by fire! Scant seconds later, a loud "whump" followed and flames shot up to the height of the treetops. Michael drew her to him. They were both trembling. It felt as though they were watching their own deaths.

"Could they have gotten out?" she asked, unable to take her eyes from the horrifying sight below them.

"Maybe—but I doubt it. They might already have been dead from the fall." He lifted her face to his and kissed her—a hard, demanding kiss that she returned in kind. It was an acknowledgment of what they'd come so close to losing.

"I love you, Andy," he said softly. "I'm sorry it took this to make me say it."

She hugged him. "I love you too, Michael. Sometimes you have to come close to losing something to know what you have."

He nodded, then led her back to the Cherokee. "I have some flares. You get them and set them up along the road in both directions while I get the flashlight and go down there to have a look."

After he found the flares and the flashlight, she saw him pick up the gun and slide it back into his holster. He saw her stare at it.

"Just a precaution. Even if they survived, they aren't likely to be in any condition to give me trouble."

He began a slow descent while she set up the flares, turning constantly to watch his progress as the flashlight bobbed its way through the dark below. Then, just as she was returning to the spot where the Blazer had gone over, a pickup truck appeared, followed only a moment later by a car. Andrea explained what had happened, omitting for now any mention of the fact that the victims had been trying to kill them. After ascertaining that she was okay, the driver of the car left to find a telephone. The two men in the pickup stood with Andy as they watched Michael's flashlight come closer to the still-burning vehicle.

"You were damned lucky," one of them remarked.

"Isn't this the spot where the Johnson kid went over?" the other one asked his friend.

"Yeah. That's why the rail is broken. Maybe we'd better go down there and give him a hand in case they're still alive."

They got their own flashlight and began to follow Michael's trail down the steep slope, leaving Andrea alone to watch the scene below her. She was trembling with cold and shock, but she never took her eyes off Michael's flashlight.

By the time the three men were climbing back up the slope, Andrea could hear a siren in the distance. And when they reached the road, the first siren was very close and another could be heard somewhere behind it.

"There was no sign of them," Michael told her. "I think they were still in the Blazer."

"Wasn't likely they were alive when it went up," one of the men said. "They'd bounced off a few trees before they hit that big old hemlock."

Andrea knew he was trying to downplay the horror of it, but she could scarcely summon up any sympathy for the Santinis, given the fact that they'd intended for Michael and her to be down there.

The police arrived, followed shortly after by an ambulance. Andrea remained largely silent as Michael told them the story. She'd had no idea what he intended to say. But he apparently had time to come up with a believable story. Basically he told them the truth, although he glossed over the reason for the "grudge" the Santinis had against Nick, and the police seemed disinclined to pursue that.

They asked her a few questions and she corroborated Michael's story. But they didn't press her, because by now she was trembling from the cold and shock. Instead, she was ushered to a warm police car while the men went back down the slope once more. By now, all that remained of the fire were a few bright orange tongues of flame.

Andrea huddled in the police car, shivering despite the warmth and feeling strangely numb. A tow truck arrived just as the men returned. The trailer was badly damaged, as was one of the snowmobiles. Thankfully the Cherokee had suffered no damage at all.

Men's voices floated around outside the car as she sat there, her thoughts gradually leaving the Santinis to focus on Val. And then a fresh wave of horror struck her. With the Santinis dead, they might never know what had happened to her!

Finally Michael came to get her and they followed the tow truck with the mangled trailer down the mountain. It had started to snow again and the flakes nearly hypnotized her as they glittered in the beams of the headlights. She was aware that they were back at the motel only when Michael came to a stop.

"Why don't you go take a nice long bath?" he suggested gently. "I have to talk to Dan and let him know what happened. Then I'll call Nick."

She nodded mutely. The details seemed beyond her now. She stumbled out of the Cherokee and started toward the motel. But then Michael was there, his arms around her. He helped her into the room, then turned on the water as she fumbled her way out of her clothes, accepting his help with that, too. When she was immersed in blessedly warm water up to her neck, he kissed her and said he'd be back soon.

Andrea leaned back and closed her eyes, then opened them again quickly as images of the fire came back to her—the death that had been meant for them.

She felt herself separating a part of herself from what had happened. As a psychologist, she knew this was a common reaction to trauma, but as a woman, she was horrified that it was happening to *her*.

She thought about Michael—about his cool, calm manner even in the face of death. It disturbed her to think he could be that way, because it seemed to suggest that the gulf between them was very wide—perhaps too much so.

Finally her thoughts turned inevitably to Val, whose body in all likelihood lay buried in snow atop a lonely mountain. She thought about all the times when she'd rehearsed some speech to her twin, using her psychological skills to say just the right words that could have brought them together again. Now those words were useless because they'd never been spoken.

She knew—and had known for years now—that the rift between them owed as much to a lifetime of built-up grudges as to her failure to save Val from the accident. How many times had she complained to her twin about her passivity, her lack of ambition? And how many times had Val resented her twin's popularity and her clear vision of her future?

The water grew cool and she had just climbed out of the tub when she heard Michael returning. A moment later, he was standing in the bathroom doorway, his dark eyes filled with concern. She felt a flash of irritation at his assumption that she couldn't cope with this, then admitted to herself that right now she needed to be taken care of.

Michael could sense the battle going on inside her—the war between her proud, independent nature and the events of the past few days that had dented that armor badly.

And he knew, too, that the worst almost certainly lay ahead of them. He was by now convinced that the Santinis had killed Val and that her body was probably buried on that mountaintop. He'd called Nick, who still hadn't heard from Val, and had done a good job in reassuring him that nothing had happened to her, and that with the Santinis gone, his problems in that regard were over.

But he couldn't lie to Andy; he'd promised he wouldn't do that again. So he held her and comforted her and later, when she wanted to, he made love to her and helped them both forget for a time.

"I DON'T BELIEVE THIS!" Andrea said as she opened the blinds and stared out.

Michael yawned, enjoying the view of her naked curves. "Believe it. Dan said we'd be getting another four or five inches. But there are rumours of a genuine January thaw later in the week."

"You won't be able to go...up to the mountain," she said, turning back to him.

He shook his head. "Not until tomorrow, probably." He'd told her last night that the police and the local search-and-rescue squad were going up there to look for Val's body. He hadn't told Nick that, of course, and he'd convinced

Nick again that he needed to stay by the phone in case Val called.

"But we *do* have to get over to police headquarters," Michael went on. "I told them we'd be in today to make formal statements."

He saw the look on her face and hurried on. "I'd go alone if I could, but you were there, too, so they need statements from both of us."

"What will you do if they press you about that 'grudge'?" she asked, coming back to sit on the edge of the bed.

Michael frowned. That particular subject had been enough to keep him awake half the night. "If I tell them the truth, it's going to be all over the newspapers and hurt Nick . . . and Val," he added hurriedly.

"It could hurt you, too, couldn't it?" she asked,

He shrugged. "It could, but I doubt that things will get that far."

"Make up something, Michael," she implored. "You've been hurt too much already—and now so has Nick."

He nodded. "Let's go find some breakfast and then get over to the police barracks. With this snow, it's probably going to take us half the day to get there."

They found a small restaurant in town where they ate largely in silence while they listened to various conversations about the accident. Michael remarked that places like this didn't need newspapers. By the time they came out, everything was old hat, anyway.

The general consensus seemed to be that city folks shouldn't venture away from home since they obviously didn't know how to drive up here in the mountains. Andrea caught more than a whiff of one of the less pleasant factors of rural life—a resentment of outsiders. The glances that were sent their way weren't unfriendly, but she suspected that behind those looks were very different feelings.

Then, as they were about to leave, someone came in with news. There might have been a murder, possibly connected to that accident up on Rattlesnake Mountain last night. Search and Rescue was going out as soon as the snow stopped. There were more remarks about the violence that outsiders brought here.

Michael paid for their breakfast quickly and hurried her out of the restaurant. "The state police told me they had five murders in this area last year. If you figure that on a per capita basis, I'd be willing to bet that rivals New York."

"Yes," she agreed. "But they don't think that way. Unless it happened right here in this town, it occurred 'somewhere else.' Their frame of reference is very narrow. I have a friend who's a rural sociologist and she's studied it."

He rolled his eyes. "Give me big bad New York anytime."

They started across the street to the Cherokee and Andrea saw the purple snowmobile parked next to them. Then she saw its owner and had to restrain a smile. Today the woman was dressed in a matching purple ski suit. She greeted Andrea as she had before, and gave Michael a careful appraisal before getting onto the snowmobile.

"Local color?" Michael asked with a grin as they got into the Cherokee.

Andrea laughed. "Where one earth could she have found a purple snowmobile?"

"Probably a custom job," Michael said as they watched her disappear down the street. "I wonder if she approved of me."

It took them more than an hour to get to the police barracks, located just off the interstate that bisected the region. Michael had warned her that they would probably be questioned separately, and that she should claim ignorance of the 'grudge' if she were asked about it. But rather to her surprise, she wasn't. The police, it seemed, were only interested in the circumstances of the fatal crash.

She learned that they hadn't as yet tried to bring the remains of the Blazer and its occupants up from the ravine. The snow was too deep and they hadn't figured out how to accomplish the grisly task. A trip down there by two investigators this morning had yielded nothing in the way of identification. There was very little to identify.

One officer told them that the force of the explosion and fire suggested that they might have been carrying extra fuel in cans, and Michael said that was consistent with his observations, as well. He'd heard several distinct explosions.

Andrea marveled at his ability to have noticed that because she hadn't. But then he was trained to pick up on such things, just as she was trained to sense the subtle nuances of speech and body language.

When they finally got back to the motel, it was Michael who first identified the truck parked in the lot. "Nick's here," he said unhappily. "I was afraid he'd show up."

Before they could wonder where he was, the door to the unit next to Michael's unused room opened and Nick came out. Andrea was as unhappy to see him as Michael was—perhaps even more so. She knew now that Nick had tried to effect a reconciliation between Val and her, and she felt guilty because she hadn't kept quiet about her "feeling" when she first met him.

"I couldn't just sit there and wait any longer," Nick said as they all went into Andrea's room. "I'll keep checking the machine in case she calls."

Andrea heard in his voice and saw in his face a hopelessness that suggested Michael's reassurances hadn't worked, and with Nick's next words she knew she was right.

"You didn't tell me everything," he said to Michael, but not in an accusing manner. "Tell me now."

So Michael did, including the fact that they were going to search for Val's body tomorrow. The conversation took a long time, because there were many details that Nick wanted to know, but when they had finished, he just nodded and then sat down on the bed and stared at the floor.

"Nick, we can't be sure that she's dead," Andrea reminded him. She meant it, because a part of her didn't yet believe it, either.

He looked up at her. "Wouldn't you *know* if she was dead? You knew about the accident and you knew about me...my past, that is. And you knew something had happened when you came here."

She understood his hope because she shared it. "I don't know," she said honestly. "When I had that feeling that brought me here, it wasn't very precise. It was just this sense that something had happened, that Val was in trouble."

"There's a difference between being 'in trouble' and being dead," he said with a harshness she knew wasn't really directed at her.

"Yes, but that's what I'm trying to tell you. The feeling wasn't that accurate." She hesitated, then went on quietly.

"I don't think she's dead, but how can I know whether that's just hope or a psychic message?"

She sat down on the bed beside Nick and took one of his hands. "No matter what happens, there are a couple of things I want you to know. First of all, I'm sorry that I ever told Val about that feeling I had about you. It was a perfect example of how those feelings can be misleading. You hadn't done anything wrong, even if the law would have judged it otherwise.

"And secondly, I want you to know that I really appreciate your efforts to bring Val and me together again. It seems that you were doing more for me than I was doing for myself."

Nick gave her a sad smile. "Someone needed to push it, Andy. I knew how it was eating at Val, but she couldn't seem to take the first step. You intimidated her, you know—not deliberately, but that didn't matter. And she needed to gain confidence first. I think she'd done that."

"Thanks to you," Andrea said.

"Thanks to our feelings for each other. She gave as good as she got. I was pretty needy myself, and she knew that."

Andrea looked over at Michael, who sat across the room, quietly watching them. She thought about the many forms that love can take. Nick and Val needed each other, while she and Michael were both complete in and of themselves. And yet they loved each other, too.

Nick saw them exchange glances and looked from one to the other. "Is there something else I don't know?"

Michael chuckled. "Remember when you told me that what I needed was someone like Andy?"

Andrea stared at them. "What?"

Nick smiled. "Yeah, I said that. And I guess I was right."

But a heavy silence fell on them again. It was impossible to be happy now. Val's absence hung over them all.

Chapter Twelve

"I'm going with you!"

"No, you're not."

"You can't stop me, Michael, so stop trying to order me around. She's my sister and I want to be there."

"I'm not trying to order you around. If you want the truth, it's going to be tough enough for me to deal with Nick if we find her—let alone having you there, too."

"And what about your own feelings—or don't you have any? Are you so in control of your emotions that finding her up there will be just another body?"

"Andy, this conversation is going nowhere fast. You don't seriously believe that I don't care about Val. Even if I didn't care about her as a person—and I do—it would still hurt to see her because it would be like finding *you*.

"I'm not going to apologize for controlling my emotions. I was trained as a cop. If this was a different situation and we were dealing with some nut, *you'd* be the one in control and I'd probably be freaking out."

"I doubt that very much," she said, turning away from him. "I just can't stand the thought of being cooped up here all day waiting for...news."

Michael circled her waist and drew her back against him. "I know that, but can't you see my point, too?"

She sighed. "Yes, I suppose I can. Nick is close to cracking up already."

"Don't worry, I'll be there for him."

He gave her a quick kiss and left the room to join Nick, who was waiting in the parking lot. Andrea watched as the two of them got into the Cherokee and drove off. Michael's last words were ringing through her head. He'd be there for Nick, all right—just as she *hadn't* been there for Val.

How she wanted to escape from this nightmare! They'd stayed up half the night, going over and over everything. None of them would say it, but they all knew they were searching for some reassurance that they wouldn't find Val's body up on the mountain.

She kept saying that it seemed strange that the Santinis had been able to find her in such a short time after both they and Andrea herself had been searching for her.

Michael said that it was certainly possible that the snow-mobile Steve had heard either wasn't the Santinis at all or was one of them trying to cool off after the argument she'd overheard.

Nick said that if Val had been clever enough to have escaped from them once, she wouldn't be likely to get herself caught again.

In the end, though, it all meant nothing, because if Val wasn't dead, then where was she? If the Santinis hadn't killed her, had she taken her own life?

I can't stay here, she thought. *I've got to do something— anything.*

She looked out the window again. Traffic seemed to be moving at normal speeds on the highway. They'd had another four inches of snow, but after the previous storm, that seemed like nothing. Maybe she should try to find herself a jacket to replace the one the Santinis had made off with. The prospect for locating anything decent didn't seem very good, and it felt wrong somehow to indulge in a foolishness like shopping now, but at least it would get her out of here.

So she put on the old hunting jacket and the ill-fitting boots and drove into town, then parked in the middle of the small downtown district and began to check the stores. She found a pair of duck boots easily, and told the clerk to throw away the ones she was wearing, then continued her search for a jacket.

As she walked along the street, she saw people staring at her. At first, she thought it was the jacket, and then she realized that she stood out in this small, closed community and they probably knew or guessed that she was involved in the crash and the possible murder. She hadn't seen a newspaper, so she didn't know what it said, but as Michael had pointed out, newspapers here were all but superfluous.

She finally found an inexpensive ski jacket in bright pastels and discarded the hunting jacket, as well. Then she glanced at her watch and saw that she'd managed to kill only a little more than an hour.

The day was cloudy but not too cold, so she walked the length of the business district and then found herself at the edge of an old residential neighborhood. Huge old trees formed a bare-branched canopy over the street, which was lined with big old homes. The street was empty of pedestrian traffic, so she decided to go for a walk there. The stares she'd been receiving were beginning to get on her nerves, which were frazzled enough as it was.

About half the houses were obviously in need of major repairs, but some had been either well-preserved or renovated. The neighborhood reminded her of the one she'd grown up in, although it had been much better kept. She felt a comforting familiarity as she walked along, staring at turreted Victorians and solid, square federal-style houses.

Lost in memories of her childhood, she didn't hear the engine until it was nearly upon her. Then she turned and saw the purple snowmobile. This time, the lady added a purple-and-green scarf to her ski suit and it blew out behind her as she sped toward Andrea, then slowed when she came abreast of her.

"Well, you must be feeling better," the woman said cheerfully. "A bit of fresh air always helps."

Andrea frowned in confusion. At first, she thought the woman might know something she didn't. Could the search party have returned already—and not found Val? But that was impossible.

Then, suddenly, it struck her and she felt almost dizzy. This woman had greeted her three times now in a very familiar manner, and it had simply never occurred to her that she might be mistaking her for Val.

"Why did you think I wasn't feeling well?" she asked cautiously as her heart leaped into her throat.

"Well, because you said so, of course—when I came over earlier this morning..." The woman's strong voice trailed off slightly at the end as she stared at Andrea. She was looking very hard.

Andrea returned her stare, afraid to let herself hope. For all she knew, this woman might be the town crazy. Given her attire and the purple snowmobile, that was a distinct possibility.

"I think you might have mistaken me for someone else," she said cautiously.

The woman's eyes left her and darted to a point up the street. "Is it possible?" she asked as a smile creased her weathered face.

"Is *what* possible?"

"Are you twins? I thought she was here alone. Have you two been playing games with me? I had twins once when I was still teaching, and they were always pulling the wool over my eyes."

She continued to stare hard at Andrea and then began to nod. "You *are* twins. I can see the difference now."

"Where is she—my sister?" Andrea asked breathlessly, now feeling so dizzy with relief that she had to put out a hand to brace herself against a tree.

"You mean you don't know?" the woman asked. "Are you all right? You look as pale as she did this morning."

Andrea started to repeat her question and the woman pointed up the street. "She's staying at Annie Duncan's house—right next door to mine. She said she didn't want anyone to know she was there, but she couldn't have meant *you*. It looks to me like she needs someone. She hasn't really confided in me, although I've tried to help."

The woman pointed to the seat behind her. "Get on, then, and I'll take you there. She's Valerie and you're . . . ?"

"Andrea," she managed to reply as she climbed onto the snowmobile. "Who is Annie Duncan?"

"She owns the house, but leaves for the winter. Annie goes to stay with her daughter and son-in-law in Florida."

The woman started up the street, shouting over the whine of the snowmobile. "She rents out rooms sometimes—to hunters and to people visiting family in town. It's such a big house, you see. And she's taken in teachers and nurses who move into the area—just until they get settled. Houses like that are very expensive to keep up, you know."

Andrea murmured her understanding. Someone *had* mentioned to her that there was a woman in town who took in roomers and that she was gone for the winter.

"But how did Val . . . ?"

"Annie's daughter brought her here. She didn't say how she'd met her—just that she needed a place to stay for a while. I keep an eye on the house for Annie, you see. Here we are.''

She slowed and turned into a driveway. Before them stood a huge old Victorian in need of a paint job, but otherwise sound.

"Did you say you saw her this morning?"

The woman nodded. ''I went over to see if she wanted a ride into town or needed me to get anything for her. Poor dear. She probably hasn't been out at all since she got here.''

Andrea got off the snowmobile and found that her legs were actually shaking. She turned to the woman and thanked her.

"You're welcome. I hope you can cheer her up.'' She waved and roared off.

Andrea went slowly up the steps onto the front porch, still not quite able to believe that she would find Val here. Her fingers were shaking uncontrollably as she pressed the doorbell and heard it ring inside.

There was no response, so she rang it again, straining to hear any sounds inside. Relief began to turn to fear again. What if Val were sick, or what if she'd come too late?

She walked along the big front porch that wrapped around both sides of the house, trying to peer into windows. But the drapes were all drawn. There were steps at the side, too, so she ran down them and hurried around to the back of the house through knee-deep snow.

There was no bell at the back door, so she began to pound on it with her gloved fist. "Val! It's Andy!"

She tried to see into the kitchen, but the only window had a set of wooden shutters on the inside that were closed. She was about to pound again when the door opened.

"Andy?"

"Val!"

There was only the briefest of hesitations before they rushed into each other's arms, tears wetting their cheeks as they hugged each other tightly. Then Val looked around warily.

"Is Nick here?" she asked fearfully. "Does he know where I am?"

Andrea winced inwardly at the fear in Val's voice, but she was able to reassure her twin honestly that Nick didn't know where she was.

Valerie's gray-green eyes still darted about nervously before she drew Andrea inside. "How did you find me?"

Andrea decided for now to give her the short version. "The Purple Lady. I never learned her name."

Valerie smiled. "It's Anna Moore. She lives next door."

But her brief smile drained away quickly and Andrea was stunned to see how pale and thin she was. It reminded her that while the search for her twin was over, the problems were not.

"She told me that the daughter of the owner brought you here. But how did you know her?" The question wasn't exactly a high priority at the moment, but Andrea was keenly aware of the delicacy of the situation. She could not afford to make a false step now.

"I met her after I escaped." Valerie stopped, frowning suddenly. "How did you know to look for me here?"

Andrea heard the suspicion in her voice, along with the rising fear. "It's a long story, Val. I did some detective work—and then got lucky."

"Where's Nick?" she asked in a taut voice.

"He's here—in the area, I mean. But he doesn't know where you are." Andrea thought about Michael and Nick up on the mountain, searching for Val's body.

"We've got to get out of here," Val said, "before he finds us."

"Then let's go. We can go to my place." Andrea knew this was no time to begin the explanations. Val was close to being hysterical, and she needed to feel safe before she'd be ready to listen.

"My car is parked downtown. It's not far."

"I don't want to be seen," she said stubbornly.

"Then I'll go get the car and bring it back here," Andrea replied soothingly. "Just promise me you won't disappear again."

Val nodded and Andrea was forced to accept that. She left and jogged down the street, trying to figure out how to let Michael and Nick know what had happened. When she reached the downtown area, she searched for a pay phone, then called the Robertses, hoping to leave a message with them. But there was no answer.

She got into her car and dug through her purse for a notebook, then wrote a hasty message, folded it and put it into her pocket. All the way back to the house, she worried that Val might have taken off again. But when she pulled into the driveway, Val opened the front door and ran to her.

Andrea backed down the driveway, then stopped. "We should let Anna know that you're leaving, shouldn't we? She said she takes care of the house."

Val was crying silently, but she nodded and pointed to a smaller house next door. "That's her house."

Now comes the tricky part, Andrea thought as she started up the other driveway. "I'll tell her," she told Val as she came to a stop.

"No, let me do it," Val insisted. "She's been really kind to me and I just want to thank her and ask her to thank Susie."

Andrea just nodded, wishing that their parents hadn't impressed upon them the importance of good manners.

Anna came to the door and Andrea decided to make one last, desperate attempt. The men would be back before they reached Connecticut, and even then she doubted that she would be able to call.

She pulled the folded note from her pocket and opened the window, waving it while Val's back was to her. Anna obviously saw her because she waved, but she had no way of knowing if she understood. The only thing she could do was to drop the note into the snow beside the driveway and hope that she would retrieve it and see that it was delivered to Michael.

The drive back to Connecticut was the longest of Andrea's life. Val cried and started to talk, then broke off to sob some more. Andrea waited to hear the story before she could try to persuade Val to listen to the truth.

"A man called me. He wouldn't give me his name, but he said that he had some information about my husband that I should know. I probably would have hung up on him, except that I thought Nick was having an affair, and I figured maybe this was the husband or the boyfriend of the woman he was... seeing."

When she stopped with a quiver, Andrea asked her what made her think Nick was having an affair.

"He...he was acting *different,* Andy. He just wasn't *there* a lot of the time. I mean, he was there physically, but not emotionally, you know?"

Andrea nodded. In all likelihood, Nick was just preoccupied with the business. If she recalled correctly, the time when he was supposed to have started this "affair" coincided with the time when they were trying to get the contract for landscaping at the new research park. But she didn't tell Val that—not yet.

"Anyway, he wouldn't tell me anything over the phone. He said we needed to meet and talk things over. So I agreed to meet him out at this truck stop near the interstate where no one would know me.''

She drew in a ragged breath. ''But he didn't want to discuss *this* affair. It was something else—much worse. Nick's a murderer, Andy! *That's* what you saw in him. *That's* what he was hiding. He killed this man's sister. She was having an affair with him, but she wouldn't leave her husband. He killed them *both!*''

She subsided into sobs again as Andrea wondered whether she should try to tell her the truth now, or wait until she was calmer. She was about to give it a try when Val continued her story.

''This all happened about five years ago, and the police never caught Nick because he must have left New York.

''I just freaked out and ran out of the restaurant. He followed me and got into my car. And then he pulled out a gun, and said that they were taking me with them—that Nick had to pay for what he'd done. His father was in another car and he followed us.

''So they took me to their hunting camp. I was totally out of it by then. I just wanted to die. But then I heard them talking about a deal they'd made with Nick for a half-million dollars, and I realized that when they said they wanted to make Nick pay, *that's* what they meant.

''We didn't have that kind of money, Andy—but I knew how Nick could get it. He'd just taken out a big insurance policy on me, so if they killed me, he'd have more than enough money. Maybe they'd even worked out a deal before, and that was why Nick took out that policy.''

She turned to Andrea, tears streaming down her face. ''What am I going to do, Andy? He's already killed two people—and now he wants to murder *me.*''

Andrea saw an exit up ahead and took it, then parked at the edge of a gas station lot. ''What you're going to do is listen to me. You probably won't believe me right away, but just think about what I'm going to tell you, because it's the *truth*."

Then calmly and carefully she told Val all of it. Val kept shaking her head, but Andrea plowed on, confident that sooner or later, her sister's good sense would return and she'd start to question her own assumptions.

When Andrea had finished, she looked longingly at a nearby pay phone. Michael and Nick would probably be back by now. But she had no way to make a call without arousing Val's suspicions.

So they drove on to Connecticut and reached Andrea's home at dusk. The farther they'd gotten from Nick, the calmer Val had become. She even agreed to go out to dinner at a charming, informal place Andrea frequented.

Val was just as pale and still jumpy, but Andrea began to hope that she could convince her of the truth. She was worried about what Michael and Nick must be thinking, but her top priority at this point was her twin.

MICHAEL STARTED WORRYING the moment they pulled into the motel lot and he saw that Andy's car was missing. A fine mist had begun to fall, and with the dropping temperatures the roads would soon be icy.

The search party had spent hours digging through snow, but in the end, they'd found nothing. Michael had told Nick that was good news, but Nick was just as worried. And when he'd asked Michael what they could do now, he had had no answer for him.

Where the hell was Andy? The woman was driving him nuts. Maybe he should have taken her along so he could at least keep an eye on her.

At least, he thought, trying to put a positive spin on it, the Santinis couldn't be after her.

He wondered if they'd gotten the bodies out of the charred wreckage yet. The state troopers said they were sending a team down there sometime today.

"Where's Andy?" Nick said as they started toward the rooms.

"Who knows?" Michael said shortly. "She does what she wants to do."

Nick gave him the first smile he'd seen and shook his head. "You've got it bad. Made any wedding plans yet?"

"Things haven't gotten that far, but knowing Andy, she'll let me know when she's ready to talk about it. Or maybe she'll just go ahead and set the date without bothering to consult me."

Both men turned at the sound of a snowmobile approaching.

"What the hell?" Nick said as he gaped at the vision in purple.

"That's the local color," Michael told him as the woman parked the snowmobile and started toward them.

"Is one of you named Michael?" she asked.

"That's me," Michael said as she produced a piece of paper.

"Then this is for you."

She handed him the note and took off. Michael unfolded the small piece of paper, then read it aloud.

"'Found Val. She's okay. We're going to my place. Don't call. Will be in touch.'"

The two men stared at each other. "How did...?" "Where...?" They both stopped and Nick began to grin even as the tears started spilling from his eyes. Michael draped an arm across his shoulders as they walked toward their rooms.

"This is kind of humiliating, you know," he told Nick. "*I'm* supposed to be the private eye and I've been outdone by a college professor."

"LISTEN TO ME, VAL! There wasn't any affair and the Santinis lied to you. Michael told me the whole story and I believe him."

"Why should you believe him?" Val persisted. "After all, he's Nick's best friend."

"Do you love Nick?"

Val shrugged. "I *thought* I did."

"Well, you sure have a strange way of showing it. Give him a chance."

"*You're* the one who said there was something bad in his past."

Andrea winced. "I know I said that—and I was right. He made some mistakes—but he's *not* a murderer and he loves you."

"I can't believe you're taking his side."

"It isn't a question of that. I'm only thinking of you, Val. You've got to give him a chance. At least talk to him—or speak to Michael if you're not ready to talk to Nick."

Valerie stared at her. "Is there something going on between you and Michael?"

Andrea groaned inwardly. There it was—the one question she didn't want to answer right now. "Yes, well, sort of. We've been too busy looking for you to have much time to sort it out."

"Nick said once that you two would be perfect for each other."

"What do *you* think?" Andrea asked curiously.

"I don't know. It seems to me that both of you are the kind who don't really need anyone."

"There are different kinds of love," Andrea replied, recalling her earlier thoughts on the subject.

"Then you're *in love* with him?"

"Um, well, maybe. But we're supposed to be talking about you and Nick now." She went to the window. "Let's go for a walk. I need to stop by my office and pick up my messages, anyway."

Val agreed, but Andrea could tell that she'd lapsed back into a blue mood. Still, she thought that she was making some progress. As for herself, she was somehow managing to curb her impatience. It was strange how patient she could be with clients, but when it came to her own sister...

They left the house. Andrea explained that there was a pathway that had once been a railroad they could take to get to campus. As they went around the side of the house, she saw her neighbor peeking out from behind her lace curtains. The woman was such a snoop. It was the only thing Andrea disliked about living here. It seemed she couldn't make a move without attracting her attention.

She smiled, thinking that she'd *really* given her something to watch now. The woman probably thought she was seeing double.

They made their way along the old path toward campus. There was very little snow here and what there was had been packed down by others who used this path regularly for jogging and walking.

Campus was quiet, although the students would be back within a day or two. They encountered no one as they made their way across the woodsy campus. The administration building was on the far side and there would be people there, but this corner was empty.

Val started to ask her about her classes, but Andrea could tell that it was just polite conversation. Still, she was content with that. Even though they'd been arguing most of the time, the old closeness was back.

"That's the psych building over—"

Andrea's sentence was left unfinished as her words were shattered by a gunshot. Both women turned to see a man emerge from the woods behind them.

"No!" Andrea said, even as she grabbed Val's arm and broke into a run.

They were both silent as they ran toward the psych building. Knowing it would probably be locked, Andrea was already fishing through her purse for her key chain. Another shot ran out as the man continued to run toward them, gaining rapidly.

They reached the door. Andrea tried it and, finding it locked, put her key into the lock with trembling fingers. She knew now what must have happened, but not until they were inside the building did she say it.

"It's Santini—the younger one! He must have followed us." She relocked the door and started up the stairs to her office.

"But you said they were dead!" Valerie protested in a trembling voice.

"We thought they were. But it must have been only the father in the Blazer."

She unlocked her office door and ran to the phone. But even as she began to punch out the numbers, it went dead.

"What's wrong?" Valerie asked.

"He must have cut the line outside," Andrea said, her mind already working out a plan. They had to be alone in the building. If anyone else was here, the door downstairs would have been unlocked.

Then both women cried out involuntarily as they heard the sound of glass breaking on the first floor.

"Come on! There's a tunnel!" Andrea grabbed Val's arm and urged her to the door, then stopped in the hallway. There was no sound below, but she knew he wouldn't have any trouble finding her. Her name was on the building directory right near the door.

"This way," she whispered, pointing toward the rear stairway. "Be as quiet as you can."

They could hear him coming up the front stairs as they reached the fire door to the back staircase. There was no way to close it quietly, so she was sure he'd know where they'd gone. Her only hope now was the tunnel—if it was open!

By the time they reached the basement, they could hear his footsteps above them. The basement was a maze of storage rooms and a few small offices used by grad assistants. She rounded a corner and started for the door at the end that led into the tunnel. Behind them, she could hear him trying various doors.

The door to the tunnel was open, and after they'd gone through it she closed it as quietly as she could, hoping it would take him a while to find it.

The purpose of the tunnel was to carry the steam pipes that heated the older buildings on campus, but it was wide enough to walk through and was frequently used by faculty to get from their offices to a neighboring classroom building in bad weather.

Andrea kept looking behind her, but saw nothing. Then they were through and out into the classroom building. A phone, she thought. Where is there a phone?

She spared a moment to glance at Val and wished she hadn't. Her sister's face was deathly pale. "He's going to kill us," she whispered.

"No, he isn't! Take off your boots so he won't hear us if he comes through the tunnel."

Carrying their boots, the two women ran up the stairs to the first floor. Andrea looked around for a phone, but could find none. Surely there must be one somewhere in the building, but she had no time to conduct a search.

They stopped in the building's entryway as she tried to decide whether they could risk going back outside. There were no other buildings close by and they would be too exposed. They had to stay here.

She tried the doors of the first few classrooms and found them locked. And then she heard the sound she least wanted to hear—the dull metallic clunk of the exit door from the tunnel. Val grabbed her arm in terror.

"Top floor," Andrea whispered. "Be quiet."

They ran in their stocking feet up the stairs. The building was four stories high, with ten to twelve classrooms on each floor, and rest rooms. It would take him a while to find them, and in the meantime, surely someone would have heard those shots and called the police. But even as Andrea prayed for that, she thought about the distance to the administration building. Her only hope lay in the possibility that there was a maintenance crew or stray faculty member close enough to have heard the gunfire.

By the time they reached the top floor, badly winded, Andrea could hear faint sounds below. He was apparently trying various doors. Would he guess that they'd come all the way to the top? If she'd thought of it, he might have, too.

At the end of the long corridor was the smoking lounge. By now, Andrea was convinced that they would have to do battle with him and her mind had turned to the search for a weapon. The first thing she saw as they entered the lounge was the big, bottom-heavy pedestal ashtrays. She picked one up. Val frowned at her uncomprehendingly.

"He's going to come up here," she whispered. "We need to be ready for him."

"But he has a gun!"

"Then we have to catch him by surprise." She scanned the room even as she heard footsteps on the stairs somewhere below.

"Get behind that sofa!" she ordered Val.

"What are you going to do?"

But Andrea didn't answer because they both heard the heavy fire door at the far end of the hall open with a clang. He wasn't even trying to be quiet—but then why should he? He was armed and he knew they weren't.

She motioned for Val to get behind the sofa, then climbed up onto the back of another sofa that sat just around the corner and at right angles to the hallway. She needed height. The ashtray was very heavy and she knew she was going to have trouble swinging it.

She crouched there, bracing the steel column of the ashtray on her shoulder, wondering if she had the strength to swing it and hoping that he would be close enough for her to strike him when he reached the entrance to the lounge.

Through her mind ran all the things that would never happen if this didn't work. No more time with Val. No Michael. She'd read that people facing death saw their lives pass before them—but what she saw was a future she might not have.

He was coming down the hall, still trying various doors. The weight of the ashtray was digging painfully into her shoulder. Her hands were clammy as she gripped the rounded top.

She saw his shadow first—followed by a hand holding the gun. And then she swung the ashtray!

He fell forward with a heavy grunt and the gun clattered to the floor. But she'd overbalanced and she tumbled forward, too, landing half on top of him. She'd managed to strike only a glancing blow, and she felt him moving beneath her. Ignoring the sharp pain in her shoulder, she lunged for the gun, just as he tried to reach it, too.

Val came running out from behind the sofa and nearly stumbled over the gun before realizing what it was. She picked it up just as Santini went for it. He knocked her over, but she kept her grip on the gun, and by now Andrea was grabbing at him from behind.

The gun went off! The sound was deafening, but didn't quite cover the sound of shouts from somewhere below. Val screamed, and for one heart-stopping second Andrea thought she'd been shot!

But then they both stared in horrified fascination as Santini bent over double and fell. A bright red stain was spreading across his chest.

Trembling herself, Andrea still gathered her shaking twin into her arms. "It's over, Val. I heard someone downstairs. We're safe now."

Still locked together, they both moved away from the body on the floor. Then, just as they reached the entrance to the lounge, Andrea saw a dark figure in a shooter's crouch at the other end of the hallway.

"Don't...!"

"Andy?"

"Michael?"

He came running toward her, and a moment later Nick was following along after him. Even when they were there and all four of them were embracing clumsily, she couldn't believe it.

Then there were sirens outside and, soon after that, more shouts. Michael led her to a sofa and said he'd be right back. Nick was still holding Val, trying to lead her from the room and the sight of the body.

Andrea watched them as a welcome numbness came over her. Not even the sight of the spreading pool of blood beneath the inert body could rouse her from her sudden stupor.

Was Michael really here? she asked herself over and over. Then, staring at Nick again, she knew he must be.

And a few minutes later, he was there again, this time with an entire squad of police in tow.

"THE STATE POLICE didn't get around to calling me until this morning, but they discovered yesterday that there was only one body in the wreckage. And they also said there'd been a report of a stolen car.

"I tried to call you right away, but you weren't answering." Michael gave her a reproachful look. "So I called the police here and gave them a description of both men, because no one knew at that point which one was still alive. And I also gave them a description of the stolen car."

"They found the car abandoned in a shopping center not far from here," Nick put in. "But they didn't find it until it was too late—or nearly too late." He drew Val closer, as though he was still worried she might vanish again.

"Anyway," Michael continued. "We got here as fast as we could—which was just after you two had left to walk to campus."

"But how did you know we'd gone over there?" Andrea asked.

"Your neighbor told us. She said she'd seen you leave. And then she saw someone following you. She came out while I was trying to decide if I should break into the house. I knew your car was in the garage."

"He already had his set of lock picks out when she came over." Nick grinned. "It's a good thing we look like such fine, upstanding citizens."

Andrea looked at Val as she watched Nick. It was impossible to guess whether or not she thought her husband was a "fine, upstanding citizen." She still appeared rather dazed, which Andrea supposed was how she herself was looking, too. Neither of them had yet faced what had happened.

Nick and Val sat together on the sofa—but apart. Nick held her hand, but there was an odd formality about it that reminded Andrea of old family pictures.

"Now it's *your* turn," Michael said. They were sitting on the love seat that matched the sofa. His arm was curved around her shoulders and their fingers were laced together. If Val and Nick projected an uneasiness, the two of them presented the opposite picture—of a couple totally comfortable with each other.

Andrea had no idea if Val had noticed this, but Nick certainly did. Several times, she saw him looking from her to Michael with a certain pride, and she recalled that Val had told her Nick said they would be "perfect" for each other.

"What happened up there?" Michael asked. "I told the police that we'd all be down to the station to give statements as soon as possible."

Andrea and Valerie exchanged looks, and then Andrea started to explain. But before long, Val was finishing her sentences and she was finishing Val's.

"I can't believe I actually *killed* someone," Val said in a quavery voice as their recitation wound down.

"What you'd better believe is that if you *hadn't* killed him, he would have murdered *us*," Andrea stated firmly, even though she knew that both of them would have to live with that memory for the rest of their lives.

Michael watched her trying to help Val with her brave words. But the hand he held in his was ice cold. He knew she was going to be needing him just as much as Val needed

Nick right now. The difference between them was that Andy would never admit it.

"I think we should get down to the station and get this over with," he said, getting up and drawing Andy to her feet.

"THEY TREATED US like criminals!" Andy stated angrily as they all left the police station. "Either that, or they're all afflicted with a hearing loss. How many times should we be expected to answer the same question?"

Michael smiled at her indignation. "Until they're sure you've told them all there is to tell."

"They were just doing their jobs, Andy," Val said placatingly.

Michael was thinking that he'd certainly seen the differences between the two women on full display during the interviews. Val had patiently, if rather tremulously, answered the same question again and again. Andy, on the other hand, had at one point reached over and snatched away the pen the officer had been toying with, telling him that he obviously couldn't write and listen at the same time. She'd already given him her response once—and that was enough. If he wanted to hear her answer again, she told him, he could just play the tape after they'd gone.

"I'm just glad it's over," Val said with a sigh that was half sob.

Andy embraced her twin. "It *is* over, and something good has come of it. I have a sister again. You'll stay with me tonight at least, won't you?"

"Uh, I thought Val and I would stay at the inn, Andy. We'll see you tomorrow before we leave."

When Andy started to look as uncertain about that as Val did, Michael stepped up and wrapped an arm around her shoulders. She turned to him for a moment, then turned back to Val and Nick.

"I'm sorry. I wasn't thinking. I know you two have a lot to talk about. We can all have breakfast together tomorrow morning."

But as Nick and Val walked away, Michael saw that Andy had a doubtful expression on her face. He took her shoulders and turned her in the other direction.

"Come on, Tiger, before they decide to arrest you, after all."

"For what?" she demanded.

"Either for obstruction of an investigation—or for the far more serious offense of trying to obstruct a second honeymoon."

She smiled, but she still turned around to watch Nick and Val crossing the street to the inn.

"I WOULD NEVER have taken you for the hot-tub type." Michael grinned as he stepped naked into the swirling waters, carrying two glasses of wine.

"I'm not. I rarely use it. It came with the house." She reached up and took the one wineglass from him. After sipping for a moment, she leaned back and sighed.

"Do you feel like we're going to have to start all over again? I mean, we've been focused on those two ever since we met."

"Not entirely." He smiled, staring at her breasts that bobbed just above the waterline. "I think we can sort of pick up in the middle and go on from there."

She sat up and caught him staring at her. "I wonder if this thing can be put to some use other than soaking." She smiled.

"Oh, I think that's entirely possible," he replied lazily. "But there's something I have to ask you first."

"What's that?" she asked with a trace of exasperation.

"Speaking as an expert in human behavior, what do you think is the minimum appropriate amount of time between when two people meet and when they decide to make it permanent."

Her slight frown vanished and a seductive smile took its place. "I think that two people who know their own minds could probably cut that time to a couple of months."

He slid over and drew her onto his lap. "I really don't need that much time. I love you, Andy. It only took me a couple of days to figure that out."

She kissed him. "I love you, too, but just to cushion the shock to our families, we might want to wait at least a month."

Epilogue

Andrea stood at the window, staring out at the fields, where feathery plumes and spiky green things rippled in the breeze. Spring had come late this year, but never had it been more welcome.

"Michael, get out of here! I told you it's bad luck to see the bride before the ceremony!"

Andrea turned at the sound of her twin's voice and found Michael standing in the bedroom doorway, his formal white shirt open at the neck and cuffs.

"For a matron of honor, you're turning into a real tyrant, Val." He grinned. "You wouldn't let me see her last night, either."

"You were supposed to be having a last bachelor fling with Nick," Val replied archly.

Michael rolled his eyes. "Some 'fling.' I kept expecting him to get out a pair of needles and start knitting booties or whatever."

"Michael!"

"What are you talking about?" Andrea asked, her gaze going from her future husband to her twin.

"Uh-oh. I'm outta here!" Michael disappeared in a hurry, but Val and Andy's mother took his place.

"I should have taped his mouth shut instead of asking him to promise he'd keep quiet. This is supposed to be *Andy's* big day."

Andy's smile widened and she hugged her twin. "You've just made my 'big day' even better."

Val grinned. "Well, I'd planned to at least wait until after the ceremony to make the announcement. But since Michael ruined that, I'll just tell you *all* of it. He doesn't know it yet, but . . ."

"Twins!" Andy and her mother exclaimed simultaneously.

"Twins, it is." Val laughed. "Maybe Nick had better teach Michael to knit, too—just in case."

* * * * *

HARLEQUIN®

INTRIGUE®

REBECCA YORK'S

PEREGRINE CONNECTION

The much-loved, critically acclaimed
PEREGRINE CONNECTION
by Rebecca York is back!

Harlequin Intrigue is delighted
to make this stellar series available once more. In 1986,
Romantic Times awarded Rebecca York with a Lifetime
Achievement Award for Best Romantic Suspense Series
for the PEREGRINE CONNECTION.

These reprints are special Intrigue 10th-anniversary
treats for the legions of Rebecca York fans—fans who
have made her ongoing Intrigue series, "43 Light Street,"
instant bestsellers!

Discover the PEREGRINE CONNECTION—three
stories of danger and desire...as only Rebecca York
can tell them!

#298 TALONS OF THE FALCON November 1994
#301 FLIGHT OF THE RAVEN December 1994
#305 IN SEARCH OF THE DOVE January 1995

Don't miss any of them!

Where do you find hot Texas nights, smooth Texas charm and dangerously sexy cowboys?

Crystal Creek reverberates with the exciting rhythm of Texas. Each story features the rugged individuals who live and love in the Lone Star state.

"...Crystal Creek wonderfully evokes the hot days and steamy nights of a small Texas community...impossible to put down until the last page is turned." —*Romantic Times*

Praise for Bethany Campbell's *Rhinestone Cowboy*

"...this is a poignant, heart-warming story of love and redemption. One that Crystal Creek followers will wish to grab and hold on to." —*Affaire de Coeur*

"Bethany Campbell is surely one of the brightest stars of this series." —*Affaire de Coeur*

Don't miss the final book in this exciting series. Look for **LONESTAR STATE OF MIND** by BETHANY CAMPBELL

Available in February wherever Harlequin books are sold.

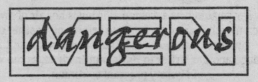

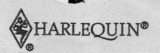

HARLEQUIN®

Deceit, betrayal, murder

Join Harlequin's intrepid heroines, India Leigh and Mary Hadfield, as they ferret out the truth behind the mysterious goings-on in their neighborhood. These two women are no milk-and-water misses. In fact, they thrive on

MISCHIEF & MAYHEM

Watch for their incredible adventures in this special two-book collection. Available in March, wherever Harlequin books are sold.

REG4